the Bookseller's Daughter

BOOKS BY DANIELA SACERDOTI

The Italian Villa

The Lost Village

The Italian Island

GLEN AVICH QUARTET

Watch Over Me

Take Me Home

Set Me Free

Don't Be Afraid

SEAL ISLAND SERIES

Keep Me Safe

I Will Find You

Come Back to Me

DANIELA SACERDOTI

the Bookseller's Daughter

bookouture

Published by Bookouture in 2023

An imprint of Storyfire Ltd.
Carmelite House
50 Victoria Embankment
London EC4Y 0DZ

www.bookouture.com

ISBN: 978-1-80314-641-6
eBook ISBN: 978-1-80314-640-9

For Alison Duff

CHAPTER 1

NEW YORK, 2022

"You at the gallery already, Francesca?" Isaac asked.

I could hear him shuffling papers in the background. I imagined him holding the phone between his ear and his shoulder, forehead wrinkled, busy as always. Not long ago, whenever he talked to me, he stopped everything and gave me his full attention. Now, I was an afterthought. After all, I wasn't his fiancée anymore, and not his girlfriend either.

After ten years, in the middle of planning our wedding, he'd decided he *cared* for me, but he didn't *love* me, and that we needed a trial separation. I would remain his best friend, his special friend, he'd told me. I was in pieces, but had concluded that the friend status would be better than not having him in my life at all.

And no, I hadn't pressured him into marriage. I was happy the way things were. Very, very happy. I suppose it was one of those situations that naturally evolve into marriage or break-up. It hadn't gone the way I thought it would.

"Yeah, I couldn't sleep anyway. And there's a lot to do." I tried to muster an upbeat tone, even though my mood had been spiraling the last few months. I moved in the world as if my legs were stuck in thick, thick mud, and I was wearing a leaden suit of indifference.

There wasn't much to do at the gallery either. Nothing interesting, anyway. Zilberstein Gallery and Antiquities was small but prestigious, specializing in manuscripts and books. When they'd offered me a job, I thought I'd hit the jackpot, considering I'd been blacklisted in the art-dealing world. I'd spent the ten years after gaining my doctorate, which I'd achieved while working two jobs and still ending up in debt, working for Hex. Yes, *that* Hex. The nice people who turned out to have links with organized crime, a few presidents and royals, and shady characters now sprawled all over the news. Powerful people don't pay for their bad deeds; little people do. I ended up virtually erased from the art world, my reputation in tatters.

When the Zilbersteins hired me, I was beyond grateful; but it didn't take me long to realize that Cassidy Zilberstein, the boss' daughter, would grab not just the money from my work, but the glory as well. I stayed in her shadow, got paid like a personal assistant, and shared my time between office tasks and picking up Cassidy's dry cleaning.

But it was this, or change careers completely. Even if I'd given my heart's blood to Hex and had no part at all in their shady business—it didn't matter. My name had been tainted and nobody in New York would hire me, except a business who believed having an art historian and paleographer for the price of a secretary was worth being associated with a former employee of Hex.

"Don't let them eat your soul," Isaac said. He'd been supportive throughout the whole mess, even if he was swamped with work and perpetually busy. He was the reason I'd stayed in New York after the Hex debacle. Moving away would have given me better chances, but Isaac had a good job in the city, and I couldn't drag him away from it for the sake of my career.

That would have been simply selfish. I couldn't even have brought it up.

"Mmm. Easier said than done," I replied. "You know Cassidy devours souls with her morning latte."

"By the way, you had nightmares again. I heard you."

Yes, Isaac and I still lived together—thanks, New York housing market—taking turns to sleep on the couch. And, yes, it was as bad as it sounds. Lonely doesn't begin to describe it. But the place was close to his work, and I...

I wanted to be close to him.

"Yeah. Same dream." I'd been plagued by that nightmare for weeks, now. A blurry figure hunting me down while I ran, ran and slipped and fell into a pool of dark waters... Sleeping pills didn't make any difference, except to turn me into a zombie the morning after.

"That's rough. I'm sorry..." On the other side of the line, I heard a door opening and a woman's voice calling Isaac's name. It was Rowena, the colleague he shared an office with. "I've got to go. Have a good day," said Isaac.

A good day. My feet were resting on a box of wedding-themed catalogs, still under my desk because I didn't have the heart to get rid of them, and I was in the process of slotting data in an Excel document, which was marginally better than washing coffee cups after meetings and collecting Cassidy's dry cleaning. I would have the *best* of days.

"You too."

"Oh, and Francesca?"

"Yes?"

"Fajitas tonight, what do you say? We haven't had them in ages..."

A tiny bubble of joy went *pop* in my heart. We used to have Mexican every Wednesday—always the same chicken fajitas we'd ordered on our first date, but were too nervous to eat. Since we'd broken up, all our little traditions had disintegrated, even if we still lived together. Isaac said that we'd got stuck in a rut, that routines were stifling. I didn't think there was much stifling happening in a Mexican takeout, and I'd loved all our little habits. Maybe this was a good sign?

"Sure. I'll stop at the restaurant on my way back."

"Cool. Don't make it too late, I have a big day tomorrow."

Isaac preferred eating early; I preferred eating late. So, we usually ate dinner early. "Understood." I put the phone down, feeling warm and unreasonably happy. I knew that it probably didn't mean much to him—*it's just a Mexican dinner, get a grip, Francesca!* But maybe it was a little step forward?

I exhaled. Hoping so hard was too much to bear, but losing hope was worse. Isaac was the lynchpin that kept my life together. Without him, I was adrift. And even if living together while not *being* together could be torture, I was so very grateful that at least he was still in my life.

Yep. Pathetic. Only last night I'd told my sister, Sofia, as much, and the look in her eyes had spoken volumes. She'd never liked Isaac, which had always been a thorn in my side, but now she *despised* him. I could still hear her words. *"Grateful?* The guy left you practically at the altar, and *you're grateful he's still in your life?"*

I suddenly remembered I was supposed to meet her after work that night. But Isaac needed me home early for our Mexican dinner. It was a dilemma. I could almost hear Sofia's response: *You need to go home to the guy who left you and broke your heart? The guy who has you sleeping on the couch but still calls you every day at work?*

I texted Sofia to meet me a little earlier, dragged myself through a few hours of wrestling with Excel, and finally gathered my stuff to leave early. Nobody would notice anyway. Cassidy was doing her thing—probably having brunch and calling it PR—and Zil was working on acquiring some manuscripts from a private collection based in a place called Santa

Caterina, in Italy—a task way too interesting to be given to me. Apparently, the owner of the collection was difficult and strange, Zil had told me while his mustache was covered in a bright green pomade that apparently was the ultimate mustache conditioner. I'd kept a straight face, honed to perfection through many years of working in art.

"These manuscripts have all been illuminated by women," he'd said to me. "Which, as you know, was not rare as such, because..."

"It's reasonable to think that in medieval times women did work on writing and illumination," I finished for him, positively drooling for the chance to use my hard-earned knowledge.

"What's remarkable about these is that they're all *signed* by the women who worked on them. And a few of them are by... wait..." He checked his notes. "Hypatia? No, Ip..."

"Ippolita?" I exclaimed. "*The* Ippolita?" She'd been the Abbess of Oswen and a polymath: poet, composer, herbalist, mystic... She was my *idol*. I know it's not that common to have an abbess from medieval times as your role model, but welcome to the weird and wonderful world of paleography, the deciphering and examining of ancient manuscripts.

"Apparently so."

I was so overwhelmed with desire to take over from Zil, acquire those manuscripts, see them, touch them (with gloves, God forbid) that I'd stood there, mute. All that came out was: "Can I help?" in a feeble voice.

"Sure. You can finish those Excel thingies so I'm free to take care of this properly."

"What I mean is..."

"I know what you mean. And do you think they want to be in any way connected with Francesca Lombardo from Hex?" He shook the papers he had in his hand.

That had been the end of the conversation. I wouldn't bring

it up again. Every time I was reminded of my tarnished reputation, another little bit of my heart crumbled.

———

Sofia was meeting me in a bar that the post-work crowd flooded
every day of the week, but at this time of day was almost empty.
I spotted her at once, her mane of black hair down her petite
back, perching on a stool. We kissed and moved to a table near
the window.

Seeing her felt so good. We didn't meet up as much as we
used to, because I tried to avoid the Isaac-related guilt trip. Her
negativity toward him had driven a wedge between us. She was
smiling now, her dark eyes looking at me, a question in them.
And maybe a little bit of pity.

I hated being on the receiving end of that look. "How have
you been?"

"Yeah, okay. Busy. You?"

"Same. Sofia, I can't stay long, I need to bring an early
dinner home..."

My sister's face fell. "You need to bring *him* dinner."

"Well, we are roommates, we're having dinner together..."

"You hate eating early. And we arranged this thing last
week. Isaac says *jump*, you say *how high*..."

"Sofia, please."

"Please? You know I'm right."

Yes. I knew she was right. I shouldn't drop her to go home to
Isaac. Yet what if tonight was the night we came a little closer
again? "Look, can we just have a nice time now, you and me?"

"*Time?* You just said you have to go early."

"Not that early. You hungry?" I smiled, trying to climb my
way out of the hole I'd fallen into. Again. In the first ten
minutes of us meeting.

We ordered Campari and cheesy chips to share and picked

at them. Small talk followed: formal, distant. We were both entrenched in our positions. She didn't like Isaac when we were together and she hated him now. She wanted me to leave him behind and never look back. I wanted to marry him.

So, yeah.

"Look, Sofia. We might as well address the elephant in the room."

She looked at me, and all of a sudden her wide dark eyes were veiled with tears. I swallowed. My big sister never cried.

"Why do you still live with him? Why do you cling to him this way?" she said, and her long earrings tinkled gently. She always wore dangling earrings: they played hide and seek in her long, dark hair.

I loved her so. "It's hard to explain..."

"Oh, no, Francesca. It really isn't. It's not hard to explain and it's not hard to understand! He *left* you. He's having you sleep on the couch. And *he's* the one who broke up with *you!*"

"We take turns on the couch," I specified.

"Oh. It's all good, then!" She was gesticulating like our mum did when she was very angry or very happy. "Francesca. He just needs you for your share of the rent!"

Those words were like a knife in my heart. Especially because, deep down, I knew they were true.

Sofia was looking out the window, a stormy cloud on her brow. Now my eyes were filled with tears too. At that moment, my phone squeaked—I'd assigned elk bellows from Cassidy —*Cassidy emergency*, the message would laconically say—and mouse squeaks to notifications from Zil.

I rolled my eyes. "I have to go."

"Who was that?"

"Not Isaac. It was Zil."

"Mmm." She eyed me.

"I promise you!"

"You don't have to go every time they snap their fingers.

We've only been here for half an hour, Francesca... Come on, stay a little longer. I promise I won't mention him again. I'm sorry."

"I really have to go. There's some sort of Cassidy-related emergency. I need to help Zil sort it out."

"She probably needs you to get a last-minute hairdresser booking."

I finished my Campari quickly. "Probably."

"And this is what you went to school for. This is why you're up to your eyes in student debt. This is what you dreamed of doing."

"This is a stepping-stone," I repeated for the millionth time, maybe not so much for Sofia's sake, but for mine. How many girls and women in this city were thinking or saying something along those lines, at that very moment? A crappy apartment, a job below your qualification, a boss who thinks a short skirt is his cue to put a hand on your knee. *Just a stepping-stone, things will change.*

But do they ever?

Sofia's eyes were dark. "You've been on your stepping-stone for five years, Francesca."

And like so often happens when someone throws the truth in your face—a truth you're unwilling to acknowledge—I lost my temper.

"You know what, Sofia? I'm tired of your nagging. Every. Single. Time. We. Meet. My fiancé, my job. Everything I do and everything I am, you *despise*! I can't take it anymore!"

The words had come out before I could even think. I hated it when it happened: it was like there was this bottomless hole of rage inside me, and sometimes I couldn't push it down any longer. Like a sleeping volcano, it erupted when I least expected it. My hands were shaking, and I'd probably turned scarlet. I could feel curious eyes burning on my back; the bartender was watching us too. I was mortified.

"I've known you since you were born, Francesca. I remember you from *before*," Sofia whispered.

"Before what?"

"Before Isaac. Before Hex. Before the Zilbersteins' crap. You didn't let *anyone* treat you like a doormat. Remember how Dad tried to put you off going to university? Working-class girl from Queens flying all the way up to a PhD? He didn't think it was even possible. He believed you'd end up in debt with nothing to show for it..."

"He was right!" That was my self-pity coming out. Self-pity and anger: a toxic combination if ever there was one.

"Rubbish. I was in *awe* of that girl. My clever, beautiful, stubborn little sister. I don't know where she's gone! And now, you're... you're a doormat's doormat!"

"You *know* what happened. I was accused of fraud. *Fraud*. At the age of twenty-four by people who mingled with politicians and millionaires. And I was innocent. I *proved* I was innocent. But mud sticks." Our heads were close together now, and we were shout-whispering.

"What happened wasn't your fault. You were employed by fraudsters. You could have fought for your name. But you gave up, and you know very well why."

"I had to keep it quiet for Isaac's sake, his job, his reputation..." I hissed. "I couldn't make a fuss."

"Your name was dragged through the mud and you didn't want to make a fuss *because of Isaac*. Then you didn't move away *because of Isaac*. And then Isaac left *you*."

We lowered our heads at the same time. Sisters: same mannerisms, but a gulf of misunderstanding between us.

"I'm just trying to rebuild my life, Sofia. If you want something, you need to stick with it. I'm clawing my way back, can't you see? Not that you'd know anything about staying power." I bit my lip. Why, why did I say that? My sister had gone through a painful divorce. She'd taken it hard, of course. And now there

I was, throwing that back at her face, as if it'd been her fault... I couldn't have sunk any lower. "Sofia, I..."

She pivoted on her stool, turning her back to me. "I think you better go, Francesca."

"I'm sorry, I..."

"Just. Go."

I found myself on the sidewalk, swallowed by the city: the scent of blooming summer buried under hot asphalt and fumes, the noise of traffic and the bright lights, and people, hundreds, thousands, hundreds of thousands of people. For a moment, a mind-blowing, clear-as-day moment, I knew that I had to do something, anything, to get myself out of the muddy bog my life had become. Change jobs. Stop trying to fix the unfixable. Move out, move away...

And then my phone vibrated in my hand, and it was Isaac sending me the sticker of an animated taco jumping around, followed by a smiley emoji. He was waiting for me. He *needed* me. And the moment passed.

I replied to his text:

Slight delay, won't be long x

I pushed it all to the back of my mind and hurried on... but first I turned around to see Sofia. She looked so despondent, both hands around her Campari. Just then a couple holding hands passed in front of the bar window and hid her from view.

I swallowed the guilt and reminded myself that I was right. I had a plan, I would stick with it and get my life back.

For now I'd walk to Cassidy's upmarket condo, fix her emergency, take a cab to the Mexican restaurant near our apartment, grab dinner and walk the few blocks home. I'd eat with Isaac like old times, the two of us—maybe watch an old black and white movie, listen to our neighbor practice his cello... Perfect.

I'll call Sofia tomorrow, I thought, as I navigated the small crowd on the sidewalk, and we'd make peace. We always did. Squabbling and reconciling were a kind of tradition for us.

I silenced the little voice inside me that said something was different about this argument, that the things we'd said might cut so deep as to separate us, if not forever, at least for a long time.

My phone squeaked another few times. Zil was practically begging me to run over. Poor Zil—nobody, not even someone as slimy as him, deserved the plague that was his daughter. Cassidy had her father wrapped around her little manicured and bejeweled finger and she knew how to use that power to her best advantage.

I just had to hold on a little longer, and everything would sort itself out, I repeated to myself as I increased the pace. Zil would see that I could do so much more than filing and making coffee, and Isaac would recognize that he made a *monumental* mistake, that we were soulmates and meant to be together, and the wedding would be back on.

Thanks to my patience, and sacrifice, and endurance, my life *would* get back on track.

You just see.

CHAPTER 2

NEW YORK

I ran past the uniformed porter with a flying *hello*—I'm sure he shot me a look of sympathy—pressed the gilded button in the elevator, and there I was, in the marbled hall. Cassidy's maid, Penelope, was waiting for me at the front door. She was a *saint*. I didn't know how she'd put up with Cassidy's demands for so long.

The irony of that particular thought wasn't lost on me.

"Oh, Miss Lombardo!" she said as soon as the elevator door opened. "At last! She's going crazy!"

I'd asked Penelope to call me Francesca more times than I could remember, but she never did, so I'd decided to reciprocate. "*Miss Torres*, I came as quickly as I could," I said, trying to look concerned and quite failing. I *was* concerned—but for Penny, not for Zil and his spawn. "What *awful* predicament awaits me?" I whispered in a dramatic tone.

The shadow of a smile hovered on Penny's lips for a fraction of a second. Cassidy's emergencies were always trivial, especially when it came to the many social events she organized. Once, she'd sent me halfway across town because the caterers' napkins were the wrong shade for the color scheme she'd chosen. *Not sage green—pea green!* But where she was an ultra-perfectionist when it came to the appearance of things, substance didn't matter much to Cassidy. I'd had to rewrite a crucial piece of copy presenting our new exhibition because she couldn't be bothered stringing five sentences together, *and* spell check, having just signed her name at the bottom. Therefore, I could pretend to take this call seriously for the sake of my job, but believe it was an emergency, as in a real-world emergency? Nah.

I was surprised when Penny led me to the kitchen, which was not a room Cassidy often used. Cassidy was leaning on the marble island, her face in her hands, glossy strands of balayaged hair threaded in her fingers. Zil, a small, twig-like man with an overbite and a black mustache that would have been in fashion a hundred years ago, stood beside her, his features morphing from pity to terror (of his daughter), and back. I waited in the doorway, striving to look sympathetic.

"Penny said Cassidy needed a hand with..."

Cassidy lifted her head and screeched, "I'm going there right now!"

I winced at the sight of her face. She had raccoon eyes, tears and mascara streaming down her cheeks. Her makeup was always perfect. A drama queen she might be, but she looked seriously upset this time.

"I'll go to Aruba and tear that little bitch apart with my own hands!"

Oh. It was a Grayson-related issue. Her philanderer of a boyfriend. How could she put up with his behavior, still? I could never take all this shit from Isaac.

The Murano glass lamp above the kitchen island made something glitter on the marble. Cassidy's engagement ring, a pink diamond she'd shown me a hundred times, lay abandoned.

"She got an anonymous email," Penny whispered in my ear. "Grayson's in Aruba with a girl..."

Oh. He was supposed to be at a work convention. I knew that because I had to sit through endless calls between them while I was performing my usual mind-numbing tasks.

"A bitch! Not a *girl*, Penny! A *bitch*! She sent me pictures of them! Look, wanna see?"

She brandished her phone toward us, and we shook our heads in unison. We really *didn't* want to see. There was another bout of tears, with Zil fumbling and hovering over his daughter and not quite knowing what to do.

"Francesca," Cassidy finally said, jutting her chin and trying to look proud—an attempt made vain by the mascara running down her cheeks. "I want you to book me a flight."

Zil was all in a flutter. "Sweetheart, you can't leave now. We have the Santa Caterina trip booked..."

Ah, the Santa Caterina expedition! My heart positively swelled with desire. Ippolita Von Oswen's work... I would have given my right arm to take care of the deal. I was way more qualified than Cassidy to appraise the manuscripts. Damn, I was way more qualified than Zil himself, though admittedly I didn't have his experience in acquiring goods. I even spoke fluent Italian, not so much thanks to my Italian mom, who'd endeavored to make us as American as the Founding Fathers and therefore refrained to speak her mother tongue at home—make of it what you will—but to my studies. It was a little rusty, but viable.

But it was always a member of the Z family who took part in this kind of sourcing trip. I was usually left in New York "to hold the fort," i.e., perform menial tasks.

"Oh, Daddy, who cares about those stupid manuscripts! Grayson is the love of my life!" Cassidy cried.

Wow. This was out of character. Cassidy always cared about the deals they made because she loved money. She might have seemed vapid, but when it came to amassing silver and gold in her Gringotts account, she was not vapid at all.

"You're better off without him, sweet pea..." Zil stuttered.

"He *betrayed* me." The ice in Cassidy's tone sent shivers down my spine. I wouldn't want to be in Grayson's shoes. Though, to be fair, she had her reasons. The glimpse I'd caught of the damning pictures was a pretty accurate portrait of the situation. Cassidy really was heartbroken; I felt almost sorry for her... though I would have felt worse if she'd ever treated me like a human being.

There was a pause in the conversation, punctuated by Cassidy sniffing and Zil shuffling in place. Every bit of him was quaking. "Sweet pea, you know I can't fly. I have a *complete and utter* phobia."

Cassidy's answer was to grab her phone and throw it across the room against the massive fridge, where it bounced and fell on the ground with a sickly crack.

I gathered all the courage I had and threw caution to the wind. "*I can go to Italy.*" My voice seemed to echo in the room, as if I'd shouted in a church.

They both jerked to look at me, like velociraptors. Maybe Cassidy's glossy tresses would fan up and out like a dinosaur in *Jurassic Park*, and she would jump on me.

It was much like earlier, with Sofia, when words had come out before I could think. It was probably International Impulse Day. But my confidence was growing. "*I can go,*" I repeated. "I'm sure I can handle it. I speak fluent Italian..."

I was desperate to go, but then I thought about leaving Isaac when things were so messy between us. *Things aren't messy. He broke up with you.* I heard Sofia's voice in my head, and my heart tightened. However, whether I had been impulsive or not, it was too late. I couldn't take my words back.

"Thanks for choosing this time to remind me how very smart you are. I'm sorry if I didn't go to university. I'm sorry if I don't speak any foreign languages!" Cassidy looked at me as if she were a puppy, and I'd just kicked her.

Penny gave out the most imperceptible of sighs.

"I'm sure Francesca didn't mean to belittle you, sweet pea. She knows that when it comes to public relations, you're beyond compare. The Zilberstein Gallery would be nothing without you, my dear."

"I hope she does," Cassidy hissed, as if I weren't there. "The Santa Caterina trip is off the table. If I'm not going, nobody's going. It's not happening. Francesca, book me a flight to Aruba. Now."

Okay. Enough was enough. "Book it yourself, Cassidy," I snarled. Another for International Impulse Day.

There was a collective intake of breath. I could feel Penny's eyes burning into me. Zil looked at me in horror, though he seemed more frightened *for* me than outraged *at* me.

Shit. What had I just done? I'd lost my job, most likely: better to turn around and go, before Cassidy's wrath hit me.

I was about to, when she said, "Francesca, wait."

I stopped, standing as rigid as a nutcracker. Words of apology were poised on my tongue, but they refused to come out. The other Francesca, the angry one that lived in my head, seemed to have had enough, because I found myself unable to apologize.

"I'll book the flight myself," Cassidy said.

"Oh. Okay. Good."

"But can you at least book my hairdresser?"

I went without another word.

———

"She really asked you to book her *hairdresser*?" Isaac said while laying out our small feast on the coffee table.

"Yep. I never met anyone as shameless as Cassidy, I swear."

"You couldn't make it up. And did you make the appointment?"

"No. I'd lost my job already, no point in further humiliation."

He cleaned his fingers, covered in hot sauce, on a napkin. "Do you regret it?"

"Oh, God, I do. I should have stayed quiet and booked that damn plane. I'd done things like that a million times before. Why did I refuse?"

I was so mad at myself. The day had been a complete disaster. Falling out with Sofia, messing up at work. For years I'd put up with their crap and waited for my moment. And now, in a fit of temper, I'd wasted all my efforts. Why oh *why*? Ugh. I stood to grab some soda from the kitchen and found myself resting my forehead against the cupboard, in a moment of complete and utter despair. Isaac tapped me on the shoulder. It was force of habit, I suppose, because I found myself in his arms, and he squeezed me, just like he used to.

"It will be okay," he whispered, cradling me. He smelled of cedar shower gel, of fajitas and of Isaac.

"Mmm." With my face hidden in his chest, it felt as if everything would be okay. Maybe everything would fall back into place, somehow. If Isaac loved me, then...

"We need to keep you in good form. If you lose your job, who's going to pay your slice of rent?"

I tried to laugh.

I couldn't.

CHAPTER 3

NEW YORK

The phone rang in the middle of the night. I rolled over and nearly fell off the couch: I'd forgotten it was my turn to sleep in the living room. Isaac had said that he would have left me the bed because of all I'd been through that day, but he had a string of meetings the next day, so he needed to be well rested.

When I saw Zil's name flash on the screen, I was instantly awake and sober. The moment had come. I was about to be fired officially. At... I looked at the time... two in the morning? Maybe he got the tip from the CIA—get them in the small hours, when they're at their most vulnerable.

"Hello?" I sat up, my hand on my forehead. Ugh. I wished I hadn't had that third... no, wait, *fourth*... glass of wine.

"Hello, Francesca. Zilberstein here. *Mhmhmhmh.*" He made that weird Zil noise, as if his mustache was threatening to fall off and he was trying to keep it in between his nose and his lip. "I'm sorry to bother you so late." He was apologizing? Really? On the other hand, it kind of made sense. Zil had a horror of conflict. His tone was to soften me, so I would go quietly and not make a scene.

"I suppose I won't be getting references, then?" My tone was flippant, but my stomach had sunk so low I could feel the wine sloshing in my ankles. Better to just get it over and done with. Ten years of work wasted. Ten years of work down the drain because I'd lost my patience with someone who truly, truly had it coming. Well, now I could say my piece. Tell him where he could shove his job, and...

"No, no. Forget about that. Cassidy... she can book her own flight," he said, his voice shaking a little. "And her own hair-dresser too."

This sudden stance surprised me. He was *terrified* of Cassidy. "She can?"

"Absolutely. Well, maybe Penny can do the hairdresser. Anyway. Francesca, we need you. *I* need you."

He needed *me*? This was quite the development. "Er... Zil?"

"*Mhmhmhmh.*" Oh, he really was unhappy. The mustache thing was in overdrive. "You're going to Italy."

He wasn't making any sense. Who talks about work stuff at two in the morning? Maybe he was drunk.

"Look. Can we just finish this here?" I spoke. "It's just protracted agony. I'll come and get my stuff tomorrow, and..."

Wait a moment. Did he say what I think he said?

I'm going *where*?

The noise of a lonely car came and went under my window, breaking the silence of the night.

"Sorry, what was that, Zil?"

"The Santa Caterina manuscripts. There's going to be an auction, or something along those lines—the owner wasn't forthcoming."

Oh. I thought the deal was done if our appraisal of the manuscript had a positive outcome. In layman's words, if we liked the goods. That wasn't the case?

"But the owner, Signora Lavinia, wants you. And you only to attend this auction."

"What? Why me?"

"I have no idea. She said she never wanted Cassidy in the first place, that she was about to tell us so, and that she also didn't want me. She wanted the Francesca Lombardo listed in our portfolio. So it turns out that my utterly deluded daughter is free to run after a loser in blooming Aruba." *Blooming.* When he was angry, Zil turned British. He probably thought British fury was more sophisticated than American fury. "And I don't have to Zoom my therapist for those extra sessions in order to be able to fly. Just thinking of being stuck on a plane... HMHMHHHH."

Had I just been given the chance to acquire some of Ippolita's illuminations?

Could I do it? Could I take on this responsibility? What if I disappointed everyone?

Panic and joy mixed up inside me and I was about to come out with my own Zil noise, albeit I lacked a mustache. But the other Francesca, the girl I was before being kicked down the curb by life, the girl who'd barked at everyone out of sheer frustration, had the upper hand.

"Sure, Zil. I'll go to Italy, appraise the manuscripts, and if I greenlight them I'll win the auction and bring them home."

There was an audible sigh of relief on the other end of the line. "Thank you."

And that made the first time that Zil ever thanked me for anything.

"You really can't elaborate more on why this Signora Lavinia asked specifically for me?"

I could picture him shrugging. "I explained that Cassidy couldn't make it over, and asked if she could possibly wait for us. Like I expected, she said no. Other dealers are looking at the collection and they'll join her in Santa Caterina for those dates, so there couldn't be any delay. Then she ended the call, quite abruptly. She was smiling, though. A fascinating woman, if I may say so." Zil had a slightly dreamy tone when he said this. "I did say you're only an assistant"—*With a PhD, thank you very much*—"but she insisted. She wants you. I have no idea why. Do you?"

I sensed suspicion. If he was implying that I'd been dealing with the Signora behind his back, he was wrong. "No."

"I'm sure you're aware how much we need this."

Oh, I was. I'd seen the accounts. And Cassidy's extravagance was eating away not only at the gallery profits, but at the family's wealth as well. I knew that the Zilbersteins were sitting on a time bomb set to go off sooner rather than later.

"I'll go," I said, trying to convey that I was doing them a favor, and hiding how intensely I wanted this. I *coveted* this trip. If I closed this deal for Zil, maybe my past employment would be forgotten.

And my life would kick into gear again.

———

I awoke after two hours of agitated sleep—agitated *good*, as opposed to agitated *terrible* like I'd so often had recently. Isaac was in a rush to get to work, so I didn't have time to give him the news. I was so excited that I could make sense of things around me even before my first coffee. I had to tell Sofia! If she still wanted to hear my good news, after our argument, I thought dejectedly.

Between getting ready, stopping for a latte to go and arriving in the still-deserted office, I tried and tried to get in touch with my sister, but Sofia wasn't answering the phone. I knew her just as well as she knew me: I'd gone too far. Oh, I was so fed up with people telling me I was doing everything wrong! My job, my fiancé...

My *ex*-fiancé.

But look at me now—my first chance to climb back after I'd fallen so low. I would succeed and acquire the collection for Zil; Isaac would realize the mistake he was making and come back to me; Sofia would quit trying to be the eternal big sister and stop micromanaging me.

"Morning, did you book the flight?" Zil called out to me, making his way across the office in his hurried little steps. "I mean the flight to Italy! Not Cassidy's!" His face went from white to red to white again and, God, I loved having power over him for once.

"I'm about to," I said, refusing to stoop and play with him even a little. Even if I would have enjoyed that immensely.

"Thank God. That *Siniora*—"

"It's Signora."

"—is a hard nut to crack."

"Good for her," I said.

Zil looked at me for a long moment. The balance of power had shifted, and we were both aware of it.

"Yes. I suppose so," he said, then he almost *ran* to his desk and back to me. "Here's the catalog. It's a little shabby, but ignore that, trust me."

I slipped the folder in my bag, refrained from smiling a catlike smile and threw a glance toward the ceramic wood stove —handcrafted in Austria—that sat in the corner. Our uber-stylish Manhattan office had been designed to resemble a 1930s European hotel—it went beyond kitsch to a whole new level of edgy. The stove hid a working cooker where every morning I made coffee with a cafetière—no Starbucks for the Zilbersteins. But this morning, Zil made his way over to the cafetière.

"How do you take it?" he asked.

The sheer *glee*. "It's okay. I have a lot to do to organize the trip, so if you don't mind, I think I'll go."

"Mhmhmhmh. Of course."

He did look a little miserable and, power dynamics or not, I don't like seeing people miserable.

"Look. I know how to do this. I know my stuff. I speak the language. I'll charm the hard nut... the Signora, I mean. I'll bring home the deal. Don't worry." I almost touched his arm, but the look of horror and the shudder of his mustache stopped me. I took a step back.

"I have all faith in you," he said with a tragic smile that denied his words. I could read the question in his eyes: *Why the hell did the woman ask for you?*

A couple of subway rides later I was in front of my family home, a semi-detached house whose sage-green façade hadn't changed since the sixties when my parents had moved in. Both my grandparents' families had emigrated from Italy after the war. We lost our grandparents early in life, and then our parents.

Sofia wasn't taking my calls, and as much as my pride wanted to just leave without saying goodbye, or send a surly text from Italy, I couldn't just go and let things fester between us. I missed her already.

I knocked on the window and waved, sheepishly. I could see her in the living room, surrounded by brown boxes and craft materials. My sister had a small business making fabric flowers so lovely and perfect, they seemed real.

She raised her head and, though she didn't smile, I knew her enough to sense she was glad to see me. And, in fact, ten minutes later I'd joined her on the floor, helping her pack orders. She wouldn't change her mind about what she believed I should do, and I wouldn't apologize for defending my life choices, but as sisters we still stood side by side against the world.

"So... I'm going to Italy as soon as I can find a ticket. For work," I said. I was wrapping some beautiful silk anemones in tissue paper and I could barely contain my delight.

"You are? But that's wonderful!"

The genuine joy on her face touched me. I knew she always wanted the best for me.

"It's the first proper assignment I've got from Zil."

"What happened? What made him see the light?"

"Well, there's this manuscript collection we hope to acquire. Cassidy has some drama going on with her boyfriend..."

"The nice lady who has you collecting her dry cleaning?"

"That's the one. So, she has stuff going on, and Zil offered to go even though he has a phobia of flying, but the owner of the collection asked for me."

"Does she know you?"

"I don't think so. I mean, if she knew me from my previous job, she wouldn't ask for me, given Hex's reputation."

"What they did has nothing to do with you!" My fiery sister always got incensed whenever my former employers came up.

I couldn't even be bothered being angry anymore. "I know, but there you go."

"Is this place you're going to far from Mom's village?"

"Oh, yes, what was it called? Lodego? I don't know. Zil mentioned it's somewhere in northern Italy, so around that ballpark, but I need to check. It's sad we don't know much about it."

"I suspect there were some bad memories there, because our grandparents didn't talk about the Old Country at all. And Mom and Dad were careful not to instill any sense of homesickness in us. They wanted us to feel rooted here."

"And do you?" I asked.

My sister played with a golden ribbon, threading it around her finger. "Yeah. Completely. You don't?"

I said nothing. I'd felt rooted too, before Isaac left me. Now I was floating, and not in a good way.

Sofia, of course, read my face. "Oh, Francesca. If only you could see what I see."

I looked away. The moment was too raw, too intimate: I was afraid I would cry. "What do you see?"

"An amazing woman who deserves better. So much better."

Silly tears began to veil my eyes. Darn. I had to defuse the moment. "Hey. Want to see what I'm going to Italy for?" I said and got up to grab my bag.

"Absolutely!" Sofia had always taken an interest in my studies and work. She didn't share my love of academics, but she'd always been supportive of my endeavors, especially the artistic side of things.

I sat back down beside her among the silken flowers. This was the first time I'd seen the catalog. Zil and Cassidy hadn't bothered to even show me before. I opened the envelope and marveled when, instead of meeting the smooth, almost liquid surface of a typical gallery brochure, I was met with a rough, almost coarse surface.

I raised my eyebrows. Really?

"Well," Sofia said. "It's very... retro. It's just appearances, after all." She shrugged at my puzzled expression.

But in the art world, in New York like everywhere else, appearances were almost everything. Yes, substance mattered, but it had to be wrapped in achingly-on-trend paper with an equally voguish bow. If the first impression wasn't good enough, there wouldn't be a second one. Anything that represented our gallery, from brochures to catalogs to our social accounts, had to look perfect. But what I had in my hand was a set of photo-copies held together with staples. I didn't even know anyone still did that. Hadn't photocopiers gone the same way as faxes?

"Wow. This looks like something I could have put together in middle school." I thumbed through the papers—some were in color, even if the quality was still appalling—and the manu-scripts seemed stunning, from what I could gauge. Some of the pages had a little handwritten *Ippolita* thrown in the bottom corner. I could see why Zil would be desperate to acquire them —what I couldn't see was why the Signora had been so careless in presenting them. My fingertips were already black with ink.

I frowned. Fraud was part and parcel of art dealing, as hard to avoid as weeds in a garden. Could it be...?

No. Zil was experienced, savvy, and sly enough to see possible deceit everywhere. And he'd trusted this woman and her grainy photographs, and her weird request for me, and for me only. I doubted that Zil's judgment could have been clouded by Cassidy's drama. He wasn't my kind of person, but I trusted his vision. Also, if you wanted to scam someone, you would do it better, I concluded, wiping my fingers on my jeans.

"If it all turns out to be a damp squib you still will have gone to Italy. I'm so jealous!" Sofia said and gave me a mock thump on the shoulder.

I leaned away from her, laughing, the catalog—if you could call it that—in my hand. A piece of paper fluttered out and fell on my knees. It was an envelope, complete with stamp and words printed in capital letters. I followed them with my finger and murmured, "*Verificato per censura.*"

Sofia scooted closer. "What's that? What does that mean?"

"It's a letter. That means it was checked by *censura*, censorship. I'm pretty sure it was sent during the Second World War."

"Wow. Does this have something to do with the collection?"

"I have no idea. Let me see... It's in Italian. *To Agostina Mirabella, Mother Superior of the Sisters of the Immaculate Heart of Mary,*" I translated for Sofia, squinting a little as I read —the ink was faded and blurry in places, with bits of discoloration dotted here and there.

"Sounds grand," Sofia said. "Open the envelope!" She shifted herself to sit on her heels.

I did so, and found a heavier, creamier piece of paper— whoever wrote this had access to good stationery even in times of war. I read the letter aloud, translating as best I could as I went along.

February 1944
   Palazzo Masi
   Venezia

Esteemed Reverenda Madre Agostina,
   My name is Helèna Masi, and I owe my life to you. I'm sure you remember the little Hungarian girl you saved that night in Viliany, and brought back to Italy with you.

This sounded like the beginning of a novel!

Your kindness was matched by Conte and Contessa Masi's generosity, who, as you know, took me in. I'm now twenty, and I have lived with them all this time. Sadly, the dear Contessa passed away, and for grievous reasons it's impossible for me to stay here at Palazzo Masi. I'm alone and without a family or friends. I'm searching for a quiet, peaceful place where I can spend these uncertain times of war and unrest. I've been brought up simply, despite my adoptive family's standing in the world. I'm not afraid of hard work and I'm willing to be of help and support to whoever might need it. Contessa Masi believed it wiser for me not to receive a formal education, and only be tutored for a short time as a child, even if I was, and am, so fond of books and of writing. But even if I have little education, I'm quick to learn and I have plenty of energy! I hope the kindness you showed to me that night, maybe endangering your own life too, will once again shine upon me.

Respectfully, my kindest regards,

Helèna Masi

"A Hungarian child saved by a nun and adopted by an Italian Contessa? Is this *real*?" Sofia said.

"I don't know, but it's certainly exciting." I examined the page more closely. I wasn't formally trained to appraise pieces of recent history, but everything looked the part—the paper, the handwriting, the stamp, the words printed across it: *verified by censorship*.

"So, this Hungarian girl... Helèna... was hoping to work at Santa Caterina. Isn't that where you're going?"

I nodded. For a moment, I couldn't speak. A shiver of wind slithered in from the ajar window, and the air seemed to shift.

It was just a random letter, about a random person.

Maybe it wasn't even real.

And yet there was something about those words that seemed to seep into me, to fill me, like the sound of church bells when you're standing close to the belfry and the notes ring in your bones.

"Francesca?"

"Yes. Sorry, what did you say?"

Sofia laughed. "It's captured your imagination, hasn't it?"

"Yeah, you know me!" I thumbed through the catalog pages —I shook them—nothing. Was this all? A random letter, a piece of a bigger jigsaw I could never complete. *Helèna Masi*—a name that had floated into my life and floated out of it, and I would never know what happened to her. I was so curious. No, that wasn't the right word. The feeling that squeezed my heart right now was not mere curiosity—it was almost... yearning.

I nestled the letter in my bag and the catalog back in its folder. "I have to go," I said, as I kissed Sofia on the cheek and stood.

She stood up too, ribbons and silken bits falling off her knee, and hugged me tight. I was so glad we'd made peace before I left —though I knew she still didn't understand my choices, and never would. Not until I showed her that my singlemindedness would be rewarded.

"Take this, okay? For luck," she said, and handed me a flower she hadn't yet secured on a stem. It was a rose, made of iridescent silk, cream and pink and yellow, changing with the light.

"I'll keep it with me."

CHAPTER 4

LODEGO, ITALY

I watched the landscape run past me from the car window as we drove alongside the lake. I was enchanted. This was a place of intense beauty, of saturated colors—the waters were bright blue green, the sky azure and the hills around us were covered in that sweet, gentle green of early summer, tiptoeing out of spring...

"First time in Italy?" the driver, who had introduced himself as Claudio, asked in English. He was an older man with a baritone voice and white hair, attired smartly in a dress shirt and blazer.

The car was lush, with buttery leather seats, and Claudio was dressed in Italian couture. I could almost smell the opulence—no, I could *actually* smell it: leather, freshly pressed cotton, cologne... But then why the horrendous catalog? Why no money invested in taking proper pictures and printing them? Had Zil's famous nose failed him?

I shook myself and focused on answering the question. My mind was darting here and there, overstimulated by all the threads I was trying to follow. Once again Helèna's letter came into my thoughts—yes: in my mind, the girl from the letter and I were on first-name terms. I was dying to know more about her, and I hoped with all my heart that there *would* be more to discover. What if it was just a random vintage letter from somewhere, its protagonists forever lost?

"We're almost there. I hope you're hungry, because Lavinia loves to cook and when we have guests she goes into overdrive," Claudio said in English.

This woman was becoming more and more *fascinating*, as Zil had described her, and I was growing even more curious about her.

"*Meraviglioso, grazie*," I replied in Italian, though the traveling and the chaos of thoughts in my mind had pretty much closed my stomach.

"You speak Italian?"

"I do, though I suspect my accent is woeful!"

"Not at all," he replied kindly, as he slowed the car down through village roads.

"Are we there?" I looked around me. A row of lovely villas decorated the shoreline like a necklace, and the lake waters were almost close enough to touch, beyond the low stone embankment.

"Not yet," Claudio replied; however, he stopped the car and opened my door.

I stepped out into the pale yellow sunshine, and the scent of still waters warmed by the sun encompassed me. People dressed in light clothes strolled along the promenade and sat in restaurants and ice cream bars, and brightly painted boats bobbed on the lake. It was a small but bustling village, as lovely as a seaside resort painted on a cookie tin.

I looked around me, and a sign appeared in my line of vision, black letters on white: Lodego. *Lodego?*

My parents' village! I brought my hand to my mouth in surprise.

"*Sta bene, Signorina Francesca?*" Claudio said, a light hand on my arm.

"*Si, sì. Tutto bene.*"

What were the chances? My first trip abroad was taking me not far from my mom's village. How serendipitous. I texted Sofia:

Do you believe in coincidences? Because I'm in Lodego!

I saw that there were a few messages from the Zilbersteins, but I ignored them. I just wanted to be in the here and now, in this beautiful place that my mother's family had called home and that, by some strange coincidence, life had taken me back to.

But I couldn't help noticing that there were no calls or texts from Isaac... I swallowed the little pang of disappointment.

"Are you sure you're well, Francesca? Would you like a coffee before we keep going?"

I did feel a little lightheaded. "Do we have far to go?"

"Half an hour at the most. And our lift is here already," he said, pointing to the gleaming waters. A bright red boat, small but with exquisite, simple lines, was making its slow way toward the pier. An old man wearing a cap and a sweater, despite the sunshine, was rowing, and beside him was a small, slight woman dressed in black, her silver hair tied back—I couldn't see her properly because of the glare from the sun. Was it Signora Lavinia?

The motorboat stopped beside the pier with a maneuver so gentle that it didn't cause any waves to rise. Claudio took my luggage from the boot of the car, and we made our way down while the silver-haired woman reached us.

"Francesca, it is such a pleasure to have you here. Thank you for accepting my invitation," the woman said, as if our meeting was entirely personal, and not professional. "My name is Lavinia."

She was tiny, her head coming up to my shoulder; she

offered her hand, which was unexpectedly rough, and then kissed me on both cheeks. She smelled of roses, ever so faintly—not a chemical fragrance, but the soft scent of the petals themselves. Though she looked like a fairy, her dark eyes exuded a calm strength and self-possession. They had a depth to them, a look of compassion and patience that seemed ageless. Her calm demeanor was contagious. I took a breath and exhaled, and it felt as if my whirling thoughts had suddenly, unexpectedly, found an anchor. I asked myself how old she was—she wasn't a young woman, but her slender figure and lively eyes belied her age.

"Nice to meet you," I said.

"This is Giovanni, our groundskeeper." She gestured toward the man with the oars, and I greeted him. "How was your journey?"

"Smooth. I've had a bit of a shock, though..."

"Oh, no! Is it anything we can help with?" Her eyes went from me to Claudio, and back.

"No, no, it's a good thing!" I put my hands up. "I just realized that my mom's family emigrated to the US from here. From Lodego." I turned around, toward the houses on the lakeshore and beyond, the belfry of the church jutting into the sky, the green hills standing tall against a shining sky.

Lavinia smiled. "You must be curious to visit it, then," she said calmly, as if that wasn't a crazy coincidence. An unspoken message passed between her and Claudio as they looked at each other.

I then noticed that, along with Lavinia's stylish knee-length black dress, her immaculate hair and her cheeks rosy with blush, she wore muddy boots that looked enormous on her slender legs.

"I was just gardening, *cara*. Sorry if I look a sight," she said, following my gaze. "Let us take you to your accommodation to refresh, and then you can visit Lodego in a few days?"

"Sure, but... take me where?"

Lavinia turned toward the waters and pointed to the horizon, where a little mound of an island seemed to float. The tops of the trees and the blurry outline of stone buildings were visible in the distance, rising from the blue. "There," she said. "The convent of Santa Caterina."

Can a person explode with excitement? Because I thought I was about to. A sense of determination rose inside me. Never mind the fragrances, the beauty, Lavinia's charisma: I was here for a reason, a very real, practical reason. That little island in the distance hid the treasure that could restore my career, my life.

I would fight for it with everything I had.

———

The lake was wide and deep, and the sweet blue waters turned dark as we crossed it. The sky was now veiled; I could see a gathering of gray clouds over the hills. But for now, the sun was still shining on me as I sat beside Lavinia. After a while my excitement gave place to ease: the rhythm of the boat was cradling me, and the silence all around, only broken by the noise of the oars breaking the water, was almost lulling me to sleep. I leaned back with a sigh, as the island of Santa Caterina inched closer and closer.

"You must be jet lagged, my dear," said my host.

"I am! But I can't wait to see the collection. There will be plenty of time to sleep later."

"It takes a little while to reach Santa Caterina," Lavinia said. "We do have a motorboat, but we hardly ever use it, really. It's noisy and it bothers the wildlife. I hope you don't mind the slower pace."

"Not at all. It's so beautiful! So, if I can ask, how did you come to own the manuscripts? Especially the work by Ippolita Von Oswen."

"I don't really own them, *cara*. They belong to Santa Caterina. I'm just the caretaker."

Right. But you're about to sell them?

I was about to open my mouth to ask if she knew anything about the letter I'd found, about Helèna, but she changed the subject, her tone so smooth and fluid that it seemed a natural transition.

"I'm looking forward to showing you our garden."

"I'm looking forward to seeing it," I said, deciding to let go of my curiosity for a little while. It was clear Lavinia didn't want to talk business, not just yet. How could we, when the light was so soft and the boat was rocking us back and forth, and the shore was further and further away, as if we were leaving this world and shifting to another. "Why did you ask for me?"

"I liked the sound of your name," Lavinia replied. Her voice seemed to come from far away.

And then Santa Caterina was before us as we glided closer to the gentle, pebbled slope that was its gate. Claudio helped Lavinia and me off the boat, and there I was! The sleepiness that had come over me during the crossing left me, as if it had been an enchantment, and we were crossing into Avalon. Santa Caterina was truly a little floating pebble—the rectangular white building of the convent, surrounded by a crown of smaller stone dwellings, swallowed most of it. A stone belfry jutted out from behind the convent, surrounded by clouds that were the color of pewter. The weather had turned.

The scent of roses, made stronger by the impending rain, embraced me—and another one, sweet and light, which reminded me of honey. Gossamer white seeds blew around us, dancing with the breeze. The gray-blue sky, the whirling seeds and the convent's shifting image reflected in the water were a combination of colors and hues I'd never seen before. The scented air and the breeze on my skin were like caresses, and the simple joy of satisfied senses filled me whole. I closed my eyes for a moment to take a breath of misty air, and to steady myself on land; suddenly, I felt something tickling my nose. A small, fluffy seed had landed on my face—I held it in my open palm and watched it blow away...

"Welcome," Lavinia said simply.

I was sure it was my imagination, but it seemed to me that her greeting echoed throughout the island, a hundred versions of *welcome* coming to me from the reeds, the stones, the trees, from the women who lived here throughout the centuries. Their voices reverberated all around me, inside me. And then the spell was over, and Lavinia's words were clear above the lapping waves on the shore.

"I'll show you to your room first, so you can refresh. Maybe you can get some rest, some sleep?"

"Thank you, but I'm not that tired. I'm more than ready to see the collection."

"I'll show you around the convent, then. Are you hungry?"

Was that a yes, she'll show me the collection? Or just the convent? I gazed at her sideways. Her expression revealed nothing. She would have made an amazing poker player, I decided.

A young girl in an apron appeared out of nowhere. She introduced herself as Manuela, the groundskeeper's daughter.

"Is it only the four of you living here?" I asked Lavinia.

"Yes. We only stay in the spring and summer, though. We organize small retreats for artists, writers, scholars. Oh, and cookery courses, taught by me. But on a very small scale. We don't want the convent to become a mass tourism destination. Sometimes, precious things should stay hidden."

A smiling Manuela followed us inside the building; our steps resounded on the stone floors and echoed on the high ceilings and whitewashed walls. I'd never been somewhere so ancient before. Throughout my studies I'd longed for the opportunity to go to Europe, but I could never afford it; then, when I could have paid for the journey, Isaac preferred staying in the US. He didn't like foreign places much.

We stepped through a corridor with stone stairs on both sides, and then out into the inner courtyard, enclosed by a cloister. I gasped when I saw the garden that flourished in the center of the cloister, swollen with rose bushes and aromatic plants. Pink, orange, yellow, white, red and all hues in between, the roses grew in flowerbeds at all four sides and climbed the stone walls, to make what looked like a rose-covered room with the sky for a ceiling.

"Sleeping Beauty," I said in a low voice.

"Pardon?" Lavinia asked.

"Oh, sorry. Only, the story of Sleeping Beauty came back to me. You know, the fairy tale... a princess asleep, surrounded by roses."

"I'm glad the garden made you think of a fairy tale! I love taking care of it." So that explained her rough hands, I thought. "But I can't really take the credit for its beauty. The rose bushes have been here forever. They're hardy plants, they prosper in almost all weathers and thrive even when they've been moved a few times. Beauty is not always fragile, I suppose."

I strolled among the roses, every once in a while touching a silky petal and bending to smell their sweet fragrance. The way the space was enclosed by the cloister gave it a magical, mystical air, like a secret garden. I thought of the silken rose Sofia had given me.

"I'll show you your room," Lavinia offered, and I followed her along the colonnade until we came to the other side. "Here were the nuns' cells," she explained. "Our visitors usually stay here, and I thought it would be interesting for you. However, if you're not comfortable you can always stay in the guest room in our quarters."

The cells sat one beside the other along a bare corridor with

a window at each end. Manuela waved me inside the first one.
The room was tiny, only big enough for a bed, a wardrobe and a
tiny desk. There was a window that sat so low the grass almost
reached it. It was cozy and intimate and perfect in its simplicity.

"This is perfect, thank you."

"Are you sure? The rooms in our quarters are more...
homey, but this is far more atmospheric," Lavinia said.

"I'm sure," I said, and stepped inside. I noticed the deep
yellow candles on the desk and the box of matches.

"We have blackouts once in a while," Lavinia explained.
"The candles and matches are a must around here." She opened
a door beside the wardrobe. "We had little ensuite bathrooms
built for some of the cells," she added. The shower was so small
I'd almost have to slide in sideways.

"Small but perfectly formed," I said.

Lavinia smiled. "Here's something I prepared for you," she
said, and pointed to a bottle with a homemade label and a jar of
bon-bons in pastel colors. "Muscat wine and my homemade
sweets. These are lemon, strawberry, aniseed and honey, all
made with ingredients from the grounds. And in the bathroom
you'll also find some products I made myself."

"Oh, this is too much!" I spoke. I'd thought I was here to
woo her, not the opposite. I'd been expecting a hotel room somewhere, not that she'd go to so much trouble to put me up. "Is
there anything you can't do?"

"I can't drive," she said seriously. "And I refuse to learn to
use technology of all kinds."

"Oh," I said, taken aback by having received an answer to a
rhetorical question. Though the aversion to technology might
explain the pitiful brochure...

"We'll leave you to relax. I'll be around; come and look for
me when you're ready," Lavinia said.

"Thank you. Oh, Signora?"

"Please, call me Lavinia."

"Lavinia, when will the other bidders arrive?"

"There's only one other, *cara*. He's a little late, but I hope he'll arrive by the time it gets dark. I'm sure you'll like him."

I nodded. *There's no need for me to like him; all I have to do is get him out of the way.*

"I'll leave you to refresh, then," Lavinia said, and she and Manuela vanished. I longed to have a shower in my fairy-sized bathroom, then have a drink and a long sleep, but I was too curious about my surroundings and too impatient to see the collection. I checked my phone—nothing from Isaac, I saw, and my heart sank once more. He was busy, that was it. More messages from Zil and Cassidy, and a missed call from Zil. I couldn't face speaking to them now, in this room—I didn't want Zil's *mmmmhhhmm* or Cassidy's strident tones to spoil my peace. I had nothing to report, anyway. I texted him quickly.

The signal is terrible here.

I lied.

Everything going smoothly, 1 other bidder arriving tonight, still haven't seen collection. I'll be in touch.

I got undressed quickly and slipped into the tiny shower—the icy water made me jump out of my skin at first, but slowly it warmed up and I closed my eyes under the stream. I made generous use of the potions and concoctions Lavinia had left me: a soap that smelled of cream and roses, and thick, silky shampoo that resembled pure honey. She certainly knew how to find—and create—pleasure in little things. The tiny shower cabin became laden with warmth and scents, and only pure willpower convinced me it was time to turn off the water and go achieve what I'd come here for.

I draped myself in a soft towel and stepped out of the

shower, making a beeline for my suitcase. It was then that I stopped in my tracks. I don't know what alarmed me: maybe a draft around my shoulders, maybe the uncanny silence that seemed to have swallowed the place and encompassed it into a bubble. At that moment, as I stood, chilled, in the middle of the room, the little window grew dark and then light again, as if a shadow had passed in front of it.

I swallowed.

It was then that I noticed my door was ajar. I tiptoed across the room and tried to glance outside—a tall, dark figure almost fell on me—I stepped backward in fear, but my wet feet slipped on the stones, and the ceiling and floor almost swapped places in one quick, painful moment.

CHAPTER 5

THE ISLAND OF SANTA CATERINA

"Ouch!"

Fear sucked the breath out of me for a moment. I don't know how I managed to stay on my feet while still holding the towel around my chest. On the ground in front of me, crumpled in a heap, was a man.

"My suit!" were the first words he said.

"I'm so sorry! I thought you were..." A ghost? "...an intruder!" I finished the sentence and offered my hand, though I was embarrassed by my half-nakedness, but he refused.

"I was about to knock!"

"How would I know?" I crossed my arms as much as I could, without the towel falling around my feet. He lifted himself up, and suddenly he towered over me. "Are you hurt?" I asked.

"Totally fine. I'm not hurt at all." The grimace on his face said otherwise—the thump of his fall on the stone had been pretty loud. "But my suit is," he said, and held his elbow. White cotton with tiny stripes emerged from the rip. "This is... *was*... Armani. And it's destroyed."

I was genuinely sorry. "Can I replace it?" I said, thinking

that an Armani suit was going to clean out my miserable bank account.

"Nah, it's for the best," he said, and took off the ruined jacket. "I hate these things, anyway. I'm supposed to wear them for work. You're Francesca Lombardo, aren't you?"

"And you are?"

"Thiago Palladini," he replied, like that would mean something to me.

"Okay. And how does that relate to... oh. You're here for the collection?"

"Why else would I be on this rock? For its crazy nightlife?"

He was trying to be sour, but I couldn't help laughing. His lips curled up a little too, and I noticed they were nice lips indeed. The kind of lips you see in Dolce & Gabbana ads. In the dim light, his hair was dark copper and his eyes two pools of black... but hey, Dolce & Gabbana or not, this guy stood between me and the collection.

"Sorry, I should have known who you were," I mocked him with fake reverence.

Manuela had appeared at the end of the corridor, and she was looking at me quizzically, half-naked and wet as I was.

"Er... dinner will be served soon," she said in a small voice, her cheeks on fire. "Signora Lavinia says to bring the catalog with you. With all you found inside," she added carefully, punctuating those last words with small nods of her head.

With all I'd found inside... the letter, of course! So it *wasn't* a coincidence that I'd found it in my catalog. It was meant to be there... surely, it had to be.

"I won't be a minute," I said, trying to look dignified while wearing just a towel, with dripping hair and a little puddle of water around my feet. I stepped back into my room and almost slammed the door in that jerk's face, when I noticed there was something on my bed: the silken rose Sofia had made for me had mysteriously made its way from my bag to the top of my covers.

My heart skipped a beat, I turned around quickly, and then threw a glance in the shower room—there was nobody there. The window was closed. The rose must have fallen out of my bag when I was undressing.

There was no other explanation.

———

Twilight was taking possession of sky and land, and the landscape was melting into purples, lilacs and blues. Strings of fairy lights adorned a terrace off Lavinia's quarters, which were almost on the water. A chilly breeze blew.

"Please sit down. The Signora will be here in a moment," Manuela said and left us.

The Thiago guy and I were sitting across from each other. He sat confidently, his long legs stretched under the table and his hands on his lap. His ruined blazer had been swapped for a blue round-neck sweater. He'd gone from ultra-formal to a bit too sportwear for the occasion, but hey, he looked good, I had to admit. His burned copper and gold hair was curly, eyes deep-set, and the sullen expression on his face suited him. He'd found his match, he could be sure of that. I had no intention to make friendly conversation: this was not play, this was work... but I was curious about something.

"Where are you based?" I asked guardedly.

"In Florence," he replied as if I should have known that. Of course, who doesn't know where the Palladini art dealers come from? I rolled my eyes. Still... Florence. Images of narrow stone lanes, gold leaf paintings, the marbled Duomo and the green, many-bridged River Arno came to me. One day I would visit, I promised myself.

After that, neither of us spoke. We sat in awkward silence, occasionally glaring at each other.

After what felt like an hour, but must have been not more

than a minute or two, Lavinia, Claudio and Manuela appeared with trays of delicacies. I was starving, and everything looked delicious, but a part of me felt a pang of frustration, knowing that there was another delay before I could finally see the collection. Why did she keep putting it off?

I reluctantly admired Thiago's cool as he made small talk over spring greens risotto, veal cutlets with lemon and capers, and finally some tiny, exquisite macarons in all the colors of the rainbow, served with a fragrant espresso that gave me a new lease of life. It was clear that the stereotype of Italians putting food over business, or before most things, was true. They had it the right way, I thought, as my tastebuds celebrated.

"Are you ready?" Lavinia said over coffee. She wore an old-fashioned woolen shawl around her shoulders, and the light of the candles was reflected in her face—she looked timeless, ageless.

"To see the collection?" I said, before Thiago could speak.

Oh, I was ready. What should I do here? Show my enthusiasm? Keep cool? What would Zil do? I hated having to admit to myself that I was almost clueless when it came to this kind of business. Zil was a social player; Cassidy was ruthless. I was more used to dealing with objects than with people, I wore my feelings on my sleeves and, apart from offering more money, I had no idea how to sway the Signora to sell to us...

"Not exactly," Lavinia replied. "I meant, are you ready to talk about... the next steps? You see, the collection as such can't be seen at this moment."

My jaw fell open. I was too astonished to be bothered by the fact that I must have looked like a fish. Oh, no. Zil's nose had failed him. This was some sort of convoluted fraud.

Lavinia gazed from me to Thiago, and back. She always seemed a little amused, as if a smile was about to curve her lips, but now she truly looked like the cat who got the cream. And when she smiled, it was enigmatic, somewhere between teasing, knowing and sweet. The definition of a Mona Lisa smile.

"I'm not buying blind," Thiago said abruptly. His pale face betrayed fear. Maybe I wasn't the only one who needed this purchase so desperately.

The Signora gazed at him. *Through* him. "The collection, with Ippolita's much-coveted manuscripts, is somewhere on this island. And you will not be *buying blind*."

I found my voice. "Why can't we see the manuscripts?" I asked as calmly as I could.

Lavinia looked from me to Thiago, and then let her gaze wander on the silent waters. Everything around us spoke of imminent rain: the moisture in the air and the heavy clouds above us, almost black against the twilight, the petrichor rising from land to sky.

"Many years ago, at a time where the world was on fire, Santa Caterina and its library were almost torn down. A young girl saved them both. She hid the manuscripts where they could not be stolen nor destroyed... she protected them and paid a steep price for it."

My chest began rising and falling fast. I knew who she was talking about. I was *sure*. I leaned down to take the catalog out of my bag—I'd slipped Heléna's letter in its pages. Now I laid it on the table and met Lavinia's eyes above it.

"I believe you found something in your catalog too," she said to Thiago.

"Yes. An old letter like that one, something of no importance," Thiago said, and he thumbed the pages of his catalog to extract an envelope much like mine.

It was strange, to hear someone working for an auction house assuming that something old would be something of no importance—the tone, I thought, was somehow discordant with the circumstances.

"Would you be so kind as to read yours, Francesca?" Lavinia asked me.

I did, and when I finished, Lavinia was still wearing her Mona Lisa smile, while Thiago's face was hard, almost antagonistic.

"Signor Palladini, will you read yours?"

He unsheathed the letter from its envelope and proceeded to read in a mechanical voice, reluctantly, as if he were being put through his paces against his will and better judgment.

February 1944

Madre Agostina Mirabella

General Mother Superior of the Sisters of the Immaculate Heart of Mary

"It's the reply! The reply to my letter!" I burst out, and immediately felt the blood rising to my cheeks. So much for keeping my cool. "Sorry. Please continue."

Mia cara Helèna,

Of course I remember you! I remember my time in Hungary very well, and the tragedy that befell your village. Which was not a tragedy at all, but an instance of the evil ingrained in our fallen humanity. Not a day has gone by that I haven't grieved our failure to rescue your parents and your sister. Oh, how you cried and how you asked after them! I shall always remember the little girl you were, defenseless, and grieving...

However, it was not this humble servant of God who saved your life, but someone else, a saintly soul. Maybe one day I'll tell you the whole story.

My dear, you are a girl no more now, but a young woman,

and my heart soars in knowing you were brought up in the fear and love of God by devoted people. In these dark times, when no place on this earth seems to be spared by war, we must be mirrors to our Lord's love, and love each other even more. Please, remember that when everywhere is darkness, the light is always within you.

Speaking of practicalities, and thinking of the quiet place you are looking for, I made some enquiries and found a sympathetic (and grateful) ear in Madre Gloria, the Mother Superior of Santa Caterina, on the island of the same name. I promise you that this place is a balm for the soul, a haven of beauty and tranquility, and sheltered from this burning world. But you must know that living in the convent of Santa Caterina will be demanding! There are many tasks and duties imposed upon the sisters, who are mostly elderly. Madre Gloria is in quite desperate need of a pair of young arms to help with the daily upkeep.

If your heart feels called to this arrangement, I would be happy to write to Madre Gloria, who's eagerly awaiting news, and tell her to expect you as soon as you can travel.

I nearly forgot: you said you are fond of books. Well, not many know that the convent of Santa Caterina hosts a library rich in both modern and ancient manuscripts. I am inclined to say better this way, that few should know this, in these dangerous days. Maybe all that is precious should stay hidden, right now.

Oh... This echoed what Lavinia had said to me... that sometimes precious things should remain hidden.

My little Helèna, little no more: let me finish this letter with a word of warning. You were baptized in the true faith, but I imagine you don't wish to forget the faith of your ancestors,

2048 DANIELA SACERDOTI

*and your roots. However, keep those hidden too, in any way
you can. Please write as soon as you make your decision.*

Yours in Christ,

Madre Agostina

"Well, there you go," Thiago concluded.

"Helèna concealed those books you seek, and the knowledge of their location passed on to me. I want you to find them," said Signora Lavinia.

"What?" Thiago exclaimed.

"You mean, they're still *hidden*?" I asked. How was I going to explain this to Zil and Cassidy?

"Yes. I know where they are, of course. And we have some photographs..."

"Oh. That's why the catalog is... interesting..." I stumbled to finish the sentence.

And there it was again, Lavinia's enigmatic smile.

"A treasure hunt?" Thiago ran his hands through his hair, leaving the strands tousled. "Like being back in Scouts," he said, so wearily that Lavinia laughed.

"Pretty much."

I couldn't laugh, not even smile. The stakes were too high, and Helèna was calling to me.

"I'm not sure I like this. I thought this would be a straightforward business transaction. The highest bidder and all that. I didn't think we'd be playing a game..." Thiago grumbled.

"It's not a game," Lavinia said in her gentle voice, but the steel underneath was unmistakable.

At that moment, a roll of not-so-distant thunder filled the air, and a blade of light cut through the sky above the lake. Thiago and I jumped and cast our eyes up. Neither Lavinia nor Claudio rushed to get inside, or even moved. Manuela appeared on the doorstep, looking at us while clutching a tray to her chest. She must have been told not to interrupt and was waiting for her sign to come and clean up before the heavens opened. Even the rain seemed to be waiting for us to finish.

"But all treasure hunts have a map, don't they? And clues," I said.

Lavinia nodded and placed a leather folder on the table. She gave it to me in a solemn gesture. A sudden gust of wind made the trees rustle and the water ripple in infinite little waves, and brought the scent of roses with it, and that other honey-like fragrance I was still to identify. I untied the leather laces of the folder: inside was a book with a black cover, the spine lined with light blue fabric. The first page had a name engraved in the handwriting that was now familiar to me: *Helèna*.

"Helèna's diary!" I gasped, fanning the pages.

"And our... treasure map?" Thiago was still unimpressed.

"All you have to do is read it," Lavinia said and rose, followed by Claudio; it looked like we were being dismissed.

Thiago's face was thunderous, much like the weather. I had too many questions to be able to formulate even one, and I sat there with my mouth half-open. Manuela ran over with her tray, and the three of them hurried to carry everything inside. I was still sitting there, stunned, when a drop of rain fell on my neck and down my back, making me shiver.

"Francesca, Thiago!" Lavinia called to us. "You don't want the diary to get wet!"

The drizzle had turned into rain, and we ran inside. It seemed that Thiago and I had been left alone—alone, with Helèna.

He shrugged. "My room or yours?" His irritated air was beginning to seriously get on my nerves. He was acting like a spoiled child.

I glared at him. "Yours." I wasn't about to have a stranger in *my* room.

"Hey. You're shivering," he said. "Why don't you go wrap up, I'll make us a cup of coffee and we can start."

Oh. Unexpected kindness. "Thanks," I said tartly. "That's nice of you. I'll keep the diary."

"You don't look first, though. Deal?"

"Deal."

Twenty minutes later we were in his room—his cell, should I say, though it sounds a little weird—sitting cross-legged on the floor, the diary between us. I'd pulled on a pair of leggings and a black sweater, while he'd changed into jeans and a round-neck sweater: an ensemble that made him look younger and much less stuffy. In fact, his features were delicate, in contrast with his muscular build—*he seems so young*, I thought. I'd warmed up, but I was still chilly—another shiver traveled through me.

Thiago pulled the blanket off his bed and handed it to me. "Hot coffee just behind you," he said. With relief, I wrapped my hands around the steaming mug. "And Lavinia left sweets." He shrugged, as if to say, *why on earth did she feel the need to do that?*

"Thanks."

"We're not supposed to collaborate on this, I guess. There can only be one winner," he mused, sitting on the floor beside me. "I *must* bring that collection home."

"Hey. You don't need to justify yourself. I understand. Same here."

His eyes met mine, his eyebrows raised. Who was going to pick up the book first? He raised his chin a little, a gesture to say, *you start.* I'd been side-tracked by niceties such as coffee and a blanket and his concern over me being cold, but he was, actually, odious—just like I'd thought.

I placed the mug down with a little thud, took the book and opened it.

Hello again, Helèna. Tell me your story...

CHAPTER 6

THE ISLAND OF SANTA CATERINA

March 1944

Convent of Santa Caterina

My dearest Hanna!

Here I am! I'm sitting on a bench in front of this beautiful lake; everything I own in this world is in the valise at my feet. I'm waiting for the boatman to arrive, so he can row me over to the island. If you can call that mound over there an island... It's raining and I'm holding an umbrella and balancing this paper on my knees, and it might end up a little wet, but I'll persevere because I have so much to tell you!

I would be happy to let loose the ropes of one of these boats, and row to the convent myself: I'm certainly used to water, after many years in Venice. But it wouldn't be appropriate so I shall sit here like the good girl I am and wait. I'm trying to catch a glimpse of the convent that is to be my home—but the lake is covered in mist, and all I can see is the top of the trees in the distance, and the ghost of a belfry.

I can't believe I'm finally here. Away from Palazzo Masi

and its claustrophobia, and alone! Alone, without the burden of the Masi family to weigh me down, without having to look after the Contessa day and night and see the Conte drink and gamble away everything he owns.

Away from Jacopo...

He, too, placed a burden on me that I can't carry.

It seems to me that this is the first time since I was adopted that I have space to think and write freely like I've always wanted to. And maybe to remember more than I've allowed myself to until now, to fill in the gaps in my childhood recollections.

I wish you could see all this now. The sky is overcast, and yet it feels wide, immense, open; and the drizzle that's falling on me is washing the last few months away and leaving me ready to start anew.

If I think back to the time of the Contessa's illness, days passed so slow, and yet so quickly. Slow because the work to be done was endless. The Contessa only wanted me to look after her and her agony seemed infinite. Fast because she got worse and worse not every day, but every hour, in seemingly endless falling. In her delirium, she gripped my hand and talked about her past, about her beloved husband—whom, of course, does not deserve her love. It was heartbreaking to hear her reliving the happy moments she'd had with him when their love was blooming; and now he never even came to her room. The rare times he was home, he stood at her bedroom doorstep, and then escaped—yes, he escaped her suffering, because he's a coward.

How unfair, how sad that Jacopo couldn't be there with his mother! The Contessa complained that he'd abandoned her, but it wasn't true; it was the war that took him away, like it's taken most men and boys. Jacopo called when he could, but his training was hard and busy, and he seldom had access to a telephone. I suspect his family's name had everything to do with the fact that he could access one at all, because common soldiers don't get the privilege, I was told. To think the Contessa would have been proud to see him in his officer's uniform... but she never did.

Not long before the end, the Contessa surprised me. She grabbed my hand and held on hard, harder than her feeble strength should have allowed her.

"Forgive me," she said. Consumption had turned her voice into a raspy whisper. "Because I've been cruel to you."

At that moment, I recalled the dreadful moment when she found the letters I'd written to you, bundled them up and burned them in the kitchen stove. She made me pray for salvation and forgiveness, for having spoken to the dead. I'd performed necromancy, she told me.

I didn't know the meaning of the word, so I asked my tutoress: she said necromancy is the practice of communicating with the deceased. Nonsense, of course, because you're not dead. Also, our father told me never to meddle with that shibboleth, so I wouldn't have done it anyway: but I couldn't explain this to the Contessa.

I remembered when she made me return all my schoolbooks to my tutoress, forbade me from studying any more or even keeping a diary, and made me pray for my own salvation: apparently, I'd filled my mind with diabolical knowledge. Thirst for knowledge is the primal reason for the Fall, after all.

From that moment, I'd smuggled books into the palazzo as if I were drinking secretly or stealing what little silver the Conte hadn't pawned off yet.

Now, she was asking me for forgiveness, holding onto my hand with clammy, cold fingers, like a drowning woman. I would have liked to say, "Please don't trouble yourself with that now, it's all forgotten. You have not been cruel, you believed you had to do this to save me from damnation!" But I couldn't say that, because I would have lied. I had not forgotten.

"Please, please, absolve me," she pleaded with me again, and I could see that this was not delirium: she was speaking from the heart, her broken heart. She was truly contrite.

"I can't absolve you, but I can forgive you. Of course I forgive you," I said.

Have I really forgiven the Contessa?

Have I forgiven the people who set our village on fire?

The Contessa had ordered me to do so, because a soul burdened with anger cannot go to heaven. But anger hadn't left me—it was still there, deep inside me, smoldering like embers.

"I wish I had time to atone," the Contessa whispered, and closed her eyes with a small, labored exhale. Finally, she let herself go, her hand no longer holding mine, her head deeper into the pillow. I knew then that she had unburdened herself, that the end was not far. I was awake until the wee hours of the morning, but somehow, I dozed off just as the night was at its darkest, and when I awoke, the Contessa's heart had stopped beating. She went peacefully, thank God, after all the troubles she had in life, after all she suffered at the hands of her husband, and because of her vexed mind. With her death, the guilt and shame I was made to feel for no reason at all went as well.

I know you won't blame me when I say that together with sorrow, there was relief, for both the Contessa and me.

Not long later the Conte came home after one of his jaunts, reeking of alcohol as he always did. He must have seen the black drape hanging on our door, but not even then did he come into his wife's room, where we were praying the rosary for her soul. He went straight to his study. When Agnese walked past his door on her way to gather more candles, he asked her to send for me...

But I must stop writing now. I see a boat in the distance!

They're coming for me. Also, the paper is getting quite damp,
even under this umbrella! I shall write as soon as I can.

Yours, excitedly,

Helèna

Thiago and I looked at each other.

"The lake, the boat, this island..." I spoke. "She came the same way as us, she arrived in the same place. We're..."

"Retracing her steps," he finished my sentence. It was as if a spell of words had been cast over us, and Thiago wasn't immune to it. Maybe he wasn't as enthralled by the story as I was, but he'd lost that grumpy, almost resentful air. A mixture of daydreaming and concentration filled his eyes, and he was looking down at the floor, ready to listen intently.

I took another sip of my coffee and kept reading.

My dearest Hanna,

This will be a long letter: much has happened! Let these
letters become my first novel. I've always wanted to write, and
now that I'm out of Palazzo Masi, I finally can. The memoir of
an ordinary girl in extraordinary times, I suppose!

I'm in my cell, in my new home, the convent of Santa
Caterina. If peace was a place, this would be it. Silence
pervades every corner of the island, so small, it's like a hand-
kerchief floating on a pond. I can't wait to be able to explore it
all, but the sun has set now, and the sisters admonished me not
to go outside at night, because the shores are slippery and
treacherous, and sometimes, when the mist rises, you can't tell
water from land. It reminds me of Avalon, the mythical land
beyond the sea, that I read about in one of my smuggled books.

I smiled inwardly. I'd imagined the same thing when I arrived, crossing into Avalon...

The journey has been... eerie. Yes, that's the word to describe the atmosphere. We left the shore with a sound that was almost like a whisper. The boatman wasn't a mortal man anymore: he was Charon, the mythical figure that ferries the souls of the dead to the underworld, rowing not on water but on mist. I dropped my hand on the side of the boat, my fingers trailing the mist.

"E quindi, Signorina Masi," he said. "You're too young to be stuck in this God-forgotten place, with only nuns for company! Would you not rather be somewhere you can meet a nice man, and get married?"

I did not respond. I certainly couldn't tell him that I'd resisted marriage twice, once with a man I despise, once with a man I love, but as a brother, not a husband. And both broke my heart, for different reasons...

When I recount what happened after the Conte sent for me, my skin crawls. The memory hurts, but I need to have this on paper, to have it all out of me.

I'd barely stepped into his study when, without a word of grief for his lost wife, he said: "Marry me, Helèna," in that fervorous way he had sometimes, that conveyed not enthusiasm, but the agitation of his mind. This mood was usually followed by a morbid sadness, in an alternation that left him, and us, exhausted. But a marriage proposal, now? When I was in the middle of praying for his wife's soul? It took me a little time to even understand what he was saying: my mind could not accept the meaning of those words. It was too erratic, even for the Conte.

If it wasn't for the sadness I had inside, after seeing the poor Contessa fade away, I would have laughed in his face.

And yet, this was the man who'd let me live in his house for years. I had to at least try to be respectful.

"Signor Conte, I'm grateful for your generosity. For having taken me in. But..."

"You have repaid my generosity a thousand times by looking after my wife." *He threw a glance to the framed photograph on his desk, and my gaze followed his: a young Contessa smiles in sepia, a tilt in her chin to show her face under a wide-brimmed hat; the Conte is beside her, his arm around her waist. He's gazing at her like he never wants to look away.*

"She would have been lost without you. She's been quite insane for many years."

The Contessa was left alone to manage Palazzo Masi while her husband drank and gambled, until she couldn't even afford to heat the place, to buy enough food. The palazzo crumbled around us, its Venetian dampness deadly for the Contessa's damaged lungs. But according to her husband, she was insane. I swallowed back my anger. Oh, Hanna. There's a volcano inside me, a well of fury that sooner or later will erupt... but not then.

"I have repaid you, yes. All I want now is..."

"What? What is it that you want, my angel?"

I froze. His words were sweet, his tone subtly menacing.

"You have no family, you have no home," *he continued.* "All you can hope for is a position as a maid, or a factory worker." *He said those words as if tasting something foul, even if being a maid or a factory worker would do me just fine: it would be a privilege, earning money for my food, for my clothes, instead of being powerless and at the mercy of the Conte throwing a few liras my way.*

But the part about having no family, no home—that gnawed at my heart. Because he was right. I was—I am—thoroughly alone. You're far away, although I know for sure we'll meet again; and Jacopo...

But one story at a time.

"I can offer you a home. A position," he said haughtily, as if he hadn't squandered away his station in society. "A family." He opened his hands and tilted his head. The portrait of sincerity, of well meaning.

"You and I can't be a family, not father and daughter like we were supposed to be, let alone husband and wife!" I was nauseated at the thought. "As for the position, you have none except your name, which is now tainted too. It's just a matter of time until you lose the palazzo as well. Not that any wealth would have convinced me to marry you! You lost everything that belonged to your wife's family, and this killed her. How can you ask me to marry you now? Signor Conte. You have no shame."

I was trembling, Hanna. For my sake, for the sake of that poor woman lying dead not far from where we stood, for Jacopo, who was away with the army, and who knew if he could even give his mother her last goodbye. Jacopo, who'd seen his family name thrown in the mud, his mother consumed by heartache, and his whole inheritance lost.

"You're right, Helèna! I have no shame. I have no soul. But you... you're an angel. You have... innocence. You can save me."

"I lost my innocence when my parents were burned alive," I whispered in a tone I had never used before, so full of rage that the Conte flinched. My knuckles were white as I held onto the desk in front of me. I crossed my arms in front of my heaving chest and tucked a strand of hair behind my ear—I was unkempt, and the Contessa would have not liked that. "I must go. There are arrangements to be made."

The Conte's mouth opened in a silent *oh*, and he straightened himself. Now that he'd seen the person I really was, and not the blonde, blue-eyed porcelain angel he thought me to be, he didn't like me as much. The little girl he thought was innocent remembered her parents' screams, she remembered a life turned to ash, a village set on fire for no other reason than that Jews lived there. She remembered the years spent looking after a lonely woman losing her will to live, a woman who had nobody but her and a son at war.

No: I had no innocence left. Decency, yes, which was why I hadn't slapped him or made a scene, but decency was not something the Conte was familiar with.

"Does Jacopo know you intended to ask for my hand in marriage? Does your son know you want to marry your adoptive daughter?"

"You slut...!"

It was my turn to flinch. Now the real Conte was showing himself. But then, why should I have taken offense, when such an accusation held no ground? His words were worth nothing.

"Does Jacopo know?" I repeated.

"You're not the woman I thought," he said, his voice dripping with disappointment. As if it was me having distressed him. "I thought you were... serene. But you—"

"But I?" I wasn't afraid of him anymore. And I felt no need to be polite. I had no more gratitude for him. He'd lost all my respect: I owed him nothing.

He shook his head, as if he was so disappointed, he couldn't even find the words.

Strangely, it was at that moment that I noticed what a handsome, glamorous figure he still cut despite the life he was leading. He wasn't even disheveled. Not like I was, having had no time to take care of myself while I was looking after his dying wife. My hair was escaping from my bun and falling on my shoulders, and I hadn't changed in two days. I was still wearing an old skirt of the Contessa's and a shirt that had been mended more times than I could remember.

His eyes traveled the length of me, and it was him who looked at me with contempt, instead of the opposite.

The young Contessa smiled at us from the sepia photo-graph, in love and ready for a bright future: what a shame, what a waste.

I held the Conte's gaze, refusing to be flustered by the disdain I saw in his eyes. He looked away first.

And then he turned away from me, and stood at the window with its lovely view of the canal—a view that would soon be for his creditors to enjoy. I'd been dismissed.

Night fell and passed fast with the Contessa's wake, and by the time light came, the Signor Conte was gone, once again leaving the family he'd never looked after. I never saw him again: not long after I'd crossed the door of the palazzo forever, a letter from a neighbor told me that he'd looked for oblivion in the canal waters. He was gone.

In the cold dawn of that first morning after the Contessa's death, when the women who'd prayed the rosary for her finally left, I wrote the letter to Madre Agostina that led me here. The letter that set me free.

If you can ever be free of memories.

I took a breath. Helèna's words were so vivid, I could almost *see* the story unfolding in front of me.

Thiago was frowning. "No clues yet," he said.

"No, I don't think so. She's writing to her sister," I reflected. "Hanna. So she, too, escaped that terrible night of the fire."

"Helèna seems to think so. But she doesn't mention having seen her again, so who knows? Maybe it was wishful thinking on her part. The Contessa seemed to think Hanna was dead."

"Maybe. That Conte guy, though... *Ew.*"

"Yeah. Inappropriate is one way to describe him. Revolting is another. Want me to take over reading?"

"Yes, please. I'm out of breath." I desperately needed sleep, but I just couldn't drag myself away from the story. I adjusted my position, trying to make myself comfortable. The most comfortable thing would have been to lay my head against Thiago's shoulder, but obviously I couldn't do it. The whole situation was strange enough.

Thiago threw a glance at me. "You look terrible."

"Why thank you, kind sir," I hissed.

His face fell. He looked genuinely worried about having offended me. "Sorry, I... you look exhausted, that's all. Maybe you should sleep."

I pinched the bridge of my nose, resolute. Yes, I hadn't slept in almost twenty hours; no, I would not go to sleep now. "It'd be a good chance for you to get ahead," I said.

The expression on Thiago's face made me regret my words immediately. He seemed shocked I would think such a thing about him.

"I didn't mean..."

"It's okay. I must have come across as ruthless, I suppose," he said.

I shrugged, repentant. "No more than me."

The night was so perfectly still and silent, except for the tapping of rain on the windows. I pulled the blanket around my shoulders—without Thiago sitting beside me, I was cold again. He sat back down, and his warmth enveloped me. I felt the instinct to shuffle a little closer, but I recovered myself at once, and sat rigid, the blanket around me like armor.

When he began to read, in a low, warm Italian voice, it was almost like a lullaby.

... and so, you see why the ferryman who was taking me to my new life received no answer when he spoke of marriage. He kept rambling on, elaborating on why a young girl shouldn't be in so forlorn a place, but I stopped listening while we glided on the mist. Slowly, to the sound of lapping paddles, the boat came closer to land. The fog crept onto the island too: I could barely tell where the lake ended and the land began. Only

when we were almost there, I saw the convent rising out of the mist and taking shape, an austere building of gray stone, with a belfry standing sentry and one side ending right into the waters. After many years in Venice, it would be very familiar to me to look out of the window and see water.

And then I saw a line of gray figures on the shore: the sisters were there to greet me. It was as if they were pieces of mist themselves, in their gray smocks and simple gray veils, shadows among shadows.

The ferryman lifted me from the boat onto the pebbles as if I were light as a feather, and finally I could see the sisters properly. One wore a black smock instead of a gray one, I noticed—she had to be Madre Gloria, the Mother Superior. Two elderly nuns looked so alike I thought they must be biological sisters; beside them stood a young woman, small and slight like a little bird; and further on there was a tall, imposing sister with wide shoulders, strong arms and a blank expression. She disquieted me a little.

The boatman took a wicker basket from Madre Gloria—his reward—and climbed back onto his boat. He left with a curt goodbye to me, probably annoyed by what he thought was aloofness, but was, instead, the awkwardness of a girl who'd forgotten how to deal with the outside world. The reeds and rushes bounced back into place as the boat left, disappearing in the mist. Now, I had no way to leave, but I felt no apprehension, no foreboding. Even if the convent stood dark and heavy over us, even if as I turned around, there was no mainland to be seen anymore, having been swallowed by the whiteness of the fog.

I have faith in the future, Hanna—maybe because the past brought me so much sorrow, it's now time for a bit of happiness, for a bit of peace. I know that my hopes, unlike the Contessa's, won't be disappointed.

So: the sisters were studying me. I hoped against all hope that my damp hair and my beret, floppy with rain, would not make me look too shabby. I wore a deep blue woolen dress with sturdy brown shoes—the Contessa's castoffs—and a brown coat that was too big for me, but pleasantly warm. All in all, I knew I was perfectly decent: but I boiled under their gazes like an egg in a pot!

"I'm Madre Gloria. You are so very welcome," the nun in black said. *She didn't look severe, like I would have imagined a Mother Superior would be, but young and trusting—her face a perfect oval almost swallowed by huge moss-green eyes, her voice a warm alto.*

"Thank you."

"Let me introduce my daughters in Christ. These are Sister Santia and Sister Emilia," she said, *indicating the two elderly women. They were the carbon copy of one another, except one was slightly taller. Both were small and dark, with wispy gray hair escaping the veil, and hands made gnarled by age.* "Welcome, my dear, welcome," *they said almost in unison, wearing a slightly fretful expression, like perpetually frightened mice.*

"This is Sister Aurelie," *Madre Gloria continued. She was the young, slight one—she seemed no older than me, and wore a cheerful countenance. She gave me a wide, joyful grin, and I warmed to her instantly.* "And over there is Sister Giulia." *The wide-shouldered, tall woman nodded briefly. She didn't take a step toward us, but I kept the smile on my face anyway. I'll win her over, I'm sure.*

"She doesn't like talking, dear," Sister Santia—*or maybe Sister Emilia—explained.*

"Well, let's go inside. You must be cold, and hungry too! I have an urgent matter to see to, but the sisters will make you some warm milk and bread. I'll show you around in a little while," *Madre Gloria said.*

The library! Please, let me see the library! *I couldn't wait... but I perked up at the mention of food. I was starving: I* hadn't eaten properly for weeks. There wasn't much left in the kitchen of Palazzo Masi, no money to buy food, and I was too ashamed to ask anyone. I hadn't quite revealed how urgently I needed a position when I wrote to Madre Agostina.

Sister Aurelie took me gently by the arm and began to lead me toward the main building. She was leaning on me heavily, her gait uneven—I saw that her legs were twisted, and that she walked with difficulty.

I could see why I was called upon to help them. Two nuns were of an age, and the youngest impaired in her movements. Sister Giulia was probably the one who did the heavy jobs. Well, she has me to help her, now.

Sister Aurelie took me to the kitchen, struggling to walk on the pebbles a little, and then again even more on the stone steps. I glanced around me as quickly as I could, envisioning with joy the upcoming tour of the place. I was so looking forward to seeing my new home—and what a home! I'd tried to picture Santa Caterina in my mind, but I'd failed time and time again. Among the books I read in secrecy, one came to my mind: The Monk, with its description of a dark, mysterious monastery and horrifying secrets, a story that gave me terrifying, delicious shivers. But as we made our way inside, everything felt quite comfortable and homely. No scary monks here, but a welcoming kitchen with a fire that warmed the damp out of my bones.

While making small talk, Aurelie heated some milk on a stove for me, which she offered with a slice of bread. It might seem strange that the kitchen of a convent in the middle of nowhere, and a conversation with a nun, with the expanse of a lake all around us and only five human beings for kilometers around, would seem heavenly to me. But here, unlike at Palazzo Masi, I felt safe. Safe from the war as well, consuming a world far away from us.

With a sigh, Sister Aurelie let herself fall on the chair

beside me. I could see that she found walking tiring, even if she
kept a bright demeanor. She's so pretty, Hanna, with elongated
eyes, as dark as licorice, and freckles on the bridge of her nose.
When she smiles, her eyes look like half-moons.

"It's a blessing that you're here, Helèna," she said, and I
was moved by her warm kindness.

"It's a blessing for me to be here. I promise I shall be of
help."

"Help is welcome. But you know why I'm so happy you're
here? The chance to chat."

I laughed. "I beg your pardon?"

"I hope you enjoy chatting?" Aurelie said, somehow hopefully. I could see now that she must be a little older than me,
but she was so small, and her face so round and smooth, that it
was like talking to a little girl. Something in me responded to
her smile and her conspiratorial tone. I've never had a girlfriend: the Contessa would not have allowed it. I only have
you, my Hanna, though we're now apart.

"I'm a little out of practice, but I do enjoy it," I said. I
could recall endless late-night heart-to-hearts with Jacopo
when we were children—and blabbering on while we played
hide and seek in the palazzo courtyard... My heart seemed to
shrink into itself as the memories came flooding back.

"I'm so glad! Madre Gloria can be very entertaining when
she wants to, but you don't really chat with a Mother Superior,
do you? The Sisters Santia and Emilia are so old they can't
remember their names... I shouldn't be saying that."

I had to laugh. "Probably not," I replied, willing to be in
the here and now, and for the memories to disperse.

"They're lovely, they really are, but it's a bit like talking to
one of those centenary turtles I read about in my schoolbook."

I almost spat out my bread and turned around to see if
anyone heard her. "And what about Sister Giulia?" I
whispered.

"*She doesn't speak. At all. She could, if she wanted to, but she doesn't.*"

"*Oh.*"

Sister Santia—or maybe Emilia, I could barely tell them apart—pushed her wrinkly neck through the door, and I tried hard not to smile, thinking of the turtle comparison. "Madre Gloria would like to know if you're ready to be shown around?"

"*Mmm,*" *I said, chewing the last bit of bread. I'd been so hungry: now a pleasant warmth sat in my belly.*

"*There's more. For later,*" *Aurelie said kindly. She'd noticed how ravenous I was—I didn't know whether to feel grateful or embarrassed.*

Madre Gloria was waiting for me at the door we'd entered from, standing straight with her hands held together in front of her. She radiated a sense of quiet authority, softened by kindness. "Come. I'm glad you're here," she repeated. "I hope you'll call this home. As you can imagine, this place is precious to me. To us."

"*I call it home already,*" *I said wholeheartedly. Even on this rainy winter day, with a steel sky and a bite in the air, the convent and the island were full of a stark grace, and a promise of mysteries to be revealed.*

"*It's peaceful. Which is more than can be said for most places, these days.*"

"*Yes.*" *To my chagrin, my mind went to Jacopo again. Where was he? I had to face the fact that almost surely, he wasn't safe. No soldier is ever safe.*

Nothing would ever stop me from caring for him... but I didn't want to think about what happened when I saw him last.

I forced myself to come back to the present, but too late: maybe I was transparent, maybe Madre Gloria had learned to read people easily, because she asked: "Are you burdened, figlia mia?" *My daughter. The term of endearment moved me so... but I couldn't explain all that had happened. Not yet.*

"I suppose we all are, these days, Madre."

She seemed to sense my restraint. "Maybe here you'll find some peace."

She laid a hand on my arm and led me on. The main building was shaped like a horseshoe, and we'd come out one way only to re-enter from another. We walked down a stony corridor, at the end of which there was a walled garden. I couldn't help mouthing an oh. The garden was lush, full of rose bushes blooming from the bordered beds...

"The roses! They're still there," I said. "Did you see them?"

Thiago murmured a *sì*. "You can smell them everywhere. Even here. Can't you?"

I smelled the air. Roses, yes, but also Thiago's scent, warm and deep, like the undergrowth of a forest.

"These letters read like a novel, more than a letter, or a diary in the form of letters. She writes the dialogs and everything..." Thiago observed.

"She said she wants this to be like a memoir."

"Do you think it could actually be a work of fiction?"

"You mean, made up? It's possible. But I don't think so." I shrugged. I wanted it to be real. I *needed* it to be real. I was too invested for Helèna's story to be a wartime fairy tale someone made up to play a weird game with us.

"I don't know. I... I can't tell. I'm just improvising, Francesca. I don't really know what I'm doing," he said. He took his cup from the little table beside the bed and downed some coffee.

I don't really know what I'm doing. It was a strange thing to say, for someone who'd looked so focused, so professional. Armani suit and all. But then, wasn't that the lesson I'd learned at Hex? That things are not always what they seem? Thiago did seem to go from smooth to bristly every time the wind changed. Professionals are supposed to keep steady during business transactions and meetings. I looked at him from under my lashes. There was something about him that was so different from the types I'd met in art dealing, all smoothness and self-importance.

Or maybe it was just him. I had a feeling that there was more about him than met the eye. As if he'd painted over his true self, but the paint was peeling and the man he was showed underneath. Perhaps it was the way we'd been thrown together in these crazy circumstances, but I was taken by the desire to know more about him, to unravel his secrets... I felt my cheeks redden, and I was grateful for the gloom that hid it.

"Ready?" he asked.

"Ready." His voice filled the air, and I was transported away, to Helèna's world, once again.

Outside, spring was still tentative, barely showing herself after a long, cold winter. Mist and drizzle still owned the land, and only wisps of tender green grass and little fragile blooms on the trees told us that winter had come to an end. But here, in this garden, there was an explosion of colors and scents, a lushness and fullness that spoke of warmth and sunshine.

"We have to thank Sister Giulia for this," Madre Gloria said, and sure enough there she was, the silent nun, bent in two over a plant with white flowers—I couldn't name it, I don't know much about flowers at all. My knowledge stops at roses, geraniums and violets. "We have to thank her for the herbs that flavor our meals, too," she added. I could see Sister Giulia's cheeks flushing with pleasure at this compliment, but she still said nothing. Herbs or not, I was looking forward to regular meals in general.

After a nod to Sister Giulia, I followed Madre Gloria to the refectory. In the center was a horseshoe table bigger than five sisters and a hired help would ever need. "There used to be more of us," the Madre explained. "As you can guess."

"Why did they leave? Or... why did no one else come here?"

"Are you the suggestible type?"

I was taken aback. "Suggestible? I don't know. I don't think so." Probably I am, because suddenly the vaulted rooms felt chilly, desolate, our voices echoing in lonely ripples against the vaulted ceilings. It was so different from the cozy kitchen, with its stove and its soft orange glow, and its inviting smells. The kitchen and the garden were the two beating hearts of the place, I thought.

She shrugged. "Some are. Suggestible and superstitious. And they don't want to come here because of... silly notions."

"Oh."

"It's all nonsense. Forget what I said! I'm sure you can't wait to see your cell. Don't worry, cell might sound stark to a layperson, but they're comfortable little quarters, I promise."

She was right. The cells were simple, bare, each with a cot, a writing desk and a wardrobe—but the lack of adornment was restful to my eyes. I had come to loathe the decaying luxury of Palazzo Masi, with its grandeur that didn't quite succeed in hiding its decadence...

"I wonder which one was hers?" I couldn't help interrupting.

"Who knows... maybe this one? Or perhaps yours..."

We both instinctively looked around us. The rain had stopped tapping on the windows, and the silence was so thick now, it was almost solid. The air itself was full of memories of the past, years and years of women and men sleeping and praying and thinking among these four walls. The reference to superstitions and *silly notions* had chilled me. Suddenly, I remembered the shadow I'd seen earlier, after coming out of the shower.

"It feels like she's here," I whispered.

"Okay, let's not get carried away now," Thiago answered in a slightly louder tone, looking around him.

"You're spooked too," I stated.

"I'm not. I don't believe in this kind of thing. Supernatural stuff. At all." But he sent a glance toward the window before he continued reading.

... Madre Gloria's question came back to my mind. Am I a suggestible person? Because I do sense a touch of eeriness to this part of the convent. At that moment, it seemed to me that the atmosphere of the kitchen, with its warmth and comfort, had now dispersed, and the further on we walked, the more mysterious this place felt.

The cells were all in a row, but the stone walls were so thick that sounds were muffled. Spider webs hung in the corners—that was a task for me, I told myself. The air was dense here, and thinking that behind those doors were many empty rooms, stretching one after the other, made me a little nervous; it was almost as if I had the sense someone who should have been there wasn't there—or the opposite. Oh, I was getting tired and addled, and my mind was going down convoluted paths.

"It's probably not what you're used to," Madre Gloria said, startling me from my thoughts.

I felt myself blushing. "Not at all. I can assure you that life at Palazzo Masi was not sumptuous as you'd imagine. I was just pondering how many women... how many nuns must have come and gone in this place."

"Santa Caterina was built over a thousand years ago. So, a good few." Madre Gloria smiled. Our steps resounded in the empty halls as we walked down the corridor—it was colder

than outside, as if the thick stone walls retained all the heat and gave nothing back. "If these walls could speak, they would have many stories to tell. But I also like to think they would echo all our prayers throughout the ages. Right now, prayers are our contribution to the war. The way we fight, without harming anyone."

"My adoptive brother is an officer... I don't even know where they sent him, but I shouldn't complain. There are so many sisters and mothers and wives in my situation."

"Oh, my dear. Your pain matters, Helèna, even if millions feel the same right now. Every single man and woman matters. Take heart. The sisters of Santa Caterina have lived through many wars in the thousand years of our existence. This is just another. Peace will return."

A conversation I'd heard on the train to Lago Cusio came back to me: two elderly women were talking in low voices, mindful not to be overheard. I only caught a few sentences —Soon there will be nowhere safe, one of them said, and then she looked around, frightened of getting in trouble. Even just those few hours I'd spent on that train, hearing those women speak and seeing the number of men in uniform, and the over-whelming, heavy feeling of wariness and fear that soaked the place, made me even more aware of how I'd lived in a tiny, sheltered world. A world that revolved around Palazzo Masi and the Contessa's health, and her obsessions, with the only solace of Jacopo. Before he left too. Now that I'd stepped out of it, I could feel war everywhere.

"Here we are, figlia mia. This is your cell," Madre Gloria said, and showed me into the last room along the corridor...

"The last cell! That's mine! It's *mine*! I'm sleeping in her cell!" I cried out.

I expected a cynical answer from Thiago, but I could feel he was beginning to be enticed by the whole thing.

"She'll come to you while you sleep," he whispered spook-ily, and earned a thump on the shoulder.

There, I found my valise, sitting beside the cot. On the little wooden writing desk was a bunch of candles tied together with a ribbon, a box of matches, and what made me happy most of all: writing materials.

The narrow window looked out to the woods—it was so low that I could see the soil covered in leaves, some tree trunks and a corner of the lake. To see the top of the trees and the sky I'd have to lean out. It was like a burrow, warm and sheltered.

"Thank you from the bottom of my heart. For all this," I said, quite choked up suddenly. I was safe, my belly full, my tomorrow clear and filled with good works, but everything I'd been through caught up with me and brought tears to my eyes. My minuscule kingdom, where I would find peace. No more Contessa calling me all day and night, no more Conte tumbling in drunk and reeking, no more empty fireplaces and lamps without oil, dusty curtains that fell to pieces, a million porcelain ornaments that suffocated me, and old paintings watching me from every wall. This little place was quiet, clean, sparse... protected.

"I'm happy you like it, figlia mia. We all deserve a haven, a place to feel thoroughly safe."

"It's perfect," I said. I could already see myself sitting at that desk at night, to read and write at the light of a candle... how peaceful it will be!

Madre Gloria must have read my thoughts, because she said, "I left our greatest treasure for last. I was told you love reading."

"Oh, yes. Yes, I do! Who told... oh, of course. It must have been Madre Agostina."

"Yes, she told me just that about you," Madre Gloria

replied, and at that moment I was sure that she, Madre Gloria, shared my passion.

She opened one arm to lead me out of the cell. We came out in the open through a back corridor, and after only a few steps on slippery paved ground, we entered another door, this one tall and arched. I was trying to construct a mental map of the convent, but with all the twists and turns it wasn't easy. The place was gloomy and half-lit: it took me a few seconds to adjust my sight.

Madre Gloria's shoes clicked on the stones. "Here we are."

I blinked—and as my eyes adjusted, I was left in awe. At last, we were in the much-fabled library.

"Here we go," Thiago said. "Now, pay attention."

"Of course I'm paying attention!" I said, and drained the last of my coffee: *please, caffeine, keep me awake.*

Without saying anything, Thiago fished a few bon-bons from the bowl on his desk and passed them to me. A little sugar rush would do the trick.

... It was a wide, vaulted room, and every bit of space from floor to ceiling was taken by wooden shelves chiseled in flowery patterns. The shelves were full to the brim with books, and a balcony ran the length of the room to create a mezzanine where more shelves found their place. The balcony was decorated with moldings of mythological scenes, and the ceilings were painted deep blue, dotted with stars and constellations. In a corner were narrow wooden stairs that led up to the mezzanine, with an intricately carved banister.

The unique, unmistakable scent of books pervaded everything. That scent, Hanna... it's so familiar to me. Do you remember our father's shop? Do you remember the piles of books everywhere, and the smell of paper and dust and that touch of mold...

I want to recall these sensations and images and yet I recoil from them, because the memories hurt too much.

I wandered around the shelves, tilting my head to read the titles. Historia Herbarum, Il Canzoniere, Orationes Catilinarie... *twelve volumes of the* Kabbalah... Honoré de Balzac? *There were modern books as well!* Maupassant, Tolstoy, Manzoni... *My fingers ran on their spines, on the carvings of the shelves. I climbed the narrow wooden stairs to the mezzanine and stood on the balcony, looking up to the painted night sky and down to the stone floor, where Madre Gloria stood, looking up.*

"My parents would have loved this place," *I called down.*

"As close to perfection as we can come on this earth," *Madre Gloria said.*

She understands, Hanna! She feels the same reverence as me in front of this wealth of knowledge and stories. I couldn't stop scouring the books. Carmina Cantabrigiensia, Le Voyage de Charlemagne, Libro d'Ore...

"Helèna?"

Storia della Russia, La Dama Bianca, La Divina Commedia, De Officiis...

"Helèna?"

"Sorry! Sorry, Madre!"

I tore myself away and climbed down, my hand light on the carved banister, feeling its exquisite patterns under my fingers. "I can't quite believe this. It's like the answer to prayers I didn't even dare to pray!"

Madre Gloria laughed. "You really are a breath of fresh air, Helèna! Madre Agostina told me that your parents were scholars and that your family had a bookshop."

"They did, yes. I grew up with books. However... Contessa Masi, the lady who took me in after I was orphaned... I'm so very grateful to her, and I cared for her very much... but she believed that knowledge is the enemy of faith."

Madre Gloria seemed aghast. "I beg your pardon?"

I nodded in confirmation. "I wasn't allowed to read nor write anything that wasn't prayers, practical notes or lists. Not even a diary, unless it was a spiritual diary, she called it: an account of my devotions. I wrote some letters but... she burned them," I explained. "When I got older, though, I smuggled books in. I tried to learn on my own as much as I could. She believed that education is not of God." It was good to tell someone what my life had been, but I also felt vaguely guilty, as if I were betraying the Contessa somehow. I was sure that Madre Gloria would look to the Contessa's flaws with compassion, but I felt compelled to add: "She was very unhappy, and with good reason. She didn't mean any harm. I'm grateful to her."

Madre Gloria nodded, her face solemn. "It's not my inclination to speak ill of anyone. But please, forget what the Contessa taught you, because it's wrong. Faith is not threatened by knowledge. If anything, the more we know about the world, the stronger the challenges that our faith faces, the deeper, more powerful, more rooted it becomes."

Those words were a balm for my soul. In my twenty years of life, Madre Gloria was the first person who had ever contradicted the Contessa openly. The tutoress I was allowed to have for a little while disagreed with her but was forced to comply— I suppose she had to consider where her living came from. Now, at last, someone wasn't afraid to say that what the Contessa believed about the inherent evilness of knowledge was wrong.

"I never believed that. I only obeyed because she was my guardian, and because she was so very upset at anything that threatened her view of the world, and I didn't want to distress her. She was... vulnerable. Oh, I can't wait to start reading!" I exclaimed, my arms open to encompass the shelves laden with books. "At Palazzo Masi there were only scriptures, books on scriptures, and prayer books. Not even lives of saints, because they're too much like novels, apparently. It was unbelievably boring... oh, sorry!" I added quickly, realizing I'd just said that scriptures were boring. Blood rushed to my cheeks.

"The word of God is not boring, Helèna," she said in a mild reproach. "But for a child, a young person... well, I understand you needed something different as well."

"I needed an education. After I arrived from Hungary, I learned to speak Italian quickly, but writing was so very difficult! I had to plead with the Contessa for lessons. I was twelve when she decided I wasn't allowed to study anymore... to this day, I don't write as well as I should. Which is horrible because I love writing so very much."

I took a breath. It was all coming out—maybe Madre Gloria would think me ungrateful, or even a gossip, but her face exuded sympathy, and I couldn't quite stop. All the frustration and anger of the past few years came pouring out. In the back of my mind was the fear that Madre Gloria would find me bitter, but I'd repressed my feelings for so long that they refused to be locked up any longer. The more I told her, the more they came rushing out, unbridled.

"The Contessa couldn't stand me playing, because it distracted me from pondering the word of God, or having friends, in case they were a bad influence on me, but even loneliness became bearable, after a while. But I never stopped longing for books," I concluded.

There was relief in my heart, finally saying aloud what I'd been thinking, telling someone what I'd been through because of the Contessa's obsessions—but the relief was still edged with trepidation, as if she could still shame me, punish me. She was gone, I had to remind myself; these weren't secrets anymore.

Madre Gloria studied me for a moment; she was almost appraising me. I froze under her gaze. Was she angry, was she disappointed? Had I gone too far?

After a few seconds that seemed like an eternity, she produced a set of heavy keys from a pocket in her habit and led me toward the stairs. Behind them was a narrow space with an even narrower door, painted as white as the walls. It was invisible to the casual eye, and even to a more observing one...

Thiago looked up. "Could it be so easy? A hidden door beyond the stairs, in the library?"

"The library, which we haven't even seen yet."

"Maybe the hard part is finding the keys?" Thiago rubbed his forehead. "What is this, *The Hobbit*? Or are we playing *Dungeons and Dragons*? This is a joke."

"You seem quite familiar with nerdy hobbies," I teased him. "Look, you can get crabby if you want, but it's not going to change anything. Come on, let me, young man." I took the diary from him and, out of the corner of my eye, I saw a smile had won its way through his frustration.

I began to read.

Madre Gloria inserted the heavy keys in the lock, even if they looked too big for such a small entrance. She crouched and felt the darkness with her hand, and grasped a lamp and matches. In the light of the lamp, I followed her down a few stone steps —the door was so low that even I, short as I am, had to duck. Another chamber to add to the maze, this one even darker than before... The scent of damp and ancient things hit my nose, and something else, something I couldn't quite put my finger on.

Madre Gloria's lamp illuminated two rows of lecterns, with enormous tomes on top, and more shelves made of a darker wood than the one used in the library. On them, more tomes. Then, I knew then what the smell in the air was: leather and parchment.

My fingers touched the manuscripts on the lecterns—and when Madre Gloria raised the lamp over them I saw golden pages, illustrated with images of men, women and angels, and animals, and monsters... the first letter of each paragraph turned into a pattern of gold and bright colors, the others black, in a language that I didn't recognize—it wasn't the Latin I heard at Mass or I learned in prayers. It had hints of it, but the words were all squashed together and there were symbols I couldn't decipher. My chest was heaving with emotion. After a silent glance to Madre Gloria, and a nod from her, I lifted one of the books from a shelf, with immense care, and carried it to a lectern: this was full of illustrations of plants and flowers, lists of mysterious ingredients, images of roots and petals and blooms...

I wanted to see them all, I wanted to learn how to read them. I want to be one of those few people who have the knowledge necessary to decipher them, all the knowledge in the world!

I became aware that I had not taken a breath in what felt like minutes. "These illustrations..." I whispered. "Are the most beautiful thing I've ever seen."

"They're called illuminations," Madre Gloria told me. "And they're as old as the convent. A thousand years or so. What you see is gold leaf, and the other colors are made of minerals and plants."

"What language is this?"

"Forms of medieval Latin. Quite different from the version of Latin we use in our prayers, and in the Mass."

"A thousand years ago someone created all this beauty. A man or a woman, just like us... many lifetimes ago. Can you imagine? And we'll never know their names..."

"We do know," Madre Gloria said. "Look..." She pointed to a corner of the page, where a minuscule signature had been engraved.

"Ippolita Von Oswen..." I repeated under my breath. "Who was she?"

"She was an abbess and so much more. She composed music, she studied medicine and wrote compendiums on healing plants. She was a philosopher as well, a mystic, some say even a seer, through the will of God, of course. Some of these works are from her pen," Madre Gloria said.

A woman who was not denied an education. A woman of faith and *letters, I imagined myself telling Contessa Masi.*

"That's her! Ippolita Von Oswen!" I said, as breathless as Helèna had been. Thiago didn't seem to share my enthusiasm: he just looked at me. It was almost as if he didn't know who she was, or he didn't comprehend the enormity of the discovery. This guy was a mystery. "You don't know her, do you?"

"I've heard of her. But I... well, I'm more of a business side of things guy."

"Oh."

"Tell me about her."

"Really? You might regret having asked." I smiled.

"I don't think so. There's a lot I need to learn."

I studied his face for a moment, trying to understand what was behind those words. Maybe he was new to the world of art; maybe he wanted to expand his knowledge. But I couldn't help feeling that he seemed like a fish out of water. I remembered the anguished look on his face as he spoke to Lavinia. I was sure that there was a story behind his presence here, like a water-mark that I could guess at but not quite see.

"You're staring at me," he said coolly.

"Sorry! Sorry." I had to admit that the grace of his features, his high cheekbones and generous lips, the too-long burnished copper fringe, the hooded eyes that made him look a little languid, had distracted me. "Ippolita is the reason why I special-ized in Medieval Paleography. I got my degree in art, and I knew I wanted to keep studying, but I was interested in pretty much everything. It was hard to choose. Then one of my professors introduced me to Ippolita's work, and... I was in love. I never looked back."

I took a breath before I continued.

"She defied all conventions; she fought to express herself in a world that wanted to put her in a box. As a child, she had visions. Proper visions, mystical ones. She was deemed strange, of course, and sent to a convent at the age of fourteen. She hadn't even been taught to read or write, even if it would have been customary for a woman of her rank. She was fortunate, though, because the prioress of her convent, a noblewoman, took Ippolita under her wing. Ippolita learned to read and write, and to illuminate manuscripts with gold leaf.

"Her illustrations were so beautiful that scholars began to travel from all over Europe to go see them. She also taught herself to play the psaltery, an ancient instrument, and began writing poems that she then put to music. The poems were inspired by her visions. When her prioress died she was offered the chance to take her place under the authority of the archbishop, but she refused because she didn't want to be under anyone's authority. This is a woman in the eleventh century. In a completely patriarchal world."

"Brave woman," Thiago said. I gazed at him looking for sarcasm, but I saw none. "So what happened?"

"She insisted. Until she got what she wanted. She and her nuns tended to a medicinal garden, looked after the sick, and worshiped with the incredibly complex, magical music she wrote. They wore beautiful robes and jewelry, like ancient priestesses. Ippolita wrote treaties on gardening, herbal medicine, even astronomy. And all the while she continued to have these visions that were so intense they made her physically ill. I suppose today they would be classified as mental illness, but to her they were a gift, even if they caused her suffering. She said that they allowed her to see things from the light of God." My face felt warm, and I was animated, all sleepiness had gone.

"When my boss told me that some of her manuscripts were on sale, I couldn't believe it. I still can't believe there's only two of us bidding for them."

Thiago's lips opened as if he was about to say something— but he remained silent. I was embarrassed now. I got carried away, and had probably come across as a know-it-all.

"Well. Let's keep going then," I said, and resolved to keep my cards closer to my chest from now on.

> Touching Ippolita's illuminated pages, I could see clearly: I am meant to be here...
>
> Hanna! I can hear noises, the shadows made by the flickering candle seem to move of their own accord. I'm sure that the shadow against the wall wasn't there before... someone is here...

"A few ink blots," I said and bent toward the diary in Thiago's hand, tracing the page with my finger just like Helèna had done with Ippolita's work.

"Well, it's obviously a ghost," Thiago said facetiously.

I gave him a dark look. These references to ghosts were as disquieting to me as they were funny for Thiago. I hadn't told him about my sister's silken rose materializing on my bed, because one, he'd think I was crazy and, two, I'd probably put it there myself, or it had slipped out of my bag, and I'd been too jet lagged to notice or remember. But a little part of me had no explanation for it, and it haunted me.

I resumed my reading.

> What a fool I am! It was Sister Aurelie! I feel silly, now. This place can play games with your imagination, that's for sure. Aurelie brought me a coal brazier to warm my bed, a warm shawl covered in cat hairs that, she apologized, were impossible to get out, a cup of warm milk and a piece of cake. She's a

darling. However, she didn't help me get rid of the disquiet I feel in this cell, alone with the night all around me.

"I'm sorry I scared you when I came in," she said and sat on my cot with a sigh—it was clear to see that certain movements required much effort.

"Don't worry, I'm just getting used to my surroundings. The silence, the solitude. I thought I saw a shadow on the wall, and the candle was... I don't know. Strange. Ignore me, it's nonsense."

"Maybe it's not. Maybe you saw... Federica." She made a dramatic pause before saying that name and opened her eyes wide in a way that made me giggle.

"Federica?"

"Were you not told about her?"

Oh. I wasn't giggling anymore. And the knot in my stomach was back. "No? Should I have been?"

"She's the sixth sister," Aurelie replied, now deadpan, as if making small talk. "Well, I must go. Madre Gloria doesn't like it if we're not all in our cells and asleep by sundown." She placed both hands by her side, ready to push herself up.

"Aurelie! I mean, Sister Aurelie." I tried to sound dignified. "You can't mention a sixth nun and then just leave."

She relaxed and remained seated, a satisfied expression on her face. "Very well, then. A minute more. If Madre Gloria finds us, it's your fault."

"Agreed."

"Hundreds of years ago," she began solemnly. "Well, maybe not hundreds... but ages ago, there was a nun here called Sister Federica. She was unbelievably beautiful and had a merry spirit..."

"This sounds like a fairy tale, and Federica sounds more like a princess than a nun."

"Shhhhh, let me tell the story!" Aurelie chided me. "So,

Federica was beautiful, with a cheerful countenance and very devout. But one day a man whose name no one remembers came to the convent to do some work, saw Federica, and fell in love." Aurelie's expression would have looked perfect on a romantic young girl, but on a nun, it seemed a little out of place. *She looks more like a little girl dressed up in costume. When we're a little closer, I'd like to ask her why she decided to take the veil.*

"Federica was a good girl. She really was." Aurelie looked serious all of a sudden, in an almost comical way. "But the man was so insistent, and he was so in love with her... she relented."

"Oh."

"Yes! Chaos ensued! The Madre Superiora back then was a very unforgiving woman, and poor Federica was punished harshly. She was locked in her cell for days and nights! But she didn't want to give up her love. She asked to be released and set free."

"Set free? Surely she had free will, and she could choose whether to leave or not? Did she not choose to be consecrated in the first place?"

Aurelie looked down and smoothed the fabric on her poor legs. "Not everyone does, you know," she said, and her words were tinged with sudden sadness. Sitting like that, her legs dangling from my cot and her face down, the light of the candle playing on her freckles—she seemed so vulnerable... *I wondered if she'd just revealed something about herself.*

She continued her story. "The Madre Superiora alerted her family. While they were coming to get her, Federica and her love... ran. Away."

"That is romantic," I conceded.

"Not so much, because they died. Or maybe that's romantic too?"

"That's not romantic, that's tragic! What happened?"

"*Nobody knows. They vanished. Probably drowned. Then how can we be sure that Federica died?*" she asked.

I nodded.

"*Because the same night she came back, but she wasn't herself. She was very quiet, staring into space, leaving her food untouched... The other nuns thought she was troubled because of all that had happened to her. The next day, someone saw her on the shoreline... but where she stood, the water was deep. She was too far out to be touching the ground.*"

"*She was...*"

"*A specter.*"

Up to that moment, Aurelie's melodramatic expressions and her glee in recounting the details had made the story almost funny. But now that she mentioned the nun appearing as a szellem, a ghost, I felt a chill going down my spine.

Don't meddle with those things, our father had admonished me all those years ago. I wanted Aurelie to leave—no more talk of ghosts and disappearances.

She must have felt my change of mood because she took my hand. "*Did I scare you again? I'm sorry, Helèna.*" This time, she seemed mortified.

I smiled. "*Of course not. Only it's late, and we're here chatting! I'm just worried we'll be reproached for breaking the rules. I don't want to cause any trouble.*"

"*You're right!*" she whispered. "*Goodnight, dear Helèna. It was just a silly story; I really am sorry if I scared you!*" She stood, leaning on my arm. She was on the doorstep when something that Madre Gloria said, about silly notions and superstitions, came back to me.

"*Aurelie,*" I called in a hushed tone, fearing the others would hear us. "*That's not why the convent emptied, is it? The reason why there are only five of you, now?*"

"*I don't know. You'll have to ask Madre Gloria... but don't*

*tell her it was me who told you about Sister Federica! She
doesn't like us even mentioning her. She says it's nonsense."*

Then Aurelie smiled and added in another dramatic whisper, "But it's true!"

"You don't believe all this, do you?" Thiago said. He must
have sensed my disquiet, because I'd almost writhed in place,
trying to settle. The dream—nightmare, more like—I'd had night
after night, where I was drowning in dark waters, had come
back to my memory. The way the water looked, and the shadow
looming over me, now seemed like an omen of this place, of the
story I was reading.

I shrugged. "I don't know. I... I had a dream before I even
knew I was coming here. A recurring dream. I think... I know
that sounds crazy, but... I—might have seen Federica before."

"Come on!" He laughed. "Want me to check if there's a
ghost under the bed?"

Argh. At that moment, I swear I hated him. "Don't make
fun of me!" I protested.

To my surprise, he seemed contrite at the vehemence of my
reaction. "Hey. It was just a joke. I suppose it's my way to deal
with things I can't quite... explain. Scary things. And that's
what it was. Just a scary dream, you know, drowning, shadows
and all that," Thiago said. He didn't seem to be teasing me now
—he was trying to reassure me. "If you let all this get to you,
you'll be terrified. Stay in the light," he said with such a serious
tone that I had to laugh.

"What's so funny?"

"The way you said it. I don't know. I'm so jet lagged, I'm
probably just a little delirious." I lowered my eyes to the diary,
but his eyes lingered on me. "What?"

He was staring at me, his face turned toward mine in such a
way that when I, too, turned to look at him, our noses almost
touched.

That was unexpected.

And not entirely unpleasant.

For a second, we couldn't quite unglue our gaze from each other—and then suddenly we both jerked away.

"Nothing," he mumbled, and I hastened to resume my reading. A strange warmth had filled my limbs: I would just ignore it. Suddenly, a wave of exhaustion hit me. Now, reading was a struggle, and Thiago's shoulder more tempting than ever...

"Aurelie... did you choose to take the veil?" The question came out before I could check myself, and I regretted it a little. We weren't friends, yet, and I didn't want to intrude. But it was too late now.

"Of course I chose my vocation." She gave a little, brittle laugh. "My mother always said, what else could you do, if not be a nun? Who would marry you, like this?" She pointed briefly to her damaged legs. "How could you work the fields, or take washing in, or sew?" She raised her unsteady arms and cocked her head, as if what she was saying was funny. "So, I chose to be a nun."

"I see." Aurelie's faith might be real and deep, but I think it sad to take the veil if it's been given to you as your one and only chance to exist in this world.

"Goodnight, Helèna," she said in a small voice. Her almond-shaped eyes were a little melancholic, now.

"Goodnight, Sister Aurelie."

She disappeared, and then her head appeared briefly again: "Sweet dreams of Federica," she said, mischievously.

Once again, she made me giggle. And yet I couldn't stop reliving the story in my mind—the bit about Sister Federica returning from her escape, silent and dazed, as if she hadn't realized yet that she was dead. Sitting in the refectory without touching food, and then... walking on water.

I'm quite sure, Hanna, that tonight I shall dream of her standing in the lake, in a place too deep to touch the ground...

I don't remember anything after reading those words, except the soft feeling of Thiago's shoulder beneath my cheek, and my hands abandoned on my lap as sleep took me faster than it had ever done before.

CHAPTER 7

THE ISLAND OF SANTA CATERINA

The next thing I knew, there was a rhythmic noise somewhere near me—my heartbeat—no, someone knocking at the door. I sat up, confused. The light of the morning sun seeped through the curtainless window, turned green and golden by grass and leaves. Tiny dust particles danced in the rays, and I was hypnotized for a moment, until I came back to myself.

Last thing I remembered was reading Helèna's diary with Thiago, the night before. I must have fallen asleep without noticing. I couldn't even remember going to bed. Oh no. Did he *carry* me to bed? I was fully clothed, still in my sweater and leggings...

"*Arrivo!*" I called toward the door. Standing there was Manuela, fresh and smiling in a roomy black apron.

"Breakfast is served," she said. "We're out on the terrace. Oh, I see you're ready! Would you like to follow me?"

I looked down at myself. "I look ready, but I'm not! Five minutes! It's over there, isn't it?" I gestured with my right hand.

"The opposite way," she said. "That side, there's just water."

"Oh, yes. Of course." I needed to get my bearings around

the convent—just like Helèna said, it was quite the maze. I'd have to do a proper reconnoiter.

I washed and changed quickly—I needed to find Thiago and make sure he didn't read more of the diary without me. I could have slapped myself for falling asleep like that. I rushed out in the corridor while checking my phone... A missed call from Isaac! My heart soared. I must have been completely exhausted not to hear his personal ringtone—usually, I was like one of Pavlov's dogs with it. Every time it rang, I stopped anything I was doing and raced for my phone.

I called him back at once, praying the signal would be strong enough to hold the call. It rang and rang, until finally, the moment I stepped outside, his face appeared on the screen and the old, familiar tenderness made its sweet way through me. He was in bed – I'd forgotten the time difference!

"I'm so sorry! What's the time over there?"

"Pretty much the middle of the night. I'll make this short; I have a long day tomorrow. We're going out for dinner straight from the office. The whole team, I mean."

My radars went up at once. He hadn't needed to specify that. "That's good, have fun!"

"Thank you. How are things there? Wow, look at that lake!"

"Yeah... it's amazing. Look," I said, and ran the camera on the waters and sky, and then on the gray walls of the convent.

"Wow. That place looks a bit like a horror film. Dracula's mansion."

I laughed. "I know! Oh, I can't wait to be home. I can't wait to... I can't wait to see you."

He looked away, and then down. "Francesca, we talked about that. Please don't say those kinds of things..."

"Okay. Okay, sorry. I suppose friends are allowed to say they miss each other, no? And *you* did call *me!*" I tried to be light, but my heart was heavy. What was with Isaac, that every time we spent time together or spoke, I felt burdened? It used to be the opposite. He used to be my wings to fly, now he weighed me down. I was desperate to go back to the way things used to be.

"Yes. I felt we needed to talk." My heart sank. That didn't bode well. "Are you alone?"

"Yes. Are you?"

"Kind of. Look, Francesca. At this point, maybe we should give each other a little space. Interface with other people. I mean friends, I don't mean any—"

A cold, cold ice bomb exploded in the middle of my chest and spread all over. "*Interface*? Is that even a word?" I interrupted him.

"Please, Francesca."

I felt my eyes welling up. But he absolutely would not know that I wanted to cry. That my heart was bleeding. "Yes, of course. Have friends. *Interface* with friends," I said.

Suddenly, everything had lost its enchantment—this amazing, magical place, my quest for Ippolita's work, the secrets to be unraveled—and I just wanted to be home, with Isaac. I wanted to be in the past, when life was *normal*: a menial little life, the two of us, Isaac and me. Nothing special, and yet, to me, it was precious and perfect. With Mexican food on a Wednesday and black and white films on lie-in mornings and walks in the park under the same umbrella. Our neighbor's cat wandering in for treats and spending the night on the couch with us; going for a run to our local free library and jogging back with a new book; friends spilling out onto the balcony during a dinner party, coming home from work on a Friday, switching off our phones and cocooning ourselves into each other.

I longed to go back to the time *before* he'd asked me to marry him. Before he imploded when we were halfway organizing the wedding. Easy for Sofia to tell me to *set myself free*: I was in love with Isaac, and this call had colored everything blue.

I was drying my eyes after our call when I felt something

warm encompass me, and the scent of roses filled my nostrils. It was like a loving hug. I turned around briefly, and I saw that Lavinia was looking at me from the lakeshore, her face illuminated by the morning sun, her pale skin luminous against the dark waters. She wore a long green dress, down to her feet, and a necklace that reflected the light...

A few lines from a poem by Ippolita came back to me:

> *Darkness holds both death and conception*
> *From conception, birth—from birth, light*
> *The light of my soul in the light of the sun*

I'd always loved that poem, since I'd encountered it the first time in university. It spoke of hope. And seeing Lavinia there, with a halo of sunlight, had brought it back in a flash of clarity.

When I finally collected myself and could join the others, I found that a spread of pastries, jam jars, honey, a steaming teapot and a blue *caffettiera* sitting in the middle of a coffee service, like a queen among its servants, were waiting for me. Everything looked glamorous and homey at the same time. What a way to look after yourself in the morning, I considered, thinking of the cereal bar I ingested on the subway on my way to work, or the coffees in carton cups gulped down while scrolling on my phone.

"Did you make all this?" I asked with a smile that I knew didn't look exactly radiant. I was sure Lavinia had noticed the drama that had unfolded before I joined her for breakfast, and my shiny eyes. Why did she give me the impression that she always somehow knew what was going on, and even what I was thinking?

"With Manuela's help!" she said modestly. She looked immaculate and yet simple, with her silver hair piled on top of her head, discreet pink lipstick and... a blue woolen dress that came to her knees, and a tiny silver cross at her neck. Wait.

Where were the green dress and the necklace so thick to reflect the rays of the rising sun? I blinked a few times. It must have been a trick of the light.

"Do try my milk croissants. And I'm especially proud of my jam. I make it from our roses." I didn't even know it was possible to make jam from petals. I didn't think I would be able to eat anyway—my stomach was in a knot after Isaac's words.

I took a croissant, soft and fragrant, and spread it with the rose jam. Its color was so lovely that I could almost taste it *before* tasting it. It melted in my mouth. I let out a little sigh and leaned back on my chair... Lavinia's rose jam seemed to defy even heartbreak.

"So... yeah," I said futilely, thinking Lavinia would be the one to say something next. But no.

She was steady, unafraid of silence and stillness. She kept spreading jam on the croissant, perfectly peaceful. I'd never met anyone that could be so vibrant, and yet so still. How did she do it? I was either electric or exhausted, and nothing in between.

I decided to sound lofty. "Will the *other prospective buyer* join us?" Or was he roaming around the place in search of the collection, without me?

"He woke up early and went for a bike ride. I do hope he won't miss out on breakfast."

I couldn't let him gain an advantage. I swallowed my croissant and took a swig of coffee. "Would you have a bike for me too?"

"Of course."

"Thank you," I said, desperately trying not to chew and speak at the same time—terrible, terrible manners but, like I said before, all is fair in love and art dealing. I lifted my phone halfway out of my pocket to quickly glance at it before my bike ride.

"I'm not curious about other people's business," she said.

"But what's so wonderful, or necessary, in that phone that you keep looking at it?"

I raised my eyebrows. Not much wonderful had come out of it this morning. But who asks a question like that, nowadays? Seriously. We all look at our phones. A lot. Obsessively, even. Why is she surprised? Also, so much for not being curious about other people's lives!

I tried to keep the irritation out of my voice. "Well, I might get news from work..."

"But is everything not settled, with the Zilbersteins?"

"Yes, but they want to keep in touch. And my sister might need me..."

"Is she unwell?"

"No, she's perfectly well. But you never know—"

"Something might have happened between now and three minutes ago, when you looked at your phone last?"

I was speechless for a moment. "I suppose things can happen suddenly."

"So you need to keep an eye on that thing at all times in case of an emergency?"

I shrugged. I realized it sounded ridiculous. "My par... *ex*-partner could message me."

She smiled one of her cryptic smiles that would have looked condescending if it hadn't been for the warmth in her eyes, that undefinable quality of kindness that seeped from her.

At that moment, I saw Thiago's tall silhouette reflected in the water. No more need of a bike for me, then. "Sorry, everyone, I didn't realize how long I'd been away for." He leaned the bike against the terrace and joined us. "I'm starving."

I gazed at him suspiciously. I wish I'd woken up earlier, but I'd completely blacked out the night before. Last thing I remembered was... oh. I fell asleep on his shoulder.

Why was I blushing like a teenager? My eyes met his and a

fresh bout of embarrassment made me look away. He seemed bewildered.

"Not at all. Coffee and tea are still warm, and we did leave something for you. Did you have a good ride?" Lavinia asked.

The Signora had this way to mix warmth, amusement and challenge in the same expression. *This woman is powerful*, I thought, the words forming before my conscious mind could interfere. But Thiago held her gaze with equal strength.

"It was lovely," he said, and then went straight to the point. "Anyway. Francesca and I started reading the diary, and... well, it's an interesting story, but just a story. What should we—?"

"Maybe Claudio can take you out for a tour around the lake?" Lavinia ignored him. "There are a few little islands beyond us; they're deserted and very atmospheric. I can put together a picnic for you?"

"Splendid idea." Thiago almost chewed the words. He got up to stand at the banister, looking out to the water. He seemed flustered.

I fought the impulse to go to him—I was still embarrassed by having fallen asleep on him—and won. But when I was making my way toward the boat, I touched his arm, without a word, and we walked side by side.

———

Before I stepped on the boat, while Claudio and Thiago were getting it ready, Lavinia offered me a pink rose from the garden. "I'll swap that for your phone."

"What do you mean?"

"I mean, if you switch that thing off, I'll give you a rose. To put in your hair," she said.

I took off the straw hat I'd grabbed from my luggage, and bent forward so she could slip the rose behind my ear. "Agreed," I said. I switched the phone off and showed her its black screen.

"And now, you're free. For a little while, at least."

I smiled, but I couldn't help thinking that my Isaac was in there. In that phone. Which was her point, I supposed.

I felt a little more upbeat now, but the conversation we'd had—his request to put even further distance between us—kept going round and round in my head. We weren't together anymore, we were friends and roommates, and we both had to *interface* with other people. How I hated that word. No. I shouldn't lose hope. It was a passing crisis, and we'd find each other again. He was worth the pain, the wait, the humiliation. Even just *thinking* the word humiliation made me cringe. Our love *was* worth it. I had to believe.

"...If you trust me, yeah, it's no problem," Thiago was saying to Claudio when I refocused on the present situation and stopped the self-torture of recounting Isaac's words, one by one.

"Sure. Be my guest," Claudio replied, and climbed back onto the wooden pier. Thiago was at the helm. Oh, okay. So he was a man of many talents.

"You can drive boats?"

"Oh, yes. My dad taught me when I was thirteen," he blurted out, then he quickly added: "Though of course I only started when I was eighteen. The *legal* age." He clarified for my benefit, and gave me a smile that denied his reassurance. I waved to Claudio, a little unsure. I hoped I wasn't bound to be shipwrecked—was boat-wrecked a word?—somewhere.

"Of course. Where's the diary?" I asked. For an answer, Thiago patted his jacket pocket. It wasn't easy to think of Helèna's story in his hands, knowing that he might read on and discover the location of the manuscripts before I could do anything about it. I resolved that next time we separated, *I'd* be the one holding the diary.

But I couldn't hold onto unease when the lake shone in all its splendor. Last night's rain was just a memory, now: the Italian summer had reconquered her realm. I took off my sunglasses to see the real colors, and it was all too beautiful for words.

"Have you been to Italy before?" Thiago asked, but as he saw my face, he did a double take. "Oh, you've been crying?" he said, looking away, to the water and then straight ahead. It was such a direct, personal question: no wonder he seemed embarrassed.

I shrugged. "No. Just contact lens trouble."

He nodded quickly, to show he respected my silence. "So, first time in Italy, yes? You speak the language well."

"Yes, first time, and no, I don't think I speak that well at all, thank you though! You can cut my accent with a knife!"

"I like your accent."

"Why thank you. If we weren't bitter rivals," I joked, "I would think you were being friendly."

"Me? Never." He laughed. With his perfect profile, his hair caressed by the wind and strong arms loosely on the helm, he cut a figure too handsome not to be distracted by it. He wore a casual shirt, open, over a black t-shirt, and sunglasses covered his eyes. Even in the wind, I could smell his fragrance—which today, I thought, had a touch of orange flowers. In lighter times, I would have joked with Sofia about being stranded somewhere so isolated with someone who looked like that; but now, my heart ached too much to make such jokes.

Isaac might have not been conventionally attractive, but I loved him.

"That look again," Thiago said.

"What?"

"See down there? The sky over the hills." He pointed to somewhere on the shore. "The gray clouds moving over. It's like that. Clouds came over you, this morning."

I didn't think he would even notice, let alone being poetic about it. "It happens," I said.

"Whatever it is that is bothering you, I hope it goes away. I really do."

The earnestness and simplicity of those words touched me deeply. A little too deeply, because I felt a little teary again. "Thank you," I whispered.

Enough, Francesca! Whatever was happening in my personal life, I was here for a reason. I would enjoy this moment; I would live it deeply and thoroughly. I inhaled the watery air, and let the beauty around me fill my eyes and heart and mind.

Thiago led the boat all around the lakeshore, with its pebbled strands and pastel-colored villas dotted here and there like confetti. The villas were beautiful, with stone terraces right on the waters and sloping gardens exploding with flowers. Some parts were untouched, with mossy rock walls, ripples breaking on their sides, birds defying gravity with their vertical nests. After a while of swaying on the azure waters under a sunny sky, holding my wide-brimmed hat so it wouldn't blow away in the wind, even my thoughts of Isaac seemed dimmer and further away.

Then Thiago sailed us back into the middle of the lake. Here the water was deep and dark, almost black, and seaweed danced in its depths. We reached a small island, so small it was not much more than a rock, covered in trees that formed a perfect canopy on it.

"What do you think? It's a good place for a picnic," he proposed.

The idea of sitting in the sun, eating delicious food prepared by Lavinia, was a balm for my hurting heart. However, there were miles of water between us and any other human being. It was so isolated.

"Do you have your phone?" I asked Thiago.

"No. Lavinia took it from me."

I giggled. "She *took* it? Like a high school teacher?"

"Well, no. She asked me if it was alright for me to be unplugged for a while. Did you give her yours too?"

"No, I just promised to keep it off."

"Why do you think she has this thing about phones?"

"She wants us to be focused? Or find some inner peace, maybe? She did say she hates technology."

"We're doing business; we're not on a yoga retreat!" Thiago exclaimed.

"Do you think they're part of a cult and we'll be ambushed and captured and be sacrificed in a bloody ritual?" I teased him.

"You watch too much Netflix," Thiago said drily and maneuvered the boat as close as possible to the rocks, until we were almost even with a set of small, mossy steps carved in the stone.

While he did that, I had the chance to notice how agile and strong he was, and how smooth his movements on the boat were, without hesitation. I could see that he was used to being on a boat—more than you'd think a weekend sailor would be. Even his tanned complexion and the sun streaks in his hair suggested... the sea. Yes: he reminded me of someone who spent a lot of time on the sea, not in an office or a gallery, indoors. While I was lost in thought, he'd jumped up on land, and was extending his hand to me.

"Wait! Do I need to climb up there? What if I slip and end up in the lake?" I squealed. I could swim, but the water there seemed so dark and menacing, and deep. All that seaweed, cold and slimy... I was more of a swimming pool kind of girl.

But Thiago had already climbed half the steps, and he was offering me his hand, holding onto the grass with the other. The picnic basket Lavinia had prepared for us was already sitting on the rocks beside him.

"I've got you," he said calmly, confidently.

I've got you.

I don't know why, but those words had the power to calm

me. I held onto his hand and he pulled me up... straight into his arms. The pink rose Lavinia had slipped behind my ear came loose and almost fell, but Thiago grabbed it in mid-air. He slipped it back behind my ear, and the touch of his fingertips on my skin sent a shiver down my spine.

"Thank you," I said quickly; and tried to free myself from his hold—but I looked down to the water, and trembled.

"Come on. You're safe with me," he said, and kept holding my hand as we climbed.

From the top, the view took my breath away. The lake waters glimmered and sparkled, but the clouds Thiago had mentioned were marching on and gave the sky a moody, dramatic look. The island we stood on was tiny, round and topped with a thicket of pine trees that offered protection from the sun and made a sweet, swooshing sound in the wind. We entered the thicket, needles crackling under our steps and releasing a wonderful, calming fragrance.

The air was warm and balmy, and I began to feel suspended in time. On that little deserted rock I could see nothing, hear nothing of the world outside. We could have gone back to Helèna's time, or further back, to when Ippolita was illuminating her manuscripts—we wouldn't have known any different. This place was timeless. As we walked, we made small talk, flowing light and easy. It was strange, that this man who'd so irritated me when I first met him was now making me feel so at ease. I was on a rock in the middle of nowhere with an almost-stranger, and yet I felt safe.

Finally, we found a patch of fresh grass, gently sloping toward the water. We sat with our backs against the trunk of a pine tree, half in the sun, half in shade, in a perfect combination of warmth and cool.

"Hungry?" Thiago said.

"Not yet. Ready to read?" I asked. I took my straw hat off

and leaned back, my legs extended in front of me with one ankle over the other.

"I'll do the honors," Thiago offered, and I was happy to settle and just listen.

The sound of the water lapping the pebbles and birdsong were our soundtrack, as Thiago began.

Dearest Hanna,

It's the end of a long, long day. My cell is so silent and peaceful—I don't think I've ever known a silence so deep. Every evening the Contessa always wanted me to list what I was grateful for and give thanks in prayer: I often struggled to find that feeling inside me at all, let alone new things to mention. She was tired of hearing me say, "I'm thankful I'm alive, and I'm thankful for Jacopo," so I learned to list the things she wanted to hear. But tonight, my list is endless! Tonight, Hanna, I am gratitude itself.

I think of those golden illuminations, and those fragile pages with words I can't understand, but that tell me so much. It's a miracle that I ended up here, not just a coincidence. I'm sure that our parents have something to do with this, watching over us from above.

One night long ago our mother came to me in a dream. At least, I think it was a dream—I'm not entirely sure. She pointed to the calendar on the wall, to the saint day of Santa Caterina... She knew I would end up here. Maybe it was my destiny.

"That's incredible."

"It's quite remarkable, yes. If it's true."

"You still don't believe this happened for real?"

"I don't know. I mean, how can we be sure? And even if it's a real memoir, who says that everything she says in it is true?"

I sat up and crossed my legs. "I had dreams too before

coming here. Remember?"

"Coincidence. They're common themes, in dreams. Water, shadows. Drowning."

"Oh, how I hope to prove you wrong."

"Good luck, then," he said and leaned back against the pine tree.

This man made me feel safe even in these weird circumstances, made me laugh, and was a joy for the eyes, to put it mildly. But he could be so incredibly, totally and completely *irritating*.

"Can you at least suspend judgment until we know more?"

"That's what I'm doing, Francesca," he said with annoying calm, and reprised his reading.

A short time later: dear Hanna! An unplanned post-scriptum for you!

After Aurelie left I noticed I hadn't put away my valise, even though I'd unpacked my few belongings. When I lifted it into the wardrobe, something fell out: it was a green velvet sachet I'd never seen before. When I opened it, I saw it was full of golden coins, with a note from the Contessa:

Forgive me, you, who are more noble than we can ever be. This is almost all that's left. For your new life.

Contessa Masi... despite all her obsessions and her nonsensical rules, the way she deprived me of an education... her last thought for me was one of love. But how did she slip this gold into my valise, when she'd been bedbound and weak for so long?

I'll never know.

I couldn't believe she'd struggled so, especially when she was ill and we couldn't even afford proper heating, but she'd saved all this for me.

I sat on my cot, the shiny coins in my hand. My first thought was to give it to Madre Gloria, as it was clear that the

sisters too lived in dignified poverty, and I didn't want to eat at
their table and keep such wealth for myself only. But when I
raised my eyes and looked out of the window, my face reflected
in the black glass, I remembered the conversation I'd heard on
the train: "We won't be safe anywhere." These sweet sisters—
how would they fare, if the storm hit here too, in this place
where time seemed to have stopped, where history passed by
like wind on its way somewhere else, but didn't pause to make
any change?

I took the sachet and scoured my room for a safe place to
hide it, but I couldn't find any. I opened the window and
examined the wall on both sides, my torso hanging out as
much as I could risk: on the left, I felt a little nook. I slipped
the sachet in there and covered it with the loose stones. A little
nest egg for the sisters and me, whatever happens.

I must have been tired and a little overwhelmed because,
as I was closing the window, I saw something moving among
the trees, in the undergrowth. A fox, or a nocturnal bird.
Maybe a badger...

But what made my heart beat faster was not that something moved there, one of the many little creatures that came
out at night: but that it was pitch-dark, and I should not have
seen it. It was as if darkness moved inside darkness.

Federica?

At the mention of the moving shadow, Thiago and I looked
at each other. He rolled his eyes—but I got the impression that
he was, once again, a little disquieted too.

"Darkness moving inside darkness," I said quietly, and in
spite of the sunshine, with the waters glimmering under the
warm rays before me, I felt a little cold. All of a sudden, the
thicket behind us felt a little gloomier, a little noisier, with the
swooshing of branches against each other, and birds jumping
from tree to tree, and taking flight...

I'm not embarrassed to say that I moved, ever so imperceptibly, a little closer to Thiago.

"Nothing can touch us. We're under Lavinia's protection," he said grandly, and pointed to my rose. I smiled, but such absurd words made complete sense with the strangeness of the situation.

Wait—had I really hoped, for a moment, that he'd touched my rose again?

Dear Hanna,

I started my work in earnest! When I wrote to Madre Agostina that I'm full of energy and not afraid of hard work, I meant it. After morning prayers and Mass, Madre Gloria left me free to decide for myself what needed to be done first, so I elected to tackle the cobwebs and to wash the floors. And believe me, there are a lot of cobwebs and a lot of floors, here!

I was on a ladder in the dormitories, my hair gathered under a handkerchief Aurelie had found for me, when Sister Giulia came and stood looking at me in silence, her hands on her hips. It was unnerving to have someone there watching you while you're two meters from the floor on an unsteady ladder; after a few minutes, I stepped down.

"Sì, Sister Giulia?" I addressed her, a little annoyed. But her eyes told me nothing: she wasn't hostile nor pleasant. They were full of life, and yet blank, which, I understand, is an impossible combination. And yet, it was such. She gestured to follow her to the garden, which I did, and showed me how one of the outside walls was so covered in weeds and ivy that the plants were beginning to eat at the stones. All of a sudden, she looked pleading, as pleading as a very tall, very broad woman with arms as big as my legs can look.

"Of course! I'll finish the cobwebs and do this in no time," I offered.

There was so much on Sister Giulia's shoulders, as strong

as they might be, I thought. It was thanks to her that the sisters had vegetables, fruit and herbs, and she maintained a garden so lovely, it was a joy for the soul. She was also the main carer for the convent's tiny farm, which consisted of a few chickens for eggs and two goats for milk. Giulia nodded, handed me a pair of leather gloves, and left me to it.

Much, much later, I was grateful for the gloves Sister Giulia had given me. There were no more cobwebs in the dormitory and the garden wall was almost free, but my arms were in agony. The weeds were tough as ropes and I was covered in sweat, my skin scratched and red, but I would not be deterred. There was so much to do. The sisters and this beautiful place deserved better, and with three of them being elderly and one too weak, the only strong arms available, other than Sister Giulia's, were mine. I did wonder why they weren't given the resources to pay for a laborer; could it be because of the man who seduced Sister Federica long ago? Aurelie had said that he'd come to do some work in the convent... My arms were too sore for me to keep thinking. I dried my forehead with my elbow and smoothed back my hair, matted with sweat. In turning, I saw Madre Gloria standing at the window of her study, observing me. Maybe she was just making sure I was as useful as I'd made myself out to be, but there was something else in her gaze, which was too intense for a simple appraisal.

The image of Madre Gloria watching Helèna was superimposed with the image of Lavinia watching me. Lavinia too had this intense look, half caring, half appraising...

When I was almost finished and the old stones were clean again, Sister Aurelie came to the rescue with her usual cup of warm milk.

"This is so thoughtful," I said. "Thank you."

"It's just a cup of milk!" She smiled and shrugged.

"But we only have two goats and I'm lucky to get it!" I jibed, only half joking. The blue enamel mug I held in my gloved hand reminded me of another, a flowery china cup full of cocoa, smuggled from the kitchen to me by Jacopo. The Contessa didn't allow me cocoa; she said it was bad for children. But Jacopo knew how to break the rules and not be caught, and so we stood together on the balcony, as night fell on Venice, sipping our hot chocolate. I remember those days like good times, when the Contessa wasn't so ill, and the Conte hadn't gambled everything away yet. But most of all, it was when Jacopo lived at the palazzo, and it was me and him against the world. It's hard to imagine it wasn't that long ago: everything had changed so fast.

I'm only twenty, but my childhood feels like it happened in another lifetime.

I remember one night, when summer melted the air and the lights of the city were reflected on the canal—his profile was exquisite as he leaned against the banister, like a painting in a museum. Portrait of a Young Prince, the painting would have been titled. He had inherited his father's aristocratic looks, but none of the spoiled curve in the Conte's lips, or his calculating eyes; and his mother's delicate beauty, but not her sorrowful, pious expression. Jacopo was untainted. To my child's eyes, he was a hero. My protector from the Conte's rants and the Contessa's manias. The only person who was steady in a world that made no sense to me, the only one who knew what was in my heart and mind.

Aurelie cocked her head a little, and she resembled a sparrow more than ever. "You're lost in thought," she said. There's something in Aurelie that makes me want to open up. I think she reminds me of you, even if the memory is so painful, Hanna. She remained silent, waiting for me to speak, or hold it all inside. I was somewhere between the two, as the memories of what happened ebbed back to me, like a bad dream.

Jacopo arrived home just after the funeral. I hadn't even taken my hat and gloves off, and I was still bidding stiff goodbyes to the Contessa's friends, on the doorstep of Palazzo Masi. I saw him on the other side of the canal, looking at me from under a felted hat, wearing an oversized coat that swallowed him. Why was he not wearing his officer's uniform? I was about to call to him—I even raised my arm halfway, gathering a curious look from the attendees. But something in Jacopo's stance stopped me; I hurried to gain everyone's attention, so they wouldn't follow my gaze to him. Out of the corner of my eye, I saw he'd turned away—he didn't want to be recognized.

I had no idea why he didn't want anyone but me to see him, but after being brought up as brother and sister, I trusted him implicitly. Whatever his reason to remain hidden, I would aid him.

I knew, anyway, when and where he would come...

I waited up for him that night, putting to paper a garbled stream of thoughts and pacing the floor. An era in my life was finished, and another was beginning: but I was starting afresh from nothing but my own strength. I had no home, because I wasn't willing to remain at Palazzo Masi, and even if I'd wanted to, the Conte's advances had made it impossible. I had no education, no money, and the country was at war. The entire world was at war. Whatever I did next, I needed all my tenacity, of which I had plenty, and clear thinking, which at that time, I lacked. Too much had happened, and I was a tangle of emotions and grief and confusion.

It was a moonless night, and I kept a candle lit on my writing desk, its light softer than a petrol lamp, and shivered in my nightgown. I made my way out on the balcony and stood where Jacopo and I had spent so many nights talking, my anxious heart soothed by the ebbing and flowing of the water against the palazzo wall: the slow dance of the laguna. Seaweed moved lazily in the canal underneath me, and clouds sailed in the sky above me.

Finally, I saw a sàndolo approaching—the boat Jacopo used around the laguna. He tied it to the balcony and easily climbed up, having done it a million times. I threw my arms around his neck and the tears started flowing—not the composed, restrained tears I'd shed at the funeral, but the desperate ones of an abandoned child. I tried not to overwhelm him with my grief and confusion, but you know, Hanna, that Jacopo is my brother in everything but blood, and having someone to share the pain and confusion of the moment, at last, was such a relief! I had a piece of my family back. I was so choked, I couldn't speak.

"Helèna, at last. I'm so sorry I couldn't be there while Mother was ill, that you had to do it all by yourself."

"You couldn't be there. And you know how much I cared for her."

"Even if she made your life impossible?" Jacopo's hands were on my shoulders and his eyes were burning into mine. He was challenging me to put into words something that, back then, I couldn't have said aloud, bound as I was in the Contessa's stifling world.

But I couldn't deny that what he'd said was true: she'd made my life near impossible. "Even then, yes. Jacopo, don't forget that she loved you so..."

Jacopo scowled. "Did she?"

"Of course! How can you doubt that?"

His tone became tender, and the touch on my shoulders lighter. "You really don't know, Helèna?"

"Know what? You and she were close."

"We were. Before she tried to take away the most precious thing in my life."

I was lost. "Jacopo, what do you...?"

But he didn't let me finish: he found my lips with his.

I froze, unable to reject him, unable to accept the kiss. When he finally let me go, I took a step back. The room felt cold all of a sudden, and I wrapped my arms around my chest. I thought I was sleeping and any moment I would wake up because what just happened could not be true.

He called my name.

I couldn't speak. The taste of him on my lips, the feeling of his hands grasping my shoulders... This was my brother. *The man I knew and loved as my kin, my family. The man that now, as the flickering light of the candle revealed and yet hid his features, was a stranger to me.*

"Okay, this is embarrassing to read," Thiago said in a clipped tone.

"Let me," I said, hiding a smile, and I took the diary from him. It was funny to see Thiago squirming with unease. "I won't impose romantic scenes on you."

"Good," he said. "You know what? Just skip it. There are no clues at this point, I suppose."

"No way. I want to know everything. Come on, steel yourself," I joked. He was acting like a kindergarten boy, and I found it funny.

"I don't understand," I murmured. It was all I could muster.

"You didn't know? You never... you never saw my feelings for you? I've been in love with you since I was old enough to feel love! Mother made me promise I would never ask you in marriage. She said if I did, she would repudiate both of us, that her heart would be broken. Now she's gone, finally..."

"Jacopo, stop! How..." I covered my face with my hands. This wasn't happening. "I had no idea. The Contessa never said anything, as for us... I told you. We're brother and sister."

I watched as his confusion turned into surprise—and

disappointment, deep in his bones. I wanted to hold him in my arms and comfort him, like he'd so often done with me, but I couldn't anymore. He'd believed now we'd be closer than ever —but what he did had pulled us apart.

"How is it even possible, that you didn't know..."

"I can't answer that, Jacopo. Maybe I'm a fool, maybe I'm naïve. Maybe..." I frowned. "So that was why she... she kept us apart. I know she did, but she said it was because she didn't want me to distract you, that you had to work hard, concentrate on your career in the army. It made sense to me. I made sure I would not burden you with family affairs, I—"

"She wasn't worried about my career. She was concerned about me marrying a Jewish girl with no family, no connections, no social status."

I think I felt my heart breaking. I'm quite sure I heard a crack, coming from my chest. "Did she really say that?"

"Oh, yes. She didn't want the young Conte to marry someone without wealth nor title. But the worst thing for her would have been having a Jewish daughter-in-law, and half-Jewish grandchildren. She couldn't have borne that."

"I see."

"When she forbade me from asking you to marry, she also told me she had consumption. I couldn't contradict her wishes then because I knew it would kill her. So I assured her I would stay away from you. But of course, I could never do that. I just waited until my love for you would not hurt her. I understand now, it was a mistake. I should have fought for you, instead of biding my time."

"No."

"Helèna..."

"She was what she was. Generous, and loving, and hateful and horrible. She was all that."

"I love you. I always did. Ever since I met you, I knew..."

His brow was pinched, as if he was trying to decipher the situation, to unravel what just happened.

"Ever since you met me? We were children!"

"But I knew. I knew you were the woman I would marry one day. I thought you felt the same."

"Please, don't come near." My world had just been turned upside down.

"You can't possibly be afraid of me."

"What's happened to you? This is not you..."

"It is me. It's always been me."

"Your father asked me to marry him."

Jacopo stood immobile for a moment—then he lowered his chin. His hands opened and closed. There was no need to add anything else. The disgust, the repulsion I'd felt, he felt, were clear.

"And now this."

"How can you compare us, Helèna? How can you compare my father to me? That... lecher... to what you and I always had?"

"What did we have? You were my brother. I'm your little sister," I repeated.

"You're not a child anymore! How can you... how can we advance, how can we build ourselves a life if you're stuck here, in this old palazzo that's falling into the water, falling around our ears as we speak... You sit there"—he pointed to my writing desk—"writing letters to the dead! Your sister is dead. You know that, don't you?"

I didn't want to hear any more. After what he said about you, there was nothing to add. My cheeks were damp with tears, and I was cold, so cold.

I know you're not dead, my beloved sister. I know you're waiting for me somewhere, I'm sure of it, and I won't let anyone tell me any different.

When they took me to Venice, to the Masi family, I

remember what was said: she has a sister, but we couldn't find her. *They couldn't find you. Nobody said you were dead. They're two quite different things, two completely different things, to be dead and to be lost.*

"I'm sorry. I'm sorry, Helèna. I shouldn't have said that..." *He stood there, waiting for me to say that it was alright, or maybe that I saw the sense in his advances, or even that I felt the same.*

I said none of that. "Why did you not come to the funeral? Why did you hide from your family's friends?"

"I can't be seen in Venice, right now. It's... army business."

A horrible suspicion came over me. Sometimes the Conte disappeared too, so that his creditors couldn't have access to him for a while. Could it be that Jacopo was walking down the same road? I had no words to express this fear of mine. I knew that if I said it, and it wasn't true, he would never forgive me.

The world seemed to be still for the longest moment. All I could hear were soft ripples of the water against my balcony. A boat must have passed on the canal, under the moonless sky.

"Amore mio. *I'm so sorry I've upset you this way. Maybe one day... you'll change your mind. If you do, I promise I'll be there,"* Jacopo said, *and his tone was so tender, so full of love that I was brought back to the times when we stood together against our family and against a world we couldn't control or understand.*

Will I ever be free of the Masi family, my Hanna? And if Jacopo came for me—how would I feel?

Because Jacopo... is still a part of me.

I couldn't say all that to Sister Aurelie. I couldn't sum up years of life with the Masi family, giving away their secrets, and mine. I just hid my face, pretending to examine the freshly scrubbed wall, and at that moment the bell for midday prayers rang.

During meals we were asked to remain silent—even

Aurelie complied. We ate in the kitchen instead of the refectory, to save on burning wood; and while we were eating—I was devouring my soup and bread, famished after the hard morning's work—Madre Gloria kept looking at me, as if weighing me up.

Something was afoot—and I prayed I hadn't failed her, somehow, so much that she wanted to send me home. After that thought, I lost my appetite.

"Can I see you in my study, Helèna?" she said once the meal was finished.

I knew it. I tried to tell myself I was being unreasonably apprehensive. Maybe it was because I'd broken the rules the night before, chatting to Aurelie after the evening prayers? Though Sister Aurelie seemed to have escaped her wrath...

I followed her to the study and stood in silence, head bowed, waiting.

"Your poor hands! Please ask Sister Emilia for an ointment. She has every sort of remedy in her apothecary."

"I will, thank you," I said, rubbing my hands together. Despite the gloves, my hands bore scrapes and grazes from the rope-like weeds. "Madre Gloria, I'm so sorry about last night, when Aurelie and I were talking when it was silent time. I promise it won't happen again. I..."

"Of course it won't happen again." She smiled. "After a little while of waking at dawn, you'll fall asleep when you ought to."

"Yes, Madre."

"But that is not why I called you here. Helèna, I'm going to ask you a favor."

This took me aback for a moment. "Of course. Anything."

"It concerns the library. The last catalog of our books was composed half a century ago. Before our convent... how can I put it... before our numbers dwindled."

I was dying to enquire if she was referring to Sister Federica's story, but bit my tongue.

"It's a big endeavor, I know..." Madre Gloria continued.

It took me a moment to fully grasp what Madre Superiora was asking of me. "Are you asking me to catalog the books?" I brought a hand to my chest. "But I... never even went to school..."

"I am sure you can do this. It's simply a matter of recording the title, the author, the place and date of publication and the publishers on a record card. You'll then place all the cards in alphabetical order. We have all the materials, and it's a relatively simple task, but quite monumental, and time-consuming..."

"That would be magnificent!" The mental image of me sitting at a table surrounded by books, taking notes and examining spines and covers and thumbing the pages, was so similar to my memories of our parents' work that I was almost choked.

"I'm delighted. But remember, I can't dispense you from the chores you came here to do. I would rather you dedicate yourself to this, but we..."

"Please, don't trouble yourself. I understand. I'll do it in my own time. It's a privilege! Thank you, Madre Gloria!"

She tilted her head slightly. "Figlia mia... when you arrived you looked so sad. But your face, right now... it's like you're a different person."

I shrugged. "Maybe I'm just the person I was always meant to be?"

All my love on this wondrous day,
Your sister Helèna

A morning postscript, dear Hanna: I dreamed Jacopo was looking for me, and I was just behind him, but he couldn't find me... He wandered in the dark, his arms extended. In my sleep, I felt a hand holding mine—it was so real, those cold fingers *intertwined with mine... I woke up with a jolt, but of course, there was nobody there.*

And now that the dawn is still a long way away, I ask myself if I'll ever see him again: and my heart answers.

Yes, there is no doubt that I will.

"Francesca... are you alright?"

I'd dried a rogue tear with my finger. So completely unprofessional. Unacceptable. *Your sister.* Those two words were enough to make me tear up. I thought of Sofia, and suddenly I missed her so intensely that it physically hurt.

"That *was* intense," Thiago conceded.

"It was."

Jacopo's plight had moved me more than I thought. I could see Helèna's point of view, her sisterly feelings toward Jacopo. But I also knew what Jacopo was going through, the unrequited love, the yearning, the powerlessness. Thiago got up and walked a few steps down the slope. I reached him, and I stood looking out to the lake, the breeze in my hair now stronger than before, and the pewter clouds almost above us. Only then I noticed that there were tiny pastel dots in the distance—I'd lost my sense of direction with the wandering around the lake.

"Is that village...?"

"That's Lodego. Santa Caterina is behind us."

"Believe it or not, my mother's family came from Lodego. My great-grandparents emigrated to New York."

"So you're a local," Thiago said with a smile.

"In a way. Nobody in the family has ever been back, that I know of."

"You know, I have ties with this place too. Some relative of my mum came from here, but we were never big on family history, so I don't have the whole story."

"Same."

Standing here, so close to my roots, the question of why my

parents barely spoke about our family history felt pressing. Sometimes my father would make a reference or two, but my mother, never. I didn't get the impression that she had any bad memories about my grandparents, in fact, she mentioned them with great affection, and she missed them: my gut feeling was that the memories simply weren't passed down. There had been a kind of cut, of hiatus between life in Lodego and life in America, with stories and memories left to sink into the Atlantic. I couldn't wait to go to Lodego and see with my own eyes where we came from.

"So you were never here before? You seem familiar with the lake."

"I wasn't, no. And I'm not really familiar with this lake. I love sailing. I mean... I *loved* sailing. I don't do it much anymore."

He ran his hands in his hair and, for a brief moment, felt his forehead with his fingers. I noticed for the first time that he had a scar on his left temple, crescent-shaped and continuing beneath his hair. He seemed to shake himself and brought both of his hands behind his back. The way I'd seen him talking to Lavinia when he first arrived—the pained expression on his face, Lavinia's concerned look—I wondered if it was connected to this sudden sadness.

"Are you hungry?" he said quickly, cheerfully: but it was too late, because I'd already seen the shadow of pain in his eyes. It was clear he wanted to change the subject, so I obliged.

"Yes I am, actually." Helèna's story had been so compelling, only now was I returning to my body. Yes, I was hungry—and felt a little heady with sunlight, as if I'd *plugged* myself in. "I think it will rain soon," I said, lifting my head up to the sky. At that moment, a gust of wind hit us, wonderful in its freshness and laden with a watery scent.

Thiago laid the blanket on the grass, and we fished the goodies out of the box: fresh, soft rolls, cold meats and boiled eggs, containers with colorful salads, strawberries and a cake with rose icing. I took out a bottle of wine kept in a small tub with ice, and fruit juices the colors of the rainbow. A *simple* picnic, Lavinia style.

We ate in silence for a bit, until Thiago spoke. "I don't get it."

"What?"

"Everything, I suppose. This whole situation. This... treasure hunt. The way she's treating us like..." He made a gesture toward the generous spread. "Like guests."

"The way she made us switch off our phones," I added.

"Yeah. It's all so personal. And strange. Also, why only the two of us? Apparently Ippolita Von Oswald's—"

"Oswen."

Mmm. He seemed to have spent more time sailing than studying history of art. I suppose he did say he was more in the business side of things.

"Von *Oswen's* work is incredibly valuable, but there's only us two bidding for it. Well, playing treasure hunt for it. Why?"

"No idea," I said, helping myself to a slice of cake.

"You don't think it's strange?" Thiago asked.

"I do. And I'm waiting to see how it all unfolds," I said. "Come on, eat. The brain needs nutrition."

"*Si!* And cake has all the brain nutrition we need!"

After a couple of mouthfuls I began to think aloud. "I wasn't even supposed to be here," I mused. "My boss' daughter was supposed to come, but she couldn't. Just as well, because Lavinia wanted me. I wonder, would she have turned away my boss' daughter? Sent her back? I can't imagine Cassidy doing all this, anyway."

Thiago swallowed a bite. "She asked for you specifically?"

"Yep. Did she ask for you?"

"Not exactly... Well, kind of."

What did that even mean? I waited, but he wasn't forthcoming—instead, the shadow of pain came back. His features became alive with emotion, and somehow, this made him look... beautiful. And not just because of the way he looked, with those long lashes and generous lips, and the hooded eyes that made him seem perpetually languid—but because I knew I'd caught a glimpse of the soul inside.

It was as if a bridge between me and him had suddenly appeared, and I didn't want it to go. For a moment, the desire to touch his face, to hold him and make his pain go away was so strong, I froze. My gaze wandered to the sky closing in on us.

I'd just met this guy. Also, men had been pretty much invisible to me since Isaac came into my life. Now that I thought about it, everyone had been almost invisible to me since then. Maybe even... myself. If that made sense?

And it didn't feel like I'd known Thiago for mere days—it didn't feel like he was a stranger... It was then I realized that his eyes were on me, and he was studying my face. I wondered what it was that he saw, as each person perceives us in a different way: the bookish, awkward woman, or the ambitious art dealer desperately looking for a break? Someone who'd just been abandoned almost at the altar, who had tears in her eyes not long before; or the person who laughed and chatted and ate up every moment of every day? All these sides made the prism that was me. I was almost overcome with the desire that he... that he would *like* me.

I turned around and he was startled, but he didn't look away.

"Don't worry, I'm not about to go all Jacopo on you," he said in a voice that was a little lower, a little hoarser than usual. A warm drizzle began falling on us: the laden clouds had finally reached us.

"Time to go home," I said quickly, and began gathering the debris, as the rain became thicker and thicker, and washed Lavinia's rose away.

CHAPTER 8

THE ISLAND OF SANTA CATERINA

I was on the little, narrow bed that had been Helèna's, going over everything that had happened. Sofia's silken rose was in my hand.

The diary sat on my desk. I'd promised Thiago that I would not read it without him, and I didn't intend to break that promise. The phone, temporarily forgotten in between Lavinia's bonbons and the diary, started chiming. Back in New York my friends were getting out of work and hitting the subway, or the restaurants, or in Sofia's case, her yoga class. I got up from the bed and seized it—maybe it was what was happening with Isaac, maybe Lavinia's contempt for technology had influenced me, but I didn't feel quite as attached to that thing now. I had no desire to reply to anyone but Sofia... though I wasn't going to tell her about the whole *let's give each other space* Isaac situation. I knew what she would say, and I felt pathetic enough as it was.

Your pics are amazing. Making progress? she texted.

Hopefully!

She answered at once. *Heard from Isaac?*

What? Sofia never asked after *the guy*, as she called him. First his request to give each other space. Now my sister's question. My radars were in full alarm.

Yes, of course I did.

I could see Sofia was typing. Typing. Typing...
She was taking ages! What did she want to say, but wasn't saying?

Class starting. I need another picture dump ASAP.

That was not what she wanted to say. I was sure. What the hell, I had to speak to Isaac. My finger was hovering on his name as I fought against my anxious desire to hear his voice. I was about to tap the call button, when I heard a male voice calling my name. Thiago.

I opened the door with my phone in hand, half relieved, half annoyed. No: it was a good thing, that he'd interrupted me, because one, I was about to make a fool of myself and, two, I wasn't there to mope about my ex-boyfriend, but to acquire the collection.

"*Scusa*, am I interrupting something?"

"No. Nothing important." I swallowed. "The gold. We didn't check if the gold is there," I said quickly. "Come in."

I opened the window; it was low enough to jump out of—a little narrow, but I could squeeze myself through. I landed on the grass, barefoot as I was, and began to feel the stone wall with my hands.

"Anything?" Thiago asked, and leaned on the windowsill. My breath caught for a second. Framed by the window, with his burned-gold wavy hair and dark eyes he looked like the portrait of a Renaissance prince you'd see in a Florentine museum.

Wait, where did I hear that before? Jacopo. Helèna had

written that he looked like the prince in a portrait. Her words were seeping into my mind.

"I think I found the indentation, but there's nothing in it. No gold."

"I'm not surprised. Come, wear something warm and put shoes on," he replied. "I want to show you something. Oh, and bring the diary."

"It doesn't really mean anything, that the gold isn't there. Even if it's a true story like Lavinia says, it happened almost eighty years ago. Someone might have taken it," he said as we walked. "I suppose it doesn't really matter if the whole story is real or not, does it? As long as it leads us to the collection," he said. I followed him, and he led me down the corridor—not toward the terrace, but in the opposite direction.

"It is real. I know it. Where are we going? Manuela said that on this side there's only water..."

"Exactly. Look!"

We'd come to a brick wall—metaphorically *and* literally. It looked as if it would once have been one of the convent's outbuildings before the water had reclaimed part of it. The ghost of an arched door was still visible in its stonework.

"But this must be where... no. It can't be." I turned around, then back. "According to Helèna's diary, she stepped out into a paved passage, from the convent to... the *library*."

"Yes. I think it's the library too. Look, I drew a map. I don't have the best sense of orientation, but I tried." He took out a piece of paper from his pocket and unfolded it. "So this is the convent, this is the church." He followed his sketch with his finger. "Inside the convent we have the terrace, the old refectory, the cells, the inner garden, and beyond the garden Lavinia's private quarters. The library should be here." He pointed to a space he'd marked "water."

"Let's go see," I said, and we made our way out through the main door.

Twilight had turned the sky violet and lilac and pink, and shapes and silhouettes seemed to melt into each other. We walked toward the shore, where mist rose from the ground and from the water, so that the two melted into each other. Such a beautiful, yet treacherous place. One wrong step, thinking you'd land on the muddy ground beneath the reeds, and you'd slip into the lake... the thought made me shiver.

"No library building. No buildings at all," I said pensively. I turned round and round, my feet getting wet in the marshy bit between water and land. "Maybe we'll find an explanation for it in the diary. Not much point in asking Lavinia. I have a feeling she would quickly change the topic of conversation."

"She would. Here, take some bon-bons! Take some croissants! Go for a picnic!" Thiago imitated her.

I had to laugh. "Like Calypso in *The Odyssey*, keeping Odysseus and his shipmates in her enchanted garden."

"No idea what you're talking about, but... look what I found," he said, taking hold of my hand—I didn't protest—and leading me down a few steps. Among the reeds was a tiny boat, a half-walnut shell, almost.

"Wait. Are we going on the lake on *that*?" The last flames of sunset were now dying in the west, and the lilac air was turning blue: I wasn't sure I wanted to be on the water when night fell.

"Not too far from the shore," Thiago tried to reassure me. "I want to check something. Trust me."

"If I drown, I'll come back to haunt you, like Federica..." I muttered, but I still followed him, careful to rest my feet where he'd laid his own, and not lose my footing. He climbed into the boat and then helped me inside, while I held onto the diary as tight as I could. "Is this really necessary?"

"Relax." He grabbed the oars sitting inside and pushed the boat out.

I gazed toward the sky, where the first stars were beginning to peep, silver among lavender—the boat was so small that it was almost a cradle. "It's beautiful," I murmured.

"See? It was worth trusting me. Now, who's reading?"

"You," I said, and settled to listen as if it were a bedtime story.

Dear Hanna,

I've been here for a month, now. Never has my life been so peaceful, never have I felt such freedom like I do here, on a tiny island with a group of old women whose life is restricted both by their rules and by their location. Strange, I know.

And strange to feel so much peace, in these terrible times!

This is an island in more ways than one: Madre Gloria reads the newspapers—the boatman brings them sporadically —but she forbids the sisters to discuss the war, because they are not to be of the world, they're to continue working and praying: evil will never prevail. After she's read them, she scrunches up the papers and takes them to the garden, to Sister Giulia, to burn in the brushfire.

I have no desire to know what is happening out there. This is the first season of happiness I've had since forever, and I'll do all I can to keep the strife and grief of the war out of my little world.

Every day I do my chores, and it gives me such pleasure to see this convent that is our home cleaned and scrubbed and restored to order, and to help Sister Giulia with the animals and the garden. When I'm finished, I go to the library. This is my time. Sometimes I wish I could bring my pillow and blankets and close my eyes among the books... Every night is a wrench, when we're called for prayers and supper. Often I return to my books after supper, cataloging them by title, author, date and place of publication... I work with my coat and hat on, because the library is so cold. Often, dear Aurelie brings me a cup of herbal tea, to help keep me warm.

One night, on my way from the library to my cell, the night was so beautiful, so enchanted, that I had to stop on the lakeshore and take it all in. There was a perfectly round, pristine silver moon reflected on the waters and shining in the first cloudless sky I'd seen in weeks. But the omnipresent white mist that rose from the water and the land was still there, and at every step I sank into transparent snow. I began to walk along the shore, hoping to steal a few minutes alone with the lake and the moon, and left the church building behind me. I had my nose up in the air, so I didn't see a tangled bush in front of me and fell head first. I was still breathless and confused, when the ground seemed to be pulled from under me, and I rolled down a steep slope to find myself among the undergrowth of a dark thicket. I lay there for a moment, in a daze.

As absurd as it seems, it was as if a hand had landed on my back and, with a small push, helped by the inclination of the ground, it sent me rolling down. Above me, the silver moon shone silent, criss-crossed by black branches. When I finally succeeded in sitting up, a bit dizzy and sore, but with all my bones still whole, what I saw made me believe I'd ended up in a fairy tale. Just like Hansel and Gretel finding the gingerbread house in the forest, in front of me there was a tiny stone house with a baby-sized door and window—and for a moment it seemed to me that a candle was gleaming behind the glass... no—there was no candle, only the shimmer of the moon. My eyes must have deceived me.

I opened the door and stepped in, stooping to fit in the small entrance. I couldn't see well, so I took out the candle and matches I always kept in my coat pocket and lit up the scene. I saw that in the middle of the space there was an altar, with two candelabra on top: it was a chapel, then, so small that barely two, maybe three people could fit in. The silence and the light of the candle in the gloom made the *place mystical. Or magical, should I say—though I can almost hear the voice of the Contessa berating me for using that word.*

At that moment something flew across the ceiling and hit the top of my head, taking a strand of my hair with it and making me squeal—only to bump against the altar and knock down one of the candelabra. A bat, I thought. I rubbed my head and went to pick up the fallen object—but something at the periphery of my vision didn't quite make sense. I did a double take: there was an opening behind the altar, so tiny that it was barely visible. I kneeled with the candle, but the opening was so small and dark that I couldn't see what was beyond. Maybe it was just the building itself sitting on unsteady ground, with the lakeshore so close, slipping sideways and revealing its foundations? Maybe the chapel was in dire need of repairs...

I couldn't finish the thought, because something dark covered the window, and with it the light of the moon. It lingered there for a moment, and then disappeared. I heard myself gasping in fear—and then I was, quite simply, annoyed. Enough was enough. Rolling down the slope, a bat or whatever it was slapping my head, shadows appearing on the moon—there was something deliberate about all this. I'd been led here, to this chapel, to the opening behind the altar.

"Whatever you are, whoever you are, fine! I'm going!" I said aloud.

Exasperation had made me brave. I turned and kneeled on the cold ground. I knew I was being foolhardy, to say the least, but I couldn't turn away now. I felt the space with my feet—there was an indentation—a step. I had to make sure to keep the candle straight, so it wouldn't be extinguished, nor would I set myself on fire. I went down, step by step. If I fall here and break something, they'll never find me, I thought. However, I kept going—maybe because I was afraid that something else would happen in order to make me proceed. Like being hit on the head or made to roll all the way down.

I found myself in a round cellar, with walls made of compacted soil. I lifted the candle to see better and realized there was a tunnel opening on one of the walls, a pitch-black hole. After having done all this, I couldn't stop now, even if the opening was so dark, and frightening. I slipped down and landed on my feet, thankfully—but the ground was muddy, and I ended up on my knees, face to face with something white and glowing. It was a miracle that the candle was not extinguished—but what I saw in front of me made me wish it had been. Hanna, it was bones, human bones. Two bodies, lying entwined.

I think I've found Federica and her lover.

I was trying to catch my breath, when a loud, dull noise from outside made me shrink and cover my head instinctively. The candle fell and I was in darkness, alone with the lost bones. For a moment I was so frightened I could have cried, when a tiny little light, glowing blue somewhere above me, showed me the way out. Federica had led me to her remains, and now she was guiding me back onto the surface. I felt my way up and out, my arms extended, touching soil and stone.

The sisters had all run out and were standing on the shore, looking to where the terrible noise had come from. I saw Sister Aurelie limping toward the water, carrying a lamp and grimacing from the effort of hurrying, and Sisters Emilia and Santia crossing themselves. The dark hills were tinged with orange. Just as Sister Giulia and Madre Gloria emerged from the kitchen, another explosion racked the ridge in the distance —a red glow lit up the mist and the same deep, dull noise I'd heard before rumbled the ground beneath us, like a gunshot, but a hundred times louder. The orange tinge spread—now we could clearly see the flames rising to lick the sky.

"The bridge!" Sister Aurelie screamed and brought her

hand to her mouth. The hill was on fire, glowing against the black in a way that, had it not been terrible, would have been beautiful to behold.

"What happened?" I whispered to Madre Gloria, too breathless and scared to speak aloud.

"Someone blew up the railway bridge!" she cried, pale, almost gray in the light of Aurelie's lamp.

"Who could have done that?" Aurelie cried. We all huddled together, watching the glow of the flames on the horizon.

"It has nothing to do with us," Sister Emilia said, frowning, as if Aurelie's question was a threat in itself.

Madre Gloria looked on, silent. I brought my hands to my head to try to remove the cobwebs from my hair. I was trembling. We were all standing in a line, now: myself, Madre Gloria the sisters... I blinked.

I swear that for a moment there was a seventh person there with us: a dark shape that stood solid for a moment, before vanishing in the dusk light.

"Now *that's* a bombshell," Thiago said, and sat up to stretch.

The boat swayed and I panicked, trying to hold onto both sides—but I couldn't quite find my grip. I ended up against his chest, one hand around his arm, the other curled up against him. We were both startled by this development, because we froze, rigid for a moment—and then he joined his hands gently on my back.

"You're safe. I promise."

It was strange and sweet—and I didn't find it in myself to pull away. Instead, I closed my eyes, and rested for a moment. The boat was swaying gently, and being in Thiago's arms felt exactly like that—safe. But then, something else made its way inside me, a warmth I hadn't felt in a long time. A shiver traveled down my spine. Thiago bent his head toward me, and I felt his face against my neck...

I pulled away, breathless. This couldn't happen. Not now. For a million reasons.

"So, she found Federica. Buried below a chapel," I said, trying to keep my voice steady. I failed, of course, and the words came out all shaky. Thiago released me, his hands disentangling as he felt me lean back.

"Yeah. I... I'll keep on reading."

I felt cold, and quite bereft as we parted, one at each end of the boat. The stars were bright now, and the rippling waters made a sweet sound.

No talk of ghosts could disquiet me now, not any more than Thiago's closeness had.

My dear Hanna,

We've all been skittish and overwrought since the explosion, yesterday. The mist has descended on the island, isolating us from the harshness of the world, and everything feels soft and quiet. The boatman was supposed to make his monthly trip to the convent, bringing us supplies, but there's no trace of him. Sister Santia needed her medication—it can't be made in the convent's apothecary. Madre Gloria tried to call the pharmacy to ask for someone else to row it over, but the telephone wasn't working—maybe because of the explosion. Someone had to go to the mainland; Sister Aurelie volunteered at once, of course.

"Please, Madre Gloria! Let me go! Maybe I can find some real soap, and not that ashy thing we've been using!"

"Be thankful you have that ashy thing," Sister Santia said, quite sanctimoniously. "I must take this upon myself. After all, the medication is for me."

"Really, I'm more than happy to go," Aurelie insisted. She's so transparent, I had to smile. I knew she was hankering

after her favorite Miscela Leone, a dry mixture of herbs that's supposed to make our chicory taste of something more than brown water, but Emilia and Santia aren't keen on such luxuries, deeming them a waste of the little money we have. "Maybe Helèna could come with me?"

I wasn't keen on leaving my work at the library, but I would do it for Aurelie. Before Madre Gloria could express an opinion, Sister Giulia stepped forward, in her usual silence.

"E va bene, Sister Giulia," the Madre Superiora decided. Aurelie looked a little crestfallen, but Emilia and Santia seemed positively relieved, and quite satisfied that Giulia would check Aurelie's spending. It was settled.

From one of the library windows, I saw the little boat carrying Aurelie and Giulia disappear on the mist, and my stomach churned with apprehension. I wasn't surprised when, as I bent over my catalog cards, a sudden shadow darkened the window for an instant, and passed over.

"Federica?" I whispered. My heart was galloping when, at my call, the shadow darkened the window again. It was as if she was calling me out, and I followed her outside. I stood in front of the water, a hand on my forehead—what was she trying to tell me?

I didn't tell anyone about the bones I'd found in the little lost chapel. I'm not sure why. Part of me wanted to inform Madre Gloria and give them a proper burial; part of me felt that Federica had shown me where she was, but needed or wanted nothing else from me.

I looked out onto the mist. The surface of the lake was still. No sign of our boat.

An hour passed, then two, then it was time for prayers, and then our midday meal. Aurelie and Sister Giulia had not returned.

Madre Gloria disappeared to her study to try and telephone the pharmacy again. But she was barely gone, and I was helping Emilia and Santia clean up the kitchen, when Sister Giulia walked in. She had sailed on the mist, and nobody had heard her. She was pale as milk, her eyes wide. I ran to get Madre Gloria, and we stormed the silent sister with questions.

"Are you hurt?"

"Where is Sister Aurelie?"

That was the first and last time I ever heard Sister Giulia speaking. Her voice was hoarse from lack of use, and she looked pained by having to talk.

"Gone."

A hundred questions came forth, but Madre Gloria raised a hand and silenced us all. "What are you saying, Sister Giulia? How did she get lost in the village? How did you lose sight of her?"

Giulia simply stood, a pained expression on her face.

"Did someone take her?" *I blurted out.*

Giulia nodded slowly.

"Madre Gloria, please, can I go and look for her?" *I pleaded, but Madre Gloria kept her eyes fixed on Giulia.*

"Do you know who took her?" *she enquired, her words slow and loud—Giulia was in a state of shock. She didn't speak again, but simply shook her head.*

"Madre Gloria. Please, let me go," *I begged.*

"Certainly not. I will. I should have gone in the first place. How could I have been so foolhardy, with the explosion, the boatman nowhere to be found, and the telephone out of order! I've been a fool. A fool!" *I'd never seen Madre Gloria so frantic: she, who was always so poised.*

"Let me come with you," *I pleaded. I couldn't let Madre Gloria face the same danger that Aurelie had encountered, alone.*

"Get your coat," *she conceded. I was about to do so, when a suffocated prayer came from Sister Santia. With a trembling finger, she pointed to the window. A small boat, one I'd never* seen before, was floating there, unmoored. We ran out once again, and called out into the fog.

"Aurelie!"

Giulia, Madre Gloria and I ventured into the shallow water—but before we could reach the boat, Santia and Emilia's voices rose from the shore. "She's here! She's here!"

"Oh, Vergine Santa! She's drowned..." Madre Gloria cried.

I couldn't believe my eyes. I didn't want to believe my eyes.

Aurelie was lying unconscious on the pebbles, her hair fanned around her face, her skin the color of a blue egg, not quite blue, not quite white. Her thin white legs were bare, and Sister Emilia, sobbing and praying, pulled Aurelie's habit down.

Madre Gloria took Aurelie's face in her hands, and her tears mixed with the water that drenched Aurelie. "I should have protected you," she said simply.

Emilia and Santia were crying and holding each other's hands. "What could have happened? What could have happened?"

"Helèna, please help me. Let's carry her inside," Madre Gloria said.

Sister Giulia rushed in, her cheeks dry, her eyes full of pain. But the moment Giulia and I began to lift her, Aurelie made a low sound, a gurgle—almost inaudible... She was alive!

Sister Giulia threw herself on her knees and laid her lips on Aurelie—it was as if she'd sucked away the water and breathed back in air. She pushed Aurelie into a seated position and banged on her back, violently.

Aurelie vomited lake water and wheezed and sputtered. "Scar..." she half-whispered, half-gurgled.

"Aurelie, breathe, breathe!" I cried out.

We clustered around her, all of us except Sister Emilia,

who kneeled in prayer just outside the circle, her eyes closed and her hands together.

"Sca... elp..."

Madre Gloria held Aurelie to her and rocked her like a child. "Breathe, figlia mia, breathe..."

"Scarlatto," Aurelie whispered, and raised her hand toward the lake.

Madre Gloria turned to me. "Look, she's pointing to..."

To the boat. I took off my shoes quickly and stepped into the cold waters, until I reached the unmoored boat. Inside, there was a man. I had to swallow back a scream of horror: the man's face and hands were bandaged, and blood was seeping through. The explosion of the night before came back to my mind.

In that moment, I knew the war had arrived at Santa Caterina.

We brought Aurelie and the man inside and laid them in bed, in a cell each. We helped Aurelie change and gave her some hot herbal tea, and soon she was recovered, albeit pale and weak. Sisters Emilia and Santia looked after the stranger, while Madre Gloria gently questioned Aurelie and Sister Giulia.

"We were on our way back, but Sister Giulia said she'd forgotten to buy some new sewing needles, so she returned to the village and I waited for her near the boats," Aurelie told us, still a little breathless. "An old man came toward me... Well, I thought he was an old man, but he wasn't really, he just walked all bent under a big coat... I thought he had white hair, but they were bandages. He told me to be quiet, that he needed somewhere to hide, and I had to help him..."

A fit of coughing interrupted her—I gave her a sip of water, and she resumed her story.

"He showed me a knife he had under his coat, but it was clear to me that he wasn't going to use it... I told him to put it *away, that I would help him anyway. He said if I screamed, if I gave him away, they would kill him, because he'd blown up the railway bridge."*

Aurelie stopped and squeezed my hand, to steady herself. "I told him I didn't care what he'd done, that I would do my best to help. Someone was coming our way, so we had to be quick... we made it on the boat, I don't know how, me with my legs and him all wounded and bleeding. He tried to cut the rope, but he was too weak—so I did. We rowed the best we could, but I joked he'd chosen the right person to help him! He said I was as brave as a lioness," Aurelie declared, and her pride was touching.

"He asked my name and told me his: Scarlatto. Soon after, he lost consciousness. I didn't know what to do. I rowed almost all the way here..." She looked at her hands, red and blistered, and all wrinkled from being in the water for too long. "But then I just couldn't keep going. I thought the water would be shallow enough for me to walk to shore and alert you all, but I tripped and swallowed so much water, I thought I was going to die! I thought that Scarlatto was going to die! I saw black, and then, when I woke up, you were all around me..." She took a breath, followed by another fit of coughing.

Sister Giulia had busied herself with the fire, and I helped Aurelie to sit beside it. Emilia and Santia scurred in, to let their opinion be known.

"You brought danger to our door," Sister Emilia said, with Santia nodding in agreement.

I saw red. "So much for loving others more than yourself, Sister Emilia! Would you have left that man there to die?"

"He's a criminal!" Santia retorted.

"He's part of a partisan brigade. They fight a guerrilla war against the Germans and the Blackshirts. It's happening all over the country, now," Madre Gloria intervened. It was the first time I'd heard her mention anything about the war. "But

it doesn't matter who he is, or what he did. It shouldn't *matter.*
Sister Aurelie aided someone in need. It might not have been
wise, but it was her Christian duty."

Emilia and Santia were silenced, at least for now.

Muffled laments and cries came from next door: the man
was awake. "I want to see him," Aurelie implored Madre
Gloria, and the older nun nodded her permission. Sister Santia
helped Aurelie up and into the man's cell, while we waited on
the doorstep. Sister Emilia, dark in the face, murmured some-
thing about needing to get some calendula salve and hurried
toward the kitchen, while Sister Giulia had disappeared
already.

I was pretty sure the predicament of this officer required
more than calendula salve, and from the pursed lips of Madre
Gloria I could see she thought the same; but what else could
we do? Certainly not call a doctor, given the situation.

With help, Aurelie kneeled beside the bed and held Scar-
latto's hand. He was of slight build, and blond hair escaped the
makeshift bandages, made of ripped rags. What was visible of
his face was caked with blood, soot and mud. He was writhing,
only half-conscious, and the hand that Aurelie wasn't holding
was pawing at the air, as if looking for something, someone to
steady him.

On impulse, I found his fingers and curled them against
my heart. When I felt the skin of his palm, I tried to keep my
composure, but panic and disbelief were ravishing me and
blanking all thoughts.

There was a round scar on his hand, an old burn, raised
and ridged.

I knew that burn; I knew that hand; I knew that man.

His name was not Scarlatto: his name was Jacopo.

Thiago made a dramatic pause and we stared at each other.
"Oh my good God!" I whispered.

"A novel. A hundred percent, a novel. These things *do not* happen in real life."

"Why not? Jacopo could have been looking for her! My brain is melting with the twists and turns. The place she described... the little chapel! Where she fell just before the explosion and Jacopo's arrival. Where she found Federica and her lover. That could be the hiding place for the manuscripts. We need to find it."

"I think I found it already," Thiago said.

"You've been there without me?"

"No. I think *this* is it," he said and extended a hand toward the side of the boat.

I'd been holding the flashlight so that it shone on the diary. With Thiago moving, the light illuminated the water. We leaned overboard together, and what I saw was a little Atlantis: the ruins of walls and arches and paths were just beneath us, semi-hidden by seaweed.

"We're floating over it. The remains of the library, and the lost little chapel. This whole side of the island is now underwater," Thiago said. "Which is why Lavinia didn't show us the library, and why we will never find the little door behind the stairs. Because where the library used to be, now there's only... lake."

The underwater remains seemed to float in front of my eyes, like a dream only half recalled in the morning. I touched the cold water with my fingers, as if I could reach them. Maybe, if I fell in, I would find myself back in time, with Helèna...

Thiago took my hand, and gently tucked it back inside the boat. "Careful."

"Whatever was inside is lost... what a terrible shame. The books, that beautiful room Helèna described, with the carved wooden shelves. And obviously, the hidden chamber where they kept the manuscripts."

"That couldn't be the hiding place we're looking for. We know for a fact that the collection is still intact."

"True." I leaned on the side of the boat, my chin on my hands. It was such a mysterious, eerie sight. I imagined the books dissolving in the water, the paper they were made of going back to being pulp until they were all gone, the seaweed dancing among the broken shelves. What happened here? What destroyed it all?

Was Federica still lying there, forever entwined with her love?

"Can we stay a little longer?" I asked in a whisper.

"I knew you'd be sold on being here," Thiago said. I gazed at him in the half-light, and time seemed to stop for a moment. I drew in a little, shallow breath, as a wave of sweet chemicals rushed in my bloodstream. Something in his features, in his voice, seemed almost familiar to me, like a memory, or something I lost and searched for, for a long, long time.

"I'll read. You watch the stars."

"And what lies below," I replied dreamily.

I've been at his side for hours—Aurelie has now taken my place.

Jacopo Masi, my brother, the boy who was all the family I had, is here. He can't speak yet: he used the last of his strength to get here; now he's falling in and out of consciousness, and burning up. Everyone saw how distressed I was, holding Jacopo's hand and trying, and failing, not to cry. I knew that I would have to give an explanation, even if keeping our secret would have been wiser.

"Helèna..." Madre Gloria began in a whisper. "You know this man." It was a statement, not a question.

"I know it's hard to believe. But he's my brother. My adoptive brother. Jacopo Masi." Saying his name aloud made my heart gallop, as if I were putting him in danger. Which,

maybe, I was. I trusted Madre Gloria with my life, but Sister Santia, not so much. And once a secret is out, it's almost impossible to stop it from dispersing, like words in the wind. Madre Gloria came to sit beside me, and wrapped her arm around my shoulder. Her affection brought more tears to my eyes, and I let myself relax against her, the only motherly figure I've ever known. With Mother Gloria at my side and holding Jacopo's hand, it was as if I had my family around me, even if not the traditional kind. If only you could be here...

Madre Gloria was quiet, waiting for me to say more, if I chose to. With her silence, she invited me to speak more than she would have with a barrage of questions—but how could I give her an explanation for Jacopo's presence here, when I had none?

"He was away with the army... Or so I thought. I wish I could tell you more, but..." I shook my head. "I had no idea of what he was really doing. I know I'm not making sense... Please, Madre Gloria, let me look after him... don't send him away..."

"We would never do that! Even if he wasn't your brother. He's a sick man and we shall do our utmost to heal him and look after him the best we can. I promise you, Helèna."

At that moment, Sister Santia came in with a steaming cup. "Something to make him sleep," she said. Madre Gloria and I exchanged a quick glance—I was quite sure that Santia hadn't heard us, thankfully.

"Thank you. We'll let it cool a little and Helèna will administer it."

"There," Santia said and laid the tea on the windowsill. "He'll bring trouble to our door," she said. She simply had to weigh in. "He has done so already."

Madre Gloria's eyes flashed in a way I'd never seen before. "This is true. But we do not deny or offer aid to our brothers and sisters based on how much trouble it is for us, do we, sister?"

Santia was silenced once again—but I don't trust her around Jacopo.

"We'll look after him," Madre Gloria reassured me and, with one last squeeze of my hand, she left the room. I waited for the tea to cool and then gave it to Jacopo, teaspoon after teaspoon, and almost immediately, he fell into a calmer sleep. I was reluctantly grateful to Santia. When I was sure he was in a deep sleep, I went to look for Aurelie. She was still shaken, her face gray, but she, too, had been given a herbal concoction in which I suspected something stronger had been mixed.

"How are you feeling?"

"Like a sunny day." She smiled, a little wanly. "Scarlatto?"

"Sleeping, thank God. His burns must be very painful," I said, and the thought of Jacopo suffering broke my heart into a thousand little pieces. "What did he tell you, exactly?"

I had to try and understand how it all happened: one moment he was in the army, visiting Venice briefly on his way back to combat, and the next he was blowing up bridges here...

"He said he was responsible for the explosion. Him and his friends. He said that his comrades had been captured, to take him here, that is all." She scrunched her face in the effort to remember. "Oh, wait..."

"What?"

"When he started to lose consciousness... I think he called your name, Helèna. But that is impossible. How could he have known..."

The expression on my face made Aurelie gasp. "Helèna?"

"He's my adoptive brother, Jacopo Masi. I think he came looking for me."

Aurelie brought a hand to her mouth. "Does Madre Gloria know?"

I nodded. "Madre Gloria, and you. Nobody else. It must stay this way."

"Of course. Oh, when he called your name... I thought I'd misunderstood. But now I see. He said, Helèna, help me."

When I heard that, I couldn't hold my tears in anymore. I ran back to Jacopo's room and cried until I was empty, with Aurelie silently hovering on the doorstep.

Hours passed, but Jacopo would not wake. His breathing was so light, I had to lay my ear to his chest to make sure his heart was still beating. My tears drenched his sheets... Aurelie made a small cot for me on the floor beside his bed, but I ended up falling asleep on my knees, my head on his chest.

I hoped, for reasons I can't even understand myself, that Federica would come to me. I haven't forgotten our father's warning—but now it seems to me that spooks and mysteries are less frightening, less menacing than humanity's savagery, concealed beneath the thin layer of civilization. When I finally collapsed into sleep and, semiconscious, felt icy fingers braid with mine, I was consoled. "Buonanotte, Federica," I said under my breath.

I had a strange dream. Sister Giulia was trying to tell me something, but even as she opened her mouth, nothing came out. And then I read her lips: "They're here," she was saying. "They are here."

I awoke this morning to see Jacopo's eyes on me. His face was swollen and burned, but the blue of his eyes shone as ever, so light it's almost transparent—how often I looked into those eyes to find comfort! And now that same comfort was flowing from me to him. I opened my mouth to speak, but I had so much to say, and so much emotion inside me, that my mind emptied, and nothing came out.

Everything that happened the last time I'd seen Jacopo, the consternation and upset, were forgotten in a rush of sisterly love that washed everything away.

"Helèna..." His voice was raspy, broken.

"I'm here. I'm here. Are you in pain?"

"Just a little. It doesn't matter. I can't believe I'm with you! There's so much you don't know... I'm sorry I kept so many secrets from you. I couldn't be in the army anymore. It was wrong..." He sighed, a long, long sigh of exhaustion that turned into a grimace of pain. Even just those few words had drained him. "I'm sorry for all the lies... I had to... and I'm sorry for asking you... or asking..."

"Shhhhh, please, enough. Don't speak. Don't tire yourself. I'll look after you, we all will. You'll be fine," I whispered and held his hands in mine for a moment. I wanted to let some light in, so I stood to open the shutters—when I looked outside, I saw that a stately figure stood on the shore. It was Sister Giulia, staring out to the waters.

It was as if she were waiting for someone.

The image was so ominous that it seemed to me an extension of my dream. It was one of those moments when intuition is fast, and wordless, and it replaces knowledge: I was sure that this was just the beginning, that the door to our little haven had been opened to the war raging in the world and there was no closing it. I lifted myself on tiptoes and scoured the mist, but all was calm, shrouded in watery fog...

"Helèna! Someone's coming." Aurelie burst in.

I looked at her and turned around toward the window again, and I saw that beyond Giulia, the whiteness of the mist was broken by the dark shape of a boat advancing slowly. A ray of winter sunshine filtered through the fog, and I could make out soldiers carrying rifles, and on the bow of the boat an imposing man in a black coat. He seemed to be floating on the waters, like a raven.

Madre Gloria appeared framed by the door, and her calm contrasted with our panicked expressions. "We need to hide him," she said.

Jacopo understood at once what was happening and tried to sit up. "I shouldn't have come. I brought this on you..."

"There's no time for contrition, now," Madre Gloria cut him short. "We're taking him to the vestry," she called to us.

We lifted Jacopo up and slipped our arms under his, me on one side and Madre Gloria on the other, but we found that his legs could not sustain him. We dragged him while he moaned in pain, and every moan was a stab to my heart—but I reminded myself that this pain was better than being found by the soldiers approaching. I don't know where we found the strength to carry him—it could only have been desperation. In the cloister we encountered the other sisters, wringing their hands, and Giulia hurried to help us. Thank God!

The vestry is a tiny room at the back of the church, hardly ever used. Inside there's nothing more than unused pews and old vestments hung for the priests that used to visit the convent in days past. We laid Jacopo on an improvised cot made with the sheets and pillow he'd used in the cell, with some medicine beside him. I ran to get him some bread and a jug of water, and, with one last, long glance, our eyes so fixed on each other that looking away was a wrench, I closed the door on him.

Madre Gloria and I took each other's hands, and unspoken words passed between us. It was time to face the soldiers. I followed her as she strode on, back into the convent and out of the main door.

"Sisters, clean the cell up. Not a trace should remain," Madre Gloria whispered to Santia and Emilia as she passed— Santia did some quiet griping, but she was ignored.

By the time we all gathered outside, the small flotilla had come closer, gliding silently on the misty waters. Three boats, seven soldiers. A collective gasp escaped us—they were Germans. Nazis.

The memory of thundering hooves and shouts and flames rising engulfed me—my hand went to my cheek, wiping imagi-

nary ash from my face—in my mind, the unnamed horsemen who'd burned my village and murdered my parents had become one with the Nazi forces. My child's mind was not privy to the intricacies of alliances and the twists and turns of Hungarian history at that time: all I could grasp was that some people hated us Jews, and those same people had enough power, enough leeway, enough cruelty to try to destroy us. Now, Hitler's forces were doing the same. Why? Why us?

I couldn't answer now just as I couldn't as a child. I loved Hungary, I loved my country, but it had been taken from me. The Christian faith I'd been baptized into in Italy had saved my life, and I believed faith had saved my sanity—but it was so unjust that I should use it as a shield, a disguise, to not reveal who I really was. I closed my eyes, and hoped with all my heart that my Italian, with the Venetian inflection I'd learned while living at Palazzo Masi, would serve me well.

"They've come for Scarlatto. Jacopo, I mean," Aurelie murmured and stepped closer to me. She slipped her arm under mine; she was trembling.

"I don't know any Jacopo," I said. "I don't know any Scarlatto either. There are no men here, only us seven women."

"Six."

You're not counting Federica, I thought, but I said nothing.

Madre Gloria raised a hand to silence us and then stepped forward, standing in front of us as if to protect us. A small, slight woman with the heart of a heroine, I thought, while I watched her face softening in a meek smile; it had been hard and resolute only a minute before. The lioness had slipped on a sheep's clothing.

The minutes passed slowly as the boats came near, flowing silently on the water, while Madre Gloria kept that submissive smile firmly on her face. Aurelie continued her butterfly-wings trembling, while Sisters Emilia and Santia, having finished their task, gathered their hands to their chests in a sisterly knot.

Sister Giulia seemed impervious as if all that was happening now had happened before, and she'd witnessed it once already.

I thought of Jacopo, alone and in pain in that cold room, and immediately banished any thought of him from my mind, as if the soldiers could read my thoughts. Nobody ever comes here, let alone one of the men who blew up the bridge. Nobody ever comes here at all.

Finally, here they were, coming ashore with the thumping of boots and scraping of wood on the pebbles—the tall man was the first to step down, and something in his penetrating, intelligent eyes made me shiver inside. This would not be someone easy to deceive, my instinct told me.

Madre Gloria was the very image of docility. "I'm Madre Gloria Farinella, the Madre Superiora of this convent. You're welcome in this place of peace." She stressed the last two words, as if those men and peace could ever be in the same place, at the same time.

The tall man clicked his boots together and saluted. "Commander Fabian Von Siegl," he announced. At that moment, he seemed like a giant to me, head and shoulders taller than any of us. His presence was commanding—he encompassed us, and our home, with his gaze, and it seemed that he'd taken it all under his rule. I was looking up into his face but I couldn't tell his features, though he was so close, now. This man, the commander, and the other soldiers were a blur to me, with their rifles and helmets: a jumble of predators I couldn't tell apart.

He seemed a huge bat who would open its black wings and devour us all any moment now. I remembered boots just like those, and me, the little girl I was, having them right in my eyeline. Terror opened a crater inside me, a place of blind fear that knew no reasoning, only dread: the place where a child cowered as her house and her parents burned. I couldn't afford to lose my mind now. I found the little terrified child inside me *and tried to rein her in, but to no avail. The past was returning to me so real, so vivid that it felt as if it were happening all over again.*

"Be very quiet now, or they will hear us, and they will come for us. Be very quiet..." someone was whispering, while the neighing of horses and the thumping of hooves and the screams of the dead and dying drowned her words. The ash from my parents' and the other villagers' houses was falling on our hair, our faces, our hands. I was afraid that a moan would escape my lips, and then it would all be over...

Why, why had I chosen that moment to remember another piece of the jigsaw? Why were those memories coming back now, in a moment of such danger? I don't know what your memories of that night are, Hanna; I don't want to picture it. I have forgotten most of what happened; I suspect my brain thought it kinder to do so. All I could remember for a long time was the fire and our parents' faces at the window, the nun's arms around me and her hand as she took me away from the smoldering ruins. After that, there's nothing; until I walked the stone steps up to Palazzo Masi, and the Contessa let me in.

My memories begin over from that moment. Every once in a while, a snippet adds itself to my story—like the silver candelabra on a white tablecloth, on a Shabbat; skating on a frozen lake, and our mamusia making us soup and toasted bread when we returned; hanging out freshly washed sheets, and playing hide and seek with them...

And then our parents' faces tight with worry, the whispered, urgent conversation, the mention of running away. I remember crying in fear for a threat I didn't understand, and finally, that fateful night: the fire, the hooves of galloping horses...

Madre Gloria's voice broke the spell. "Helèna, would you please help Aurelie sort some refreshments for our guests? Or the best meal we can. We don't have much to offer, but..."

I missed the rest of the sentence, because my head was spinning with both my memories, and the relief that Madre Gloria had sensed my consternation and given me a way out.

The soldiers sat around our table. They were ravenous and devoured the potato soup, the bread, the cheese, chugging down the creamy milk. They hadn't parted with their weapons.

"Are you afraid of a few old women, Commander?" Madre Gloria said, eyeing the rifles.

"Afraid, no. Wary, yes. Always, in these dark times."

You made *these dark times, you hypocrite, I would have liked to say—I bit my lip.*

"Dark indeed." Madre Gloria gave the meekest smile.

"May I speak to you in private, Madre?" the commander asked. His Italian was near-perfect, though with an inflection that turned that sweet language into something hard, jagged.

"Of course," she said, and then made a small gesture toward me.

I followed. I didn't want her to be alone with that man. Madre Gloria took her place at her desk, sitting with a slightly stooped posture instead of her usual straight, strong shoulders. I was in awe of her composure and self-possession: she was giving the perfect impression of a timid, acquiescent old nun, when I knew that there wasn't a timid bone in her body. The commander studied me. It was evident that I wasn't a nun, dressed as I was in a woolen skirt and a simple jumper, a shawl around my shoulders and my hair down, kept from my face with a tortoiseshell pin—I hadn't had time to do better, that morning.

"This is Helèna." Madre Gloria answered his unspoken question. "She's a friend and companion of ours. She helps us with all the work that needs done, and believe me, there is much of it."

"It's an honor to meet you," the commander said in a quiet, even voice. He sounded different now—a little gentler. He'd

taken off the black hat with the silver wings—his hair was very dark, so black it was almost blue; his hands were hidden by leather gloves.

I froze for a moment, then composed myself and nodded. He'd mentioned honor; it must be a concept high on his list of priorities. Interesting, considering the situation.

My hands were shaking—I grasped one with the other and rested them against me. There would not be a repeat of the fit of terror I'd felt earlier. It simply would not happen again. I felt myself blushing at the thought.

"Madre Gloria, I promise you that my men and I won't bother you for long," the commander said.

Just enough time to take all we have. Or worse.

"Commander," Madre Gloria began. "I think we agree this is not the best place for an outpost. We're very much isolated here, and we have very little. We won't even be able to provide for you for long, our stores are so meager, and we have nothing of value. I struggle to understand why you decided to come on this island."

The commander regaled us with a smile. He regarded us as if every word he said was like throwing pearls to the pigs. Those black eyes, the dark hair a little too long for a man of his rank, thick and glossy with a wave to it. He'd taken his gloves off to reveal tanned, strong hands with long fingers, placed calmly on the desk. He had wide shoulders and a frame that would have been even more intimidating, had he not been so... well mannered.

And still.

How many people had this man killed, by his hand or by his orders? How many like my parents had he exterminated, like they weren't even human?

I squeezed my hands harder and looked away. I couldn't have him read my thoughts. He couldn't see the contempt I felt for him.

"I'm sure that war news finds its way to you, even in this isolated place," the commander replied. "You must know that we're close to victory…"

Something spread on Madre Gloria's face: contempt. I hoped the commander would not detect it.

"Forgive me if I interrupt you. We're women of faith. Our purpose and priority are and always will be prayer and a humble life. The things of the world are of little importance to us, aside from the work needed for our survival and dignified living. We want nothing to do with any conflict."

"Of course. However, we don't always choose to deal with conflict, do we?"

"No."

"Sometimes war is necessary."

"I beg to differ, Commander."

He appraised her for a moment—his features were fine, somehow patrician, I thought. He looked like a dark-haired Apollo: but his beauty only highlighted his iniquity.

"I'm sure you know that the railway bridge was blown up yesterday. Such violence is appalling. You certainly do not want it coming here, on this island, in these grounds. A place of faith and a place of peace. People who do such things should be kept well away from here."

"Goodness, yes!" Madre Gloria breathed.

I thought of Jacopo, wounded and cold, and alone…

"There's no need to worry about that specific threat, thankfully. They've all been apprehended." Not all, you bastard. "But nobody is safe when there's anarchy, and right now, while we're establishing control in the swiftest manner possible…" He shrugged. "Everyone is in danger. You will be grateful to know, then, that we'll be taking responsibility for the convent."

A long look passed between Madre Gloria and the commander, an unspoken exchange. Sadly for us, it was clear where the power lay. For now.

"We are grateful. Why here, Commander? Of all places?"

"I've been sent to Italy with a special mandate. My assignment is to rescue artwork, and make sure that it's kept safe."

"Kept safe... in Germany."

"Austria, hopefully."

I hoped he wouldn't notice how fast and shallow my breathing had become. The library. He wants to take it away from us.

"Please excuse me," I uttered quickly and made my way out. I leaned against the wall and closed my eyes, overwhelmed. When I opened them again, Aurelie was there.

"Aurelie?"

"I'm scared," she said, and she looked so small, so vulnerable. I composed my face quickly—I had to be strong for her, for all the sisters...

"Don't be. It will be fine, I promise," I said.

At that moment one of the soldiers came by, a small, thin man with wispy blond hair and a squashed nose. His gaze lingered on us, invasive, insistent.

"Come," I whispered, and took Aurelie away. The soldier followed her with his eyes, and I felt sick to my stomach.

"Are you sure it will be fine?" she asked in a low voice.

"I'm sure," I lied once again, because I had no idea what was ahead of us, and I knew by now that not all stories have a happy ending...

Thiago stopped reading, even if the letter wasn't finished, and laid the flashlight on his knees. Its beam, now sideways, enveloped us in a half-light.

"True," he whispered. "That not all stories have a happy ending."

I was quiet: I could feel that he wasn't done talking. And I was right. "You know, this is not... this is not my job. You probably guessed. I'm not here for myself."

I hesitated for a moment. I wanted to choose the right words. "I did think there was something you kept... under wraps."

"It's not a secret. Just... I didn't think I would want to tell you. I didn't think I would want to tell you anything, to be honest. I couldn't imagine... that I'd feel so close to you, so quickly."

My heart began to beat faster; I could hear it in my ears, above the gentle rippling of the water in the breeze. The stars shone above us; the little Atlantis slept below us.

Thiago began his story.

"The Casa d'Aste Palladini is my father's baby. He wanted my brother and me to work with him. To take over after..." He swallowed. "After he went. I never wanted to. I left for a few years, did my thing. I was a diving instructor."

"Oh! That's why you're so good with boats, and you look like you work outside, in the sun..."

"You're observant," he said, and I nodded, a little embarrassed. The semi-darkness made confidences easier, for sure. "My brother was the good son. He was my father's right hand. He had the same passion for art that you have. He was good at what he did. Excellent, really. You know, you would have liked him." He brought his hand to his temple, where a scar puckered the skin.

The way he spoke about his brother in the past tense made my heart rush again. "What happened?" I murmured.

"Good question. Something stupid happened. Something really, *really* stupid." He shook his head. "Ever been scuba diving?"

"No."

He took a breath. "Well, *every time* you dive, you must be careful. Even if you've done it a million times. You must come back up slowly, very slowly and carefully, or you can get hurt. Badly hurt. And if you're an expert diver and you're taking a beginner with you, you must watch them. You have to look after them, so they don't mess up." He took a deep breath. It seemed to me that every word he said was jagged, hurting him from the inside. "Last spring, just as the season began, my brother and I went for a dive off the coast of Sorrento. That place is incredible, you know? There are Greek and Roman remains everywhere, underwater. It's like a time machine. You get lost in the blue, and... forget." Thiago's voice caught.

"What happened?" I whispered.

"He came up too fast. There was nothing to be done. He was gone, just like that. He was my big brother, and I didn't look after him. I tried..." Again, he fingered his temple. I gathered that he must have got hurt on that occasion. His pain had been etched in his skin.

I couldn't help it—I took his hand, warm and strong, in mine. "I'm so sorry."

"Yeah. I miss him every moment of every day. And it was my fault."

"It was an accident..."

"I was responsible for him. I was the instructor. The *expert* one." He gave a bitter laugh. "My father got sick soon after. Heartbreak, I suppose. The Casa d'Aste is not doing well. I thought maybe, if I save the business..." He opened his hands. "That's why I'm here. Remember you asked if Lavinia called for me? To answer your question truthfully, no, she didn't. She called for my brother."

Now, that was a good reason to be wanting the collection. A very good reason.

"I'm sure you're making him proud."

"Proud? I have my brother's life on my conscience. I'm just trying to pick up the pieces of what I destroyed. My father says he doesn't blame me, but I don't believe him. Deep down, he believes I should have taken care of him. And he's right."

It was a moment of madness; or maybe the sanest moment

I'd had in a long time. I leaned over and took Thiago's face in my hands. And then I kissed him, soft and slow, under the silent stars.

It was one kiss, just one kiss, because he pulled me to his chest and held me tight.

"There's someone back in New York, isn't there?" he whispered in my hair.

Confusion and guilt overcame me. "It's complicated," I said.

"Not for me. When he's out of your life and your heart... if he ever is... I'll be here."

Warm tears wetted my cheeks—I couldn't believe all this was happening.

Unplanned, unexpected, was one way to put it.

"Shall we go back?" he asked.

"Yes. If you're not holding me, I'm cold," I said—and then I realized the undertone of what I'd just said, and I was embarrassed to my core.

What was I doing?

I was in such a rush to get off the boat that I almost fell on my face. Thiago had to grab my arm to hold me up, which added to my embarrassment a millionfold. He dragged the boat up through the reeds, and secured it once again with expert, quick movements. We didn't talk as we went inside—I was now shivering, and tired, and mortified.

And to my shame, I was full of longing, and yearned to be back in his arms.

Which didn't make sense, because I loved Isaac.

Didn't I?

Tears were pressing beneath my eyes once again, and I wasn't sure how long I could stop them for. I didn't know how Thiago could have unraveled me that way...

Once we got to the cells, I leaned against the cold wall. The adrenalin was leaving me, and now I was just drained. The little, almost-empty cell that had seemed like a peaceful haven not long before, now felt desolate.

"What about you? Do you have someone?" I asked.

"Not anymore. I was angry, depressed, after my brother... She couldn't deal with all that."

"I'm sorry."

"I know it's a cliché, but clearly, it wasn't meant to be."

"And is *she* out of your heart?"

"Yes. Completely."

My jacket pocket vibrated and told me I'd received a message. I was tempted to ignore it, when the familiar pattern I'd assigned to Sofia's communications made me think again. "Sorry, it's my sister."

"Goodnight, then," he said, and walked away.

I rushed inside and closed the door behind me. With an inward groan, I took refuge under the blankets, shaking from the perpetual cold inside those stone walls, and nerves. It took me a moment to comprehend the words that had appeared on my screen.

Honey, I know it will hurt, but I have to tell you. I saw Isaac downtown, he was with Rowena. I'm so sorry. I tried to phone but your phone is out of reach. Please call me when you get this. I love you x

I *knew* something had happened. My radars had been up since Sofia texted me to ask if I'd heard from him. And that whole thing from Isaac about giving each other space...

And then the picture arrived.

Unmistakable.

Isaac and Rowena holding hands over a restaurant table, eyes locked, her head tilted as if she were hanging on his every word. A little square of light, shining in the darkness to bring me despair.

I couldn't even say he'd cheated on me. It was me who had been deluded. Not wanting to accept that he'd left me for good, hoping against hope that he'd change his mind...

I couldn't look away from that picture. It broke my heart, but I couldn't look away. I couldn't hold back the tears any longer, and I went from crying to sleeping, like a little girl.

CHAPTER 9

THE ISLAND OF SANTA CATERINA

"I came looking for you, but your room was empty," Thiago said, materializing behind me with a tray in hand.

I was sitting on a rock, lulled by the sound of the water ebbing and flowing, and soothed by the gray dawn. His voice had made me jump; I'd been so lost in thought that I hadn't heard him coming. I smoothed my hair, barely brushed, and dusted my jeans. I knew I looked ghastly.

"A spot of breakfast for you. Coffee and, guess what? Croissant with rose jam, obviously."

"You shouldn't have..."

The memory of our kiss, the night before, made me blush. My heart was in chaos, somewhere between the sweetness of Thiago's lips and the wrench from Isaac and our life together. I was in between two worlds, walking on a tightrope, afraid that whatever step I'd make next, I would fall.

Thiago's eyes were kind, transparent, and showed no embarrassment nor regret. In comparison, I was in a knot of uncertainty. "I need you in good form. We have a mystery to solve, don't we?"

I need you in good form—it was the same thing that Isaac

had said to me. But the tone, the intention felt different. In fact, the same words seemed to come from two completely different places, from polar opposites. Isaac wanted me to keep going so that I could do something for him; Thiago's concern was that I would do something for myself. Isaac needed taking care of, while this almost-stranger was looking after me.

"Francesca?"

I shook myself: I'd been staring at him. "Yes... No, of course not. I was just... reminded of something. Sorry."

He laid the tray on the pebbles between us, sat down and crossed his long legs. The fancy suits were gone for good, it seemed—jeans and a simple khaki jacket suited him a lot more.

"About last night..." I began.

"Last night..." he said at the same time, and we laughed an awkward laugh.

"I didn't mean to put you under pressure," he continued. "It's just that... this is not a game for me. I mean... I haven't even *looked* at anyone in this way for a long time."

"I understand. Same for me. I..." And then it all came rushing out, in a stream of dismay. "I was engaged. He left me. I hoped we could sort things out. But now he's seeing someone else. That's all. Nothing out of the ordinary... it happens every day, doesn't it? People promise it'll be forever, and then it isn't. I know, I'm pathetic."

"I'm sorry. And you're not pathetic."

"Independent woman and all that. I should have told him to fuck off, that's what I should have done."

"True. But that doesn't mean you're not allowed to be sad."

"Yeah."

A moment of silence. *What's going to happen now? What are we going to do?* I wanted to ask those questions, and yet, I was sure there could be no answer, not now. "Let's focus on the collection," I said.

"Yes. But first, eat," he said without ceremony.

"I'm not sure if..."

"Good food is medicine for heartbreak. We Italians believe good food is a remedy for almost anything."

"Okay." I was beginning to wonder if Lavinia was a kind witch and her rose jam was part of a spell, because the scent and taste seemed to infuse strength and gratitude. Everything seems easier after caffeine, and on a nicely full stomach. "I'd like to see the church, before reading on," I said. "And the vestry, where Jacopo was hidden."

"Good idea," Lavinia said from behind us—she definitely was a witch, because I swear she'd just appeared out of thin air. "I'd love to show you. Let me take all this inside."

She left us to carry the breakfast dishes to the house, and Thiago and I exchanged a glance—Lavinia had been a discreet, gentle presence from the beginning; but this time, it was as if she'd broken a delicate, light-as-gossamer affinity between Thiago and me.

"She offered to *actually* show us something. I thought we had to find everything out ourselves," Thiago said.

I shrugged. "I suppose let's jump on any bit of information we can get."

We. Thiago and I were working as a team now. I had no idea how this would work out in the end, but I had no intention to go back on it. His presence warmed my heart.

Lavinia came back, and as we were heading toward the church together, she slipped her arm under mine.

"You know, when I was young, I was so romantic that I ended up immolating myself on the altar of love once or twice," she whispered to me out of the blue, as soon as Thiago was out of earshot. "Now, I've come to the conclusion that *joy* is the measuring index of love."

I looked at her in astonishment: she always seemed to know what was happening inside my head—it was a little unnerving.

"Life is so very short, why suffer self-imposed pain?" she added.

Why suffer, indeed? I didn't know how to answer that impromptu lesson on love, but Lavinia had already moved on, light and graceful as she always was, and was standing framed by the arched church door.

We stepped into the cold, damp air, and it took me a few seconds to get used to the gloom. Even if the sun was coming out, and it promised a beautiful day, inside was a never-ending winter. I thought of Jacopo, and how cold he must have been on those days and nights concealed from the Nazis.

"This church is over a thousand years old," Lavinia began. "Like most ancient places, it's made of layers. The original chapel was a tiny stone building, but through the centuries it was restored and partially rebuilt."

I looked around me—the vaulted ceilings were plain, the painted plaster ruined in patches. The stone altar was austere, but embellished by a marble slate and by a painted crucifix behind it. The other three sides were decorated with faded frescoes, primitive figures of saints and angels moving in what looked like a garden—maybe the Garden of Eden?

"Can we stay and read some of the diary here?" I asked.

"Legally speaking, no, because the place needs restoring and it's not completely safe. However, if you promise not to sue me if a piece of plaster falls on your head"—the three of us looked up—"then you're welcome to stay."

"We won't sue," I said. "But can't you get public funds to restore it?"

"There are more ancient churches, palaces and villas in need of restoring, here in Italy, than there are public funds," Thiago intervened.

"True, but it's not just that," said Lavinia. "Public funding would mean handing things over to strangers. And I can't do that. Once it starts, this place will lose its heart. Its original nature. Everything would be licked clean, painted white and opened to the public."

"Would that not be good?" Thiago said.

A glance passed between me and Lavinia.

"No," we said in unison.

"No," Lavinia repeated, and walked out, her heels clicking on the stone floor. "Oh, and promise you won't try to go up the belfry: the stairs are closed for a reason."

When she left, I whispered to Thiago, "But she didn't mention the *vestry*, did she?"

Thiago shook his head, and we walked along the pews, beyond the altar, to a little wooden door. I tried the handle, and it opened... but the room was empty, except for a solitary bench. The window looked onto the woods behind the convent—I leaned on the windowsill, thinking that this was what Jacopo would have seen during the days he'd spent in here.

We settled in a pew, and I pulled my jumper tighter around me against the dampness in the air.

"You want me to read, don't you?" Thiago asked.

I put on my best puppy eyes. "You have a better accent," I said.

"Fine. Here we go..."

When I joined them again, Madre Gloria was giving her best effort to lead the commander off the scent, but to no avail. "We don't have anything of value here, Commander. A few paintings in our church, some modest marbles of the kind that Italy is littered with..."

"Madre Gloria, a woman of your intelligence shouldn't lower herself to play these games. You know very well what I'm talking about."

There. The blue flame I keep hidden inside me flared up, and this time, there was nothing I could do to stop it.

"If we're not playing games, Commander," I began, my

interference gaining a reproachful look from Madre Gloria. "Then you shouldn't say you're rescuing our art or keeping it safe; you should use the correct word: theft."

The commander looked at me, surprised—maybe because of my insolence, maybe because of the way I speak. My Italian is almost perfect, and my Hungarian is half-forgotten, having arrived in this country when I was so little, but a foreign inflection still remains. I was surprised too at my audacity. I'd always been an obedient child, I'd always swallowed the anger I felt inside me, coiled up in my heart. But it seems that the longer I am away from Palazzo Masi, the more I recall of my childhood, and the less I can keep my fury under wraps. Hopefully, this dormant volcano won't end up killing me.

The commander was calm—and his suaveness, his impeccable manners, made me even angrier. "I believe there's nothing else to be said. Please, show me the Santa Caterina library."

I allowed myself to feel a little hope. Maybe he was referring to the library everyone knew about, the beautiful but certainly not unique collection that we officially housed. As much as it would be a loss for us, the books in the main collection were not the real treasure of Santa Caterina. Maybe he didn't even know about Ippolita's work, and the other illuminated manuscripts!

Madre Gloria must have thought the same, because as soon as we ended the short journey between her study and the library building, she said: "This is it," her tone sharp, conclusive, like the clicking of a stick.

To see the commander there, where I worked with all my heart and soul, was painful. I stood removed from him and felt as if, with every step he took with those heavy boots, he was trundling on my heart. When he came close to my little desk, the notebook open with my pen still on top, and the pile of books beside it, I felt my guts seizing up. Images of dancing flames and whirling smoke exploded in front of me. The books turned to ash, flying up to the sky and into my mouth, my nose —the ruins of the life we once had...

"Fraulein Helèna?"

He was right in front of me, while I felt the blood rise to my face and my heart explode in my chest. I felt my forehead and my palms wet with sweat. I blinked again and again, until I was back in the convent's library, and not in the burning house, the burning street.

"Yes, Commander?" I said, pretending I had no idea why he'd stopped there, staring at me, pretending that everything was just fine. I was surprised to see concern in his eyes. He was a monster—monsters don't have concern for the people they're about to devour. He repelled me.

He studied me for a second longer; I did my best to remain inscrutable. Then, he began wandering around, occasionally cocking his head to read the books' titles, or taking one in his hand and thumbing it for a moment. I recoiled as his hand stroked the carved shelves, as if he were touching me.

"This is all... nice," he said. "But you know it's not what I'm here for."

Madre Gloria deliberately misunderstood. "If you need a place to stay, and refreshment, it's our duty to be hospitable to both pilgrims and travelers, and I place you in the second category. I trust that you'll be mindful of the scarcity we find ourselves in..."

There was steel in the commander's voice. "Please, do not make me lower myself, and humiliate both of us, with threats. You will give me what I ask."

The frown between Madre Gloria's eyebrows was the only sign of her pain and frustration. "Forgive me, but I do not..."

"Madre Gloria. I beseech you." His tone, which was anything but beseeching, denied his words.

She looked at me, and then down. We had no choice. I

slipped my hand in the pocket of my cardigan; the key felt cold and heavy.

"We need light," I said briefly, and made my way toward the kitchen, without looking the commander in the eye. I was afraid that fear would jolt me into the past again, and make me lose control of myself.

Aurelie was washing dishes, and two of the soldiers were still sitting there, drinking the last of our chicory wartime coffee. I did my best to ignore them, but I did see that one of them was the blond soldier with the squashed nose, and that his porcine eyes were following Aurelie's every move. Aurelie and I exchanged glances—it was as if the sisters and I had lost the gift of speech, and were communicating silently in the language of weariness and fear. Aurelie threw a glance toward the church, and I knew that her unspoken words were about Jacopo. The intense awareness that he lay in the vestry, wounded and weak. Should they find him...

Once again, the fury I'd had inside me for a long time rumbled. I was like a rushing river held back by a dam, but for how long?

I turned toward the wall so the soldiers wouldn't see my face, and closed my eyes for a moment. I had to keep myself under control: if Madre Gloria could do it, so could I. Just appease them, keep them calm—like I used to do with the Contessa.

I turned around, took a match from the tin box and lit one of our lamps. I was going to cast light on our treasure, only for a predator to come and take it away... The sky weighed on me as I crossed from the main building to the library. Out of the corner of my eye I saw Sister Giulia bent over her plants, scissors in hand, like nothing out of the ordinary was happening.

"Follow me," I said to the commander, taking small pleasure in giving him an order, and led him to our secret room.

Turning the key in the lock was like opening my heart—but not of its own accord... forcing it open against its will.

Our precious manuscripts waited silently on the lecterns, my light revealing them one by one. The commander took off his long leather coat and his gloves and carefully placed them in a corner, shedding his soldier skin. He leaned over the illuminated page as if smelling a flower—his long fingers almost touched the illuminations, but not quite, hovering instead over them. In the light of the petrol lamp I could see his face was younger than I'd thought, and his features exquisite, as fine as an angel's.

An angel of death.

"May I?" he said quietly and took the lamp from me.

Madre Gloria and I stood in the gloom, very close to each other, watching him.

"We know that women did write and illuminate manuscripts," he said, as if he were holding a lecture, "but they seldom signed them. The Santa Caterina collection differs. They're signed... by Aracoeli, Carabona, Violante. And most of all... Ippolita Von Oswen. As rare as the ghost orchid."

How did he know about the collection? Was he an historian, a professor? I bit my tongue. I wanted as little interaction as possible with this man.

Madre Gloria's calm façade showed no cracks. "These books belong to Santa Caterina. They belong to the church," she said, in the meek tone she'd been wearing like a cloak.

"And this is how you keep them? In a dark, damp chamber? Do you think this is right?"

"It's all we can do now. When the war is over..."

"When the war is over, you'll all speak German, and all of this will be ours," he said calmly, matter of fact. Like there was no doubt in his mind.

I felt all warmth leaving my body, and jumped when Sister Santia, standing on top of the stairs, began calling

Madre Gloria with some urgency. Madre Gloria excused herself, and lingered for a moment, waiting for us to depart as well—but the commander did not move. Madre Gloria followed Santia, and I was left alone with him. I tried to leave too, my eyes on the wedge of light coming from the ajar door— but my body was frozen...

And then, the old hinges gave way, and the door inched its way closed.

Federica?

In a heartbeat, day had turned into night. The commander and I were left standing in the gloom. A low buzz began in my ears and the hair rose on my neck.

Someone else was there with us, and her presence was as real as the glow of the lamp in my hands, as real as the commander standing over the lecterns in his ominous uniform. A moving piece of darkness, like a shadow with its own will, appeared behind the commander, and swiftly, faster than the eye could see, she glided through the lamp. It seemed as if the shadow had taken the light itself away with her, because the light dimmed and disappeared into black. I let it fall on the floor with a yell. She was there with me: Federica.

I heard the commander drawing a breath, although he couldn't have seen what I'd seen, because it happened right behind him. I couldn't place the panting and heaving I could hear, until I realized that it was coming from me. The Helèna I used to be, the frightened child who saw everything she loved go up in flames, had once again leaped out of my conscious-ness: we were one.

"Please don't set it on fire," I heard myself whispering. I was shuddering. I raked my hair with my hands, to free it from imaginary ash.

"Fraulein Helèna, I have no intention..."

"Don't set us on fire!"

I knew I wasn't making any sense, but I couldn't help it.

My body was shaking and my skin clammy—icy and burning at the same time, if that is ever possible. I was blind and deaf to everything but my terror, my dreadful memories. I felt the commander's hand on my arm and flinched.

"Please, Fraulein. Come here. Come out."

His voice was coming from the steps. I turned to see him standing there, against the light of the open door, his hand extended toward me. But I couldn't move. I was frozen in terror, lost in the flames of my memory. Another image took shape over the one in front of me—another person, another hand, darkness all around and the cruel light of flames in the background...

"Fraulein Helèna? Helèna?"

The commander was with me in two great steps. I waited for rough hands to grab me—but there was a gentle arm around my waist, and a whisper in my ear.

"Come with me, Helèna," *he said in his heavily accented Italian. And then:* "Ne aggódj," *he whispered. Don't worry.*

Hungarian. The language we spoke at home... Our parents used Yiddish when they spoke to each other, but not to us. The familiar words jolted me out of my terror. Docile, I let the commander guide me out, into the light, his fingers light on my hips, on my arm.

My face was covered in cold sweat and tears. I was so ashamed.

"I'm sorry if I have upset you, Helèna. I don't know what happened to the lamp," *he hastened to say as soon as we were outside, his words tumbling out in a stammering Italian. He seemed almost shaken.*

I know it wasn't you. I saw what happened, *I wanted to say, but how could I have explained to him all that I couldn't explain to myself—and that no rational person would have believed, anyway?*

"You're Hungarian, aren't you?" *he asked me.*

I didn't want him to know about my origins... Was it even possible, to hide it, at this point? I found his eyes, and what I saw was unexpected. Not just concern, nor a passing moment of kindness—which, I reasoned, even the most awful person could have. But something that mirrored my experience: a wistful gaze, a sense of... regret? Nostalgia? With a certain effort, I looked away. But not down.

I didn't answer his question. My nationality was none of his business. He might have grabbed the right to sleep under our roof, eat our food, have us waiting on them like servants— and steal our one and only treasure. But I didn't owe him conversation, let alone my family history. The recommendations I'd heard all my life came back to me—never, never say you're a Jew. If they press, don't admit it. Forget about it altogether. You are Catholic, you were baptized. Forget the sweet voice of your father as he sang the prayers over the Shabbat lights that your mother had lit. Forget who your mother and father were...

But I was not ashamed. I could never be ashamed of who I was.

When you let go of your home nation, of your ethnicity, your religion, your ancestors, what's left? Only the present, and maybe, if nobody takes it away, the future.

"I need to clean up," I said coldly. The idea of stepping into the dark again to gather the pieces of the lamp terrified me. I just hoped he would forget my strange behavior. And that I would forget that he'd been oddly gentle, with me.

"I'll ask one of my men to do it," he said in Hungarian.

I pretended not to notice and made my way out as quickly as I could.

Even only in the short space between the library and the main building, the cold seeped into my bones and made the sweat freeze on my skin, but also helped restore my mind. I thought of Jacopo at once, suffering alone in the vestry—when would I be able to see him, bring him something warm to eat, make sure he was recovering? I had to be so careful. If they found him, I was sure they would execute him at once.

The mist had turned into fog, and I almost couldn't see my feet... Maybe I could sneak out the manuscripts, one or two at a time, concealed by darkness and fog? It was the perfect night to remain hidden.

I forced myself not to dwell on the fact that it would also be the perfect night to be mistaken for a foe, and be shot.

———

Dear Hanna,

I'm writing this in bed, in the middle of the night. I'm so cold, I can't stop shivering and I'm quite sure I'll never be warm again. But I'm alive. Miraculously.

While the soldiers stuffed themselves in the kitchen and the sisters had to serve them as if we were their maids, I slipped away to the church. Hidden under my coat was a parcel of fresh bandages, medicine and a little bread. The two men left as guards on the shoreline saw me, while I made a big show of wearing my Mass veil and holding my rosary. I kept my head down like someone deep in prayer or meditation. I kneeled and crossed myself, I lit a candle, I sat on one of the pews until I was sure they hadn't followed me—then, I slipped into the vestry.

Jacopo was sleeping, and I had to cover his mouth with my hand to stop him from making any noise when he saw me. His face wasn't bandaged anymore, but ruined with burns and bruises—he's grown a beard, as blond as his hair, but some-where underneath the ravages of war was the man I knew, my Jacopo! He opened his eyes, glazed over with pain and medica-tion, and covered my hand with his.

"Jacopo," I said and stroked his face.

"My Helèna..."

"We'll look after you. I promise."

"It should be me, looking after you. Where are they?"

I knew at once who he meant. "In the convent. Gobbling food like the pigs they are. They're not showing any interest in the church, don't worry."

"Are you hurt?" The words came out of his mouth with some difficulty, but overall he seemed a little more alert and rested.

I shook my head. "I'm fine. I'm going to change your bandages and give you some more medicine. Are you hungry?"

"Ravenous. But what about you? Do you have enough to eat?"

"I have plenty." I examined his face. The burns looked a little better—Sister Santia is more skillful than I'd given her credit for, because her salve seemed to have done good work in keeping infection at bay and reducing the pain.

"Whatever is in that drink, it works," he said.

"Sister Santia says it's Passiflora. I suspect that it's mostly alcohol, and that's how it takes the pain away: it knocks you out."

Jacopo smiled, but his smile turned into a grimace of pain.

"I'm sorry! Is it something I did?"

"No. It's laughing. I haven't done it for a long time and my face is not used to it."

It was my turn to laugh now—a little miracle, that we could do so in the midst of such danger. I applied the salve to all burns and wounds on his face, his arms, his chest. To see his beloved body so tortured made me want to cry—but I steeled myself.

"I'll help you relieve yourself if you want," I offered. We'd left a bowl in the corner that was already half-full.

"I'll do it when I'm alone, thanks."

"You're not embarrassed, are you? We're brother and

sister..." My voice trailed away. His feelings for me were not brotherly, I remembered. What we used to have, the innocence of our relationship, was gone forever. There was a moment of silence, and I assumed the most practical, sisterly tone I could. "There. Have some more knock-out medicine, and bread."

"I'll take the bread, but I don't want to sleep anymore. I'd rather take the pain."

"I understand. We need to get you off the island."

"No way. I'm not running away and leaving you here, Helèna. Do you understand me?" He took my wrist and looked me in the eye—I knew that there would be no negotiating on this.

I turned toward the door—there was perfect silence outside. I was desperate to steal some more time with him, even just a little. "Tell me, Jacopo. How did you end up like this? What happened? You were an officer..."

"What we were doing wasn't right. It's not right. I opened my eyes, though always too late! I joined a partisan brigade near Milan; we were all dispatched to various places. I knew you were here, and I hoped to see you... but I didn't want to put you in danger. I promise you, I didn't."

"I know. I know," I said and held his hands. I was kneeling on the floor and our entwined hands rested on his chest. The more I spoke to him, the more the Jacopo I remembered came back and filled the body of this stranger. His fair hair was now clean, his eyes the same, familiar blue, even if surrounded by dark circles. This was the boy who'd come to me when I had nightmares; this was the man I could turn to when the Contessa became too much, when everything was too much. This was the man who loved me, and who would have married me. Who still, I believed, wanted to marry me.

"It's chaos, out there. Our army is worth nothing to anyone now; we were cannon fodder for deluded leaders. The Germans seem to believe our nation is their birthright. The *new government is helpless, Mussolini is already a man of the past, and the Allies are on their way... You don't know what I'm talking about,"* he said, seeing my face.

"*We are isolated, here. We don't read the papers or listen to the radio. The commander said the Germans are winning. That they have won...*"

"*It's not true. There are partisan brigades everywhere. We're opening the way for the Allies the best we can! We blow things up, roads, bridges, anything that can slow the enemy down or damage them. Italy will be freed and then we'll be a nation again, with our own government, not just placeholders for the Germans! Even our king has sold us...*"

"*The Germans aren't winning,*" I repeated slowly, letting it sink in.

"*No. We just need to hold on. I promise you, there will be an end to all this, and we won't have to wait too long.*" He sat up, slowly, with fire in his eyes and a grimace of pain on his face. "*My comrades and I blew up the railway bridge. They were all captured and shot. I couldn't do anything to save them. I ran away... An old woman found me in the woods and cleaned me up. Without her, I would have died. But I couldn't hide in her house and get her in trouble. I was forced to return to the woods and try to survive there the best I could. I didn't think I stood a chance. I knew the wounds and the cold and hunger would kill me. I was desperate, so much that I ended up at the edge of the village. I almost didn't care about being seen anymore, because I knew that if I didn't take care of my wounds, I'd be dead. When I saw the nun there...*"

"*Aurelie.*"

"*When I saw Sister Aurelie, I was desperate. I'm so sorry I put her life in danger, on that boat—*"

"*It was Aurelie's choice and desire to help you—*"

"*I can't quite believe I'm here with you!*"

"*Me neither. It's a miracle,*" I said, and a rush of joy made my eyes fill up. Almost at once, I looked behind me. If they found him... I had to go. "Stay here. Don't make a sound. We'll look after you."

"It should be me looking after you, like I've always done! Those bastards. What do they want with this place?"

"The convent has a collection of medieval manuscripts, illuminated and signed by women. The commander wants them..." I began, but I saw that I was losing him. His eyes were glazing over once again, and the blood had left his face once more. "Are you in a lot of pain?"

"Doesn't matter," he murmured, and lay back down on the makeshift cot. I placed my lips on his forehead, gently, so I would not cause him any pain. Our roles had reversed, I thought, as I recalled a frightened child closing her eyes to sleep. with her big brother watching over her.

I left Jacopo and returned to the kitchen to help the sisters clean up after the soldiers, and then I waited for the small hours of the morning, when I knew—I hoped—that only the sentries would be awake. Two soldiers have been appointed watchmen, but they don't seem to pay much attention to what's happening in the convent: they concentrate on warding off threats from the mainland, after the bridge explosion. I pray and pray that I'll be able to save at least a few of the manuscripts.

I began hiding them, one at a time. Two are away already. I have no idea if I'll be able to hide them all, or if they'll discover me and kill me. They're in a secret place. In case these letters fall into the wrong hands, I won't say where it is. I hope that if I am discovered Federica will be there and come to my aid.

"Of course she won't say," Thiago cried out in frustration. "That would make it too easy!"

"She hopes Federica will come to her aid. Do you think... I mean, do you believe Federica is... *real?*"

Thiago shrugged. "I think this is an old place, full of creaks and nooks and crannies, shadows and shades. Helèna heard that story about the nun who went missing, and her imagination did the rest. Nobody pushed her down the slope; she slipped. Nobody was there with her and the commander in the library."

Of course, Thiago was right. He had to be. I had to keep rational, instead of letting the whole atmosphere get to me, turning the shadows I saw into ghosts.

"There's a quote at the end of the letter. A poem, maybe?" Thiago said.

> *And when you see, you'll see*
> *That you can walk on water*

"It's a poem by Ippolita," I explained. "One of her most famous ones."

Thiago pretended to keep reading. "*Just because I want to make things really hard for Francesca and Thiago...*"

"Stop it!" I laughed. "Oh..."

"What?"

"Remember what Aurelie said about Federica's ghost? That she walked on water."

"Back to the ghosts again," Thiago said with mock exasperation.

At that moment, Manuela called us for lunch on the terrace and, reluctantly, we interrupted our reading. "I wonder if she was brought up here... if she spends a lot of time on the island."

"Who?"

"Manuela. Maybe she'll help us fill in some gaps."

"Hope springs eternal!" Thiago said, and tucked the diary safely away.

CHAPTER 10

THE ISLAND OF SANTA CATERINA

Lavinia and Claudio were away, so there were no formalities. We finished quickly and offered our help to clean up. Manuela wouldn't hear of it, but we left her no choice; it was the perfect moment to speak to her, alone.

"I know this will sound strange, but... have you ever seen or *felt* anything... weird, in the convent? On the island?" My wording was woeful, but I didn't know how else to articulate something like this.

"What do you mean, Signorina? Weird... Like what?"

"It's difficult to explain. A shadow. The shadow of a nun... or perhaps of a girl?"

"Not anymore, no."

"Not *anymore*? But you used to?"

"When I was little, yes." Manuela's cheeks reddened. "We used to spend every holiday here. My parents have worked for Lavinia for as long as I remember. And every time I came here, I saw her. It was lonely, to be here for weeks and weeks without any other children nearby. She was my imaginary friend. You know, children often have imaginary friends," she said, with a mature tone that made me smile—she must have been about sixteen.

"Yes. I saw her too. Well, I thought I saw her. Clearly it was just my imagination," I said.

"Clearly."

"All done? You ready?" Thiago interrupted us.

"All ready," I said, with one last smile to Manuela.

We sat on the terrace, a gentle lake breeze refreshing us and, as always, bringing the ever-present scent of roses with it.

"Manuela saw her," I whispered.

"Who?"

"She saw Federica."

"Right..."

His disbelieving air annoyed me. If only Federica would show herself to him, that would teach him to be so infuriatingly rational!

"Come on, we were at a crucial bit. She was hiding the manuscripts." I elbowed him not so gently, and after shooting me a dark glance, he began to read.

On my way back that first night, frightened and muddy and shivering as I was, I slipped. The lamp fell into the water, and I was in complete darkness. It was horrible, Hanna—the mud sucked my leg in, it wouldn't let me go—I fell on my face, and I tried to drag myself out of there with everything I had, my hands grasping at weeds, trying to advance on my elbows, but nothing worked. My leg was trapped in mud. I swear, it was as if the mire had a will of its own and didn't want to let me go. I know it's strange, and crazy, but I called out for Federica...

But it wasn't Federica who came to me. I saw a flashlight coming my way and trembled even more—it couldn't have been Giulia or Aurelie, or they would have carried a lamp. It was one of the soldiers. What excuse could I find for being here, alone, wandering in the dark?

I saw his boots before anything else, illuminated by the flashlight. It wasn't just a soldier, it was the commander. He lowered himself onto his knees at once, wanting to enjoy the spectacle, no doubt. I wanted to say something defiant, something scathing, but I was too terrified to speak. I felt myself slipping away, further and further, and I knew that at the end of that sliding the cold, black waters of the lake would have swallowed me, entrapping me in weeds and roots.

"How did you end up here?" the commander said calmly and took hold of both my wrists, lifting me up and out of the mud and reeds as if I were weightless. The lake reluctantly let me go with a sucking noise—it was as if it'd been trying to devour me. I shook the commander's hands off me, but I was trembling so hard that my legs gave way—he caught me the moment before I fell again, and picked me up, one of his arms around my back and one under my knees, my feet dangling, my head against his chest. I was desperate to free myself, but I found I had no strength. I'd been so close to those dark waters, and so close to being found out hiding one of the manuscripts and being shot for it, that I'd shut down.

Step after step, in almost complete darkness, illuminated only by his flashlight, he took me back. With a clipped German command he dismissed the two sentinels standing at either side of the door. The sight of their rifles reminded me again of the risk I'd taken... Drowned or shot, that night I walked the fine line between life and death.

And yet, I would do it again. And I will do it again.

"It wouldn't be appropriate for me to take you to the sisters' sleeping quarters," the commander said. "Can you walk?"

This brought me back to my senses. I freed myself from his grasp and stood alone but his arms lingered around me for a moment, which made me furious and frightened even if his *hands were light around me and not predatory, making sure I would not fall.*

"Don't touch me. Do not touch me!" I growled.

"I don't believe I've done anything to harm you." His calm infuriated me. "You'd be in the bottom of the lake, without me."

That was true, but I didn't care. I was a fury, all the terror and trauma and rage pouring out of me without control or constraints. "You scum," *I hissed. I could see nothing, I could hear nothing but my rage. The dam was gone; the river of wrath was flowing free. I know it was such a stupid thing to do, that I was putting in danger my life and those of the sisters, but it was as if my wrath had a mind of its own.*

The commander took me by the wrist again and dragged me to Madre Gloria's study. I refuse to call it his, even if he'd taken over the room. The commotion must have awoken sisters and soldiers all over the convent, but at that moment I noticed nothing. The commander closed the door, and I thought, as clear as a shard of light in my mind: I'm going to die now.

"I shall not accept your disrespect, Fraulein Helèna."

It was my anger, the boiling anger that had its roots deep, deep inside me, that answered him. And I did so in my native language, bursting out of me like water through a shattered dam. "People like you believe we are vermin! You're no different from the monsters who burned my village!"

He looked at me as if he saw me for the first time. "You are Hungarian, then."

"You knew that. You recognized my accent. My name is Helèna Szenes, not Helèna Masi. And I'm a Jew. Do you understand me, Commander? People like you burned my village of Viliany and killed my parents!" *I knew I was signing my death warrant, but I couldn't control myself any longer.* "Are you sorry you saved me, now? Are you sorry you didn't let me drown?"

The commander froze at the mention of my village, and a strange expression crossed his face. But he said nothing. Instead, he grabbed my arms. "Be quiet. Be quiet, now," he ordered.

"I will not..."

He clasped a hand on my mouth, and fear rose again inside me, making its chilly way through the rage. He stood behind me and held the back of my head against him, one hand on my mouth, the other wrapped around my waist.

"Please, stop shouting," he whispered in my ear. "Stop. I answer to my soldiers, do you understand? They will not accept that I let you speak to me like this and do nothing."

I grabbed his hand with both mine and yanked with all I had, to no avail—he let me go of his own accord. I didn't shout anymore.

"You're so generous and kind," I hissed. "Letting a Jew live instead of killing her. Or maybe I'll be made to disappear? We can all be made to disappear, don't you think? The sisters as well, Madre Gloria, everyone. Then all the books will be yours. You can set up a nice little Nazi colony!"

The commander took a step back. That was the first time I properly looked into his face, and I really saw him. He was very pale, and his features were set, as sharp as blades. He wasn't wearing his eagle-crowned peaked cap, nor carrying the stick that must have brought fear to so many people. His black, curly hair was wet with dampness, and his gloved hands and arms were sodden with mire and water. The crease between his eyebrows betrayed his anger, but his eyes were devoid of reproach—what I read in them, instead, was pain.

"You know nothing about me," he said, and left the room without a backward glance.

I was left there, drenched and trembling.

He saved my life, but I hate him all the same...

I feel so powerless right now—all I have is my pen to chronicle all this injustice.

Aurelie is here, sleeping in my bed. She looks so small. Her eyes are moving behind her eyelashes and her fingers curl around the hem of the blanket. Her pallor is such that her skin is the same color as the sheets.

Not long after I returned, I heard Aurelie coming down the corridor. I almost dragged her inside, to avoid trouble from the soldiers—but I was too late. The trouble *had just happened.*

"Aurelie! What happened? You're crying!" I dried her tears with my fingers and pulled her to me.

She was sobbing so hard that she struggled to let the words out. "The man who is always looking at me. The one with the mean eyes..." They all had mean eyes to me, but I knew which one she meant: Werner. I'd noticed him following Aurelie.

"What did he do?"

"He was standing in front of my cell. That's all. Just standing there. I thought I heard something... and when I opened the door, he was there. Looking at me."

"What did he say to you?"

Aurelie shook her head, crying too hard to be able to speak.

"What did he do *to you?"*

Before Aurelie could reply, I saw that Sister Giulia was standing just beyond the doorstep, behind us. She'd been so silent that neither of us had heard her.

Aurelie hid her face in my shoulder, her cheeks aflame—I glanced at Sister Giulia, but her face bore no expression at all. She turned around and left, as silent as she'd come.

"Nothing, yet," Aurelie whispered in reply. "But I know he will. I'm so afraid..."

I cradled her in my arms and vowed to myself that before anyone hurt Aurelie they would have to step over my dead body.

Dear Hanna,

I'm alive.

Last night I took another book, one of Ippolita's manuscripts. I carried it like I would a baby.

I was so afraid—and not just of another misstep that would plummet me in the water. I was afraid—I am afraid—because I have no idea how the commander knew I was there. What was he doing around the lake at that time? Commanders certainly don't do the night watch, and even if he did, he wouldn't go as far as the secret place. What should I do? If something happens to me, who will look after Jacopo? Who will protect Aurelie? And how much time do I have before they decide it's time to leave? I know that the commander will notice the missing books, even if I've been so very careful in camouflaging their absence.

I'll cross that bridge when I come to it. There isn't much use in worrying now, as I keep walking a fine line between life and death.

I think back on what Jacopo said: the Allied forces and the Germans are using Italy as their battlefield; the Germans are losing the battle. The question is—if they lose, and the men here go, will they keep us alive?

I'm sure they're waiting for something, preparing for something—the commander sends and receives communications through the radio, and when he's not there, one of his men keeps guard to intercept anything coming through. But what is their plan?

They have set up camp in the refectory, like mold on an apple. We take turns to serve them breakfast, while Madre Gloria looks on, her arms crossed and her face pinched with worry. I'm pretty sure she's not eating much more than milky rice once a day, to leave more for us. We're struggling to feed so many mouths, especially because some are so greedy and thoughtless. This morning, when I woke up, I found a small punnet of apricots on my desk—a gift from Sister Giulia, who was tasked with picking fruit and vegetables for our table. The apricots that grow in the thickets behind the convent are small and not so sweet, but when you're hungry, they taste heavenly. They were now in my apron pocket, waiting to find their way to Jacopo.

While I was pouring more chicory in the soldiers' mugs, I succeeded in adding, unseen I hope, a piece of bread to the modest feast I was cobbling together for him. Almost at that moment Sister Santia appeared at my shoulder and made me jump.

"You look like you haven't slept in days," she whispered.

"I haven't. Have you?"

"You weren't in your bed last night, for sure," Sister Santia said maliciously. "I saw you, last night, near the chapel. With the commander."

I felt myself blush, both with embarrassment and alarm. I don't want anyone to know what I'm doing with the books, and I certainly don't want anyone to think I'm giving myself to the commander, or anyone else.

"I went for a walk and felt unwell. The commander came across me and brought me back."

"Right. You went for a walk in the middle of the night. Well, you didn't take any vows." She sighed. "But don't forget that chastity for a woman is more precious than a jewel."

I refrained from hitting her over the head with the breadboard though, I can assure you, I was sorely tempted. "I'll make sure to keep that in mind," I said between gritted teeth.

Aurelie was about to hand the commander's tray to one of the soldiers—bigger portions, and some honey and cheese on the side—to take to Madre Gloria's study. I quickly took it from her and made my way out before anyone could protest.

I knocked at the door, balancing the tray with my other hand, and entered without much ceremony. He was standing in front of the window, his tall frame silhouetted against the lake and the sky above. An ugly metal box with buttons and wires and what looked like a watch face sat on Madre Gloria's desk: the camp radio, an object they almost worshiped, like a golden calf to leave burned offerings to.

"Fraulein Helèna. It's you," *he said in Hungarian.*

I considered feigning submission, with hands in my lap and a timid gaze—but he'd seen me furious, and he'd heard me screaming. He would never believe that I was suddenly in awe of him. But so much depended on me: Jacopo and Aurelie's safety, the books: I had to try to survive, somehow.

"I wanted to thank you for not letting me drown, last night," *I said.*

"I'm not a monster."

I pursed my lips together. "You were out in the middle of the night," *I said. I didn't really think he'd give me an answer that would be of any use to me, more something along the lines of* what I do is none of your business.

But he surprised me.

"I don't sleep much. I was in here, and..." *He shook his head.* "What if I told you I heard someone calling me?"

I said nothing.

"Were you calling me, Helèna?"

"Of course not." *I'd called Federica. I'd invoked her help. But I couldn't tell him that.*

"I went out, and I saw someone. One of the sisters. I thought it was you, but now I can see it's not possible. I heard the voice calling me over and over again, I followed the woman, but she kept pressing on. She disappeared... but then you were there."

I swallowed. Federica had heard me, after all.

"What were you doing there, Fraulein?"

I lied easily. "I was claustrophobic. I wanted some fresh air."

His eyebrows went up—he didn't believe me, of course. "Freezing, drizzly and misty. The ideal night for a walk."

I shrugged once again. "Like I said, thank you for not letting me drown."

"I accept your gratitude," he said coolly.

"And now you know that I'm a Jew. That I escaped the pogrom that killed my parents."

"Now I know, yes."

"So I'm here to ask you to spare my life once again. The sisters need me. I must take care of them. One of them in particular."

"I would have thought that someone begging for their life would do so with a little more pathos."

"I'm not begging. And there's no need for pathos. It's a yes or a no."

"Do you think I would have pulled you from the mud and water just to kill you?"

"You didn't know of my origins then."

His features seemed to rearrange themselves—suddenly, his expression had changed so much, he seemed a different person. It was as if the uniform had disappeared, and underneath was just a man. A man who'd been taken by surprise.

"I don't think you know what it's like to pretend you are someone else. All the time," he said in a low voice.

I blinked. "I was baptized in the Catholic faith. I pray and live and work in a convent. I speak Italian. But all along, I'm a Hungarian Jew. I think you'll find I do know how it feels to pretend you're someone you're not."

There was a hint of a smile on his lips. "You really are not afraid of me, are you?"

"If I were unafraid now, I would be stupid. I'm not stupid."

"*True.*"

"*So, which one is it? Will you have me shot, or will you spare me?*" I swallowed. Suddenly I was aware that my chest was heaving, and I couldn't hide it. I laid my hand on my heart.

"*You won't die by my hand or by my order. And I will protect you any way I can.*"

Thank you was on the tip of my tongue, but those two words burned too much to be said aloud. Why should I thank him, anyway—my life was not his to take!

I noticed he was staring at my waist, quite insistently. I followed his gaze and saw that the piece of bread I'd hidden for Jacopo was peeping from my apron pocket. I was mortified, that he should think I was stealing from the sisters. "*It's not for me.*"

He pushed the tray toward me. "*Take this. Please.*"

"*It's not for me, I said!*"

His eyes narrowed. All of a sudden, the commander was back. "*Who is it for, then?*"

"*For one of the sisters,*" I lied, with ease once again. It was becoming second nature, I thought with a not-too-heavy dose of guilt. "*She's fragile, and often sick. Your soldiers are eating all we have.*"

He seemed to believe me. "*I'll send someone to the village to acquire what else we need.*"

Acquire. Which meant steal. I noticed that, while talking about going to the village, he'd thrown a glance to the radio...

"*In the meantime, take this. Please, eat.*" He pulled back Madre Gloria's chair. I was hungry all the time again, like when I was at Palazzo Masi—but I would not eat while my sisters went short. I would not sit and eat as if I were a dog he was feeding out of the goodness of his heart.

I shook my head.

There was nothing left to say. It was as if the commander

had been there with me, but now he'd left for somewhere far, unreachable. His eyes were as cold as the lake waters, and his lips thin.

"You may go."

I nodded and turned around, when he spoke again.

"My mother was Hungarian," he said simply. His eyes seemed to ask a silent question of me—but I didn't know what the question was. I didn't know what to say. He didn't either, it seemed, because he looked down, and then turned away.

When the door closed behind me, I steadied myself for a moment—I was trembling. This man had my life, and those of all of us, in the palm of his hand.

"I don't think you know what it's like to pretend you are someone else." What did he mean? He wasn't pretending. He was an odious Nazi murderer, and nothing more.

To my chagrin, I couldn't bring Jacopo my small loot. The soldiers were everywhere, and the sound of shots echoed in the thickets. We were alarmed at first, but then we saw one, two, a whole group of men coming out of the trees with quails and woodcocks. By the end of the morning, the kitchen table was covered with little winged creatures and two ducks. It was a sad spectacle, but we needed to eat. In spite of our hunger, there was silence around the table as we plucked the birds. Sister Giulia came in briefly, saw the slaughter, and walked out, her cheeks red.

I kept thinking that I could steal some meat and bring it to Jacopo—how good it would be for him, recovering from his wounds!

When night finally fell, I was faced with the choice: should I try and hide another book? At the risk of drowning, or being discovered and endangering the lives of people I love? Oh Hanna: to have so much to lose, and to bet it all on a turning card!

I sat on my cot and thought of Ippolita. Of her courage and strength.

And I did it again, two of the precious manuscripts tied on my back. Step by step I walked along and back, and I didn't drown.

At least, not yet.

———

Dear Hanna,

I had a dream so intense, I had to tell you at once! Another piece was added to the jigsaw of my memories. All I could remember up to now was the flames, and our parents' faces at the window, the galloping of horses, and finally Madre Agostina's hands on me as she dragged me away. But now there's more. I was hiding my face in long, soft, black hair—but of course Madre Agostina always wore a veil, and her hair was shorn. The woman's knees, while she held me on her lap, were covered in a soft yellow fabric, and lace. Madre Agostina wore always and only the black, rough fabric that makes the nuns' habit.

I awoke with tears on my face. Those memories are excruciating, as I am sure they are for you. I long to know more. I regret, now, not having written to Madre Agostina before, not having appealed to her to tell me everything. Now that my life and that of Jacopo and the sisters are on the line, I'm not afraid anymore about what there is to find out about that night.

What I know for sure is that you survived, and that we'll meet again...

"Mmm."

"What?" Thiago asked.

"I think something is happening between Helèna and the commander."

"Nah... they're mortal enemies."

"Still. From what she writes..."

"It's you who has a romantic soul, Francesca," he teased me.

"It's you not reading between the lines, Thiago," I replied, and then wondered who I was really talking about—Helèna and the commander, or... Thiago and me?

CHAPTER 11

THE ISLAND OF SANTA CATERINA

That night, I needed a moment alone.

I had a long shower and tried to settle down to rest a little, but I couldn't relax—the walls of my room were closing in on me. I threw on my jacket and almost ran out in the summer night, warm but with a chilly bite around the edges. The sky was full of stars and an almost-full moon shone on the hills. The beauty of it all soothed my addled mind, as step by step I walked along the lake. Only the moonlight guided me until the screen of my phone lit up in the dark. It was Isaac.

A part of me simply didn't want to pick up. I didn't want to hear what he had to say; I didn't want to know. But like all things in life, I knew that facing it was better than running away.

"Hello."

"Hey."

"You okay? You sound a little strange. Tense," I said, waiting to see what he would say. A gust of emotions knocked me off my feet. It wasn't true, it was just a work dinner and Sofia had misunderstood. Photographs can be deceiving...

No. That was denial.

"God, you know me so well." A pause. A silence I didn't know how to fill. "Helèna... I met someone. I mean... I met her years ago, but only now..."

"Rowena. I know." I closed my eyes for a moment, my heart sore even with just saying that woman's name.

"How..."

I had to swallow back the impulse to scream. "New York is a big city. But you'd be surprised how small it can be when everyone hangs about the same places."

"Sofia told you."

"Yes." Though that wasn't strictly true. I suspected already, before Sofia told me that something was going on.

I saw the way she looked at you, the way she behaved when I was around. She'd brush a speck of dust off your shoulder as if you belonged to her; she'd make inside jokes followed by "Oh, don't mind us, IT humor." All the tiny little ways she tried to create a Venn diagram around the two of you, that excluded and challenged the diagram we'd made as a couple. Maybe only women notice these things; maybe it flattered you.

"You moved on fast." I was too choked to say any more.

"Francesca, it's been almost a year..."

"Did it start before... before we..."

"No. Absolutely not."

I nodded, though he couldn't see me. I covered the phone with my hand and pushed it away from me for a moment. We were friends, weren't we? He'd broken up with me, we were only friends, and it was his right to see someone new. I had to be grown up about it. Even if I was dying inside.

The summer breeze coming off the lake seemed to caress me, to comfort me, and the air was laden with the scent of roses.

"It was inevitable. And you'll meet someone too..." he was saying, when I returned the phone to my ear.

"So... what's going to happen now?"

"Look, you can stay as long as you like, but..."

Wait a minute. It was *me* who'd found our apartment. It had taken *me* an insanely long time because Isaac wanted to be as close as possible to his work—in *Manhattan*. In our price range were places where we'd have cockroaches as roommates; an apartment where you had to crawl on all fours between rooms; one where the bathroom window opened onto the neighbor's lounge; another that shared a corridor with a laundromat. Seriously, you couldn't make it up: you'd open the living room door and step into a laundromat, open the door across and you'd be in your kitchen. The landlord had assured me it was perfectly legal, of course. Every day after work, every weekend, I scoured the area in concentric circles, with Isaac's work as the fulcrum, until I landed our little miracle, the small but perfectly formed home that I'd cherished for ten years.

And now *I* had to find another place to stay?

"Francesca, say something."

"Yes. Yes, I understand."

A doormat's doormat.

"Thank you. I don't deserve your friendship, I really don't."

"Is Rowena moving in, then?"

"No! Of course not. It's way too early."

"Mmm."

"Though her lease is coming up soon..."

I squeezed my eyes shut.

Maybe I didn't even want to go back to my apartment. Because it was our apartment, mine and Isaac's. We'd had picnics on the living room floor, made love in every room, spent lazy Sunday mornings in bed with coffee and pancakes. There were tiny marks on a wall from when we'd reproduced a scene from *Stranger Things*, one Halloween, and hung colored lights everywhere. Our neighbor had a green thumb, and the perfume of her flowers and plants wafted from her balcony to ours, challenging even the city traffic—her *Passiflora* had climbed onto our railing, blooming in spring and wrapped in soft tissue in winter. The man above us was in an orchestra and practiced the viola and gave us impromptu concerts. A black and white cat came to sit on our windowsill once in a while: we'd feed her, she'd stay for a little bit then bid us goodbye to return wherever she came from. My childhood desk, the desk I'd studied on all throughout high school and that had followed me on campus, had found its perfect home in the space between the kitchen counter and the couch—like it'd been made to measure—and...

"Goodbye, Isaac."

"Bye, Francesca."

I felt physically ill and hid my face in my pillow, crying tears Isaac might not deserve, but the ten years of my life I'd given him certainly did.

After a little while there was a knock at my door—but I pretended I didn't hear. It could only be Thiago, at this time of night, and I couldn't let him see me like this. He didn't give up, though, and knocked again.

With a sigh, I got up to open the door, even if I knew my eyes were red from crying.

"Thiago, let's..." I stopped abruptly. There was nobody there. I felt the hair rise on the back of my neck. "It's a stupid joke!" I called out to nobody, my voice echoing on the stone walls.

Thiago appeared in the corridor, with shaving foam on his chin and a towel around his middle. "What's wrong? I heard somebody shouting."

"Did you...?"

He opened his hands, waiting for me to finish.

"Never mind... Can we keep going with the diary tonight?" I said.

"Sure. Just give me a moment."

I had to wrap up this whole thing, go home and sort things out with Isaac. And I didn't mean sorting out our relationship— I meant making clear to him that no, I would not leave my apartment. I didn't want to leave my apartment. Yes, there were ten years' worth of memories of us there, but it was my *home*. I would not leave him the place I'd found and kept and looked after with so much love, and that was in my name. It was mine, not his and Rowena's.

It was time for me to see life after Isaac. No, that time had passed me by already, and I'd failed to see it. But no more.

About time, I imagined Sofia saying.

My dear Hanna,

  So much has happened, I don't even know where to start.

  I was desperate to see Jacopo, but I didn't seem to be able to extricate myself from the million things that needed doing, and I wanted to keep an eye on Aurelie. The soldier who'd taken a shine to her, Werner, kept following her with his eyes, though Madre Gloria, in turn, kept him in check. I slipped out while the Germans were eating the meat they'd hunted with vegetables from our stores and fresh bread I'd just made. The lack of sleep and anxiety enveloped me like a lead suit and made my movements slow and my thoughts confused. Images of Jacopo lying there on his own, hungry, in pain, tormented me. What if he decided, against all reason, to get out of there? It would end up in his death, for sure. The more I thought about it, the more frantic I felt.

  "Madre, if you can spare me for a moment, I'll go see if the chickens have laid," I said, and grabbed the small bucket of kitchen scraps we kept underneath the sink. It was a miserable amount, and the chickens were as lean as us. Madre Gloria shot me a quizzical look—we always collected the eggs in the morning, never at this time of day.

  "Take a little moment for your devotions," she said. "But please, take this. It's so cold outside." She freed her shoulders from her black knitted shawl and gave it to me. She knew I

was going to see Jacopo in the vestry, of course, and was giving me something to keep him warm.

"Yes, Madre Gloria."

I had to stop myself from running—step after step, Madre Gloria's shawl around my shoulders, the little bucket of scraps hitting my thigh rhythmically. I opened the chicken enclosure and poured the contents of the bucket in their feeder—then I scoured the wooden cages, where my hand closed on a just-laid egg. I turned around and threw a glance toward the convent— nobody was around, not even the usual sentries. The air itself was dark, gloomy, as if night had decided to come early and push the day away.

I closed the little gate and made my way to the church. I threw another glance around before stepping in, in a way that I hoped would go unnoticed—again, I didn't see anyone. It was colder inside than outside. I rushed forward between the pews, the dark vestry door waiting for me.

My heart skipped a beat. The cot was empty.

"Helèna!" Jacopo's voice called me from the corner where he sat, his long legs extended in front of him.

"Thank God! For a moment I..."

"I couldn't lie there anymore. I'm going crazy."

"Have a little more patience. Please. They won't be here forever."

"I know. But the idea of you out there, defenseless..."

I had to smile. "I'm not defenseless. I have my wits and my sisters. Here. An extra blanket for you, from Madre Gloria." I laid the shawl on his cot. "And look at what I got you." I smiled and took the egg out of my pocket. I broke it in the bowl that Sister Santia had left. "I know what you're about to say, and don't."

"You need it more than..."

"I said, don't! Eat it. You'll recover faster..."

We were interrupted by the sound of boots on the hard

stone. Immediately, I gestured to Jacopo to stand behind the square, dark wooden panel where the old vestments were hung. He looked at me for a moment, his eyes dark—I won't hide, they were telling me. I saw his hand disappear inside the pocket of his pants for a moment and come out with a black pod that with one swift movement magicked into a blade. But what can a knife do against rifles?

He stood flattened against the wall, his knife ready. His stubbornness was maddening. I was so terrified I could have cried. But instead of crying, I gathered myself and prepared to face the soldier—or soldiers—out there.

I grabbed a pile of linen altar cloth and my little bucket, and made myself look busy, concentrated on my tasks. I opened the door and breezed out, closing it behind me. I was ready to pretend to jump a little when I saw the soldier—but I ended up jumping for real, because it was the commander.

"Helèna?"

"Yes, Commander?" I prayed that in the gloom of the church he wouldn't see my flushed cheeks.

"Where's your shawl?" he asked unexpectedly.

"I... oh, it must have slipped off. Maybe in the chicken run. I'll go see..." I headed toward the door.

I was trying to lead him out of the church as quickly as I could, but he stopped me. His fingers around my wrist were gentle—his touch had almost become familiar. Silently, he took off his coat and wrapped it around my shoulders. It smelled of leather and of something fresh, clean, like pine, or star anise.

"You're shaking," he murmured.

The silence was so perfect all around us that even the quietest whisper had an echo—or maybe it was the language he used, Hungarian, that seemed to resound from inside my head.

"I'm a little cold," I replied. It was a perfectly plausible explanation. My mouth almost struggled to form the sounds, because I haven't spoken the language for so long. Now that

the shock of the commander knowing who I was had subsided, the door of nostalgia had opened in my heart.

"I came looking for you. I want you to be in the library with me. I want you to show me your work. Can you do that?"

"You don't need to ask me. All you must do is command me, mustn't you?" The anger that rippled under my skin was palpable. And yet, it was muted, somehow. Maybe I was too afraid for Jacopo; maybe there was something in the commander's face, in his demeanor, that in that moment tamed me.

"I won't command you, no. I'm asking you if you want to."

"Yes. I do," I said, and it wasn't just because I wanted him out of there and as far from Jacopo as possible. I think it was because I wanted to keep speaking my language, Hanna. Even if I was speaking with the enemy.

"Helèna. Are you well?" Madre Gloria asked as we stepped inside on our way to the library.

I was vaguely embarrassed that I was holding the commander's coat over my back with both hands, but I couldn't explain, not in front of the commander. "Just a little cold," I repeated.

"Is there anything I can help you with?"

Where are you going with her? I want to come too, so I can protect her. *I knew this was what the Madre was trying to say, but I didn't feel threatened by the situation. I want to show him the library, I realized. I want to speak to him about the books and tell him what I know.*

It made no sense. It makes no sense, Hanna. But I had no strength left to harden my heart, if it wanted to soften.

"You're very kind, Madre Gloria. But no, thank you," the commander replied, and we walked on.

The library is like a person to me. She welcomes me when I walk in; she beckons me to the shelves, to my desk, to the papers and pen and ink, the little world I'd built for myself. If I could, I would spend my whole day here—and if I could wrap myself in a blanket and sleep among the shelves, I know my dreams would be sweet, and sheltered.

Books were the first thing I knew, after all. We didn't spend our childhood in a kitchen, or in a courtyard like most children do. We spent it in the bookshop, while both our parents worked and studied. The feeling of paper, parchment, leather was my first experience—the smell of ink and dusty pages the air I breathed. My parents' loving arms closed around me as I sat on their knee and listened to them reading.

The first time I saw the commander wandering among the books, it felt like being violated. But this time my reaction was almost hushed by all that happened. To my bewilderment and even shame, the commander had become more familiar to me, less odious. I suppose this is what happens when someone saves your life.

"I want to see the manuscripts with your eyes, Helèna. Show me," he said.

Would he notice that a few of them were missing? I'd hidden eight out of the thirteen by Ippolita Von Oswen that we owned. If he knew already which were which, he would realize at once.

I opened the door, picked up the lamp I always kept there, and stepped down the stairs with a sense of inevitability. If this was my undoing, let it be so. There was nothing I could do.

Would he know it was me, who spirited away the books? For sure. Would he kill me for it? Would he be able to look me in the eye while he took my life? Would I beg for my life?

"Show me your favorite," he said now. My favorite of Ippolita's works is an herbarium, Delectatio Hortis, in which she describes the properties of aromatic plants and gives recipes for different ailments. The illustrations in it take my breath away. But the book wasn't there anymore: it was the first I'd hidden, wrapped in cloth and burlap.

"This one," I declared almost without hesitation. I rested

*the lamp on the windowsill, not without a glance to the door—
that it shouldn't close again as if of its own accord.*

"Symphoniae Angelorum. Symphonies of Angels," the
commander read easily and fluently. *How I wish I could read
Latin and understand it, instead of laboring with the dictio-
nary and inching my way through every text!*

"You read Latin?" I asked.

*"And a few other dead languages. Before... this, I was a
scholar. I was on my way to teach history in München... It
wasn't to be."*

*I was speechless. A scholar? A professor? How could
someone with such knowledge and education lower themselves to become a brute—to hold a rifle instead of a pen? I
studied his face as he, in turn, studied the foiled illuminations
—stars and planets, mythological creatures and constellations
illustrated the music.*

"So you learned Hungarian, too?" I asked.

"No."

*His answer was so abrupt, I was quiet—it was he who
spoke again.*

*"My mother was Hungarian. She died when I was little.
She... defied my father. He sent her away, to one of our castles
in the north."* One of our castles. *I never thought I would hear
such a sentence spoken.* "She took ill. I was later told that the
place was so damp that paint peeled off the walls and her blankets were always wet. My father killed her without spilling a
single drop of her blood."

*What could I say to that? Once again, I remained quiet.
The beauty of the illuminations spoke for us, recalling a world
of harmony and peace that was lost for us both.*

*"I used to call for her in the night," he continued. "My
father hated me for it. My governess said I reminded him too
much of her. I took refuge in my books and stayed out of his*

way, but my presence still bothered him. He sent me away when I was eight."

"What was your mother's name?"

"Elizaveta. Elizaveta Rosa Garay." He murmured her name, as if tasting it, feeling it. "She and I spoke only Hungarian to each other. I hadn't spoken it in years. When I heard your accent, when I spoke to you in my mother's language... it was like coming home."

"I hadn't heard it in years either. Like I told you, I had to hide. And my parents were killed too."

"I know. Because my father was complicit in the slaughter. It was he who ordered Viliany to be destroyed. And now here I am, my father's son. Threatening your world for the second time."

His words floated on my consciousness for a little while, too strange, too alien to sink in.

"Your father gave the order?" I heard myself saying.

Once again, like many times before, the noise and chaos and terror of that night came back to me. I wasn't there anymore, in the convent's library, with the commander—but in a street lit by burning buildings, cowering among horses stomping and flashlights lighting the sky in flaming arcs. It all came back to me with a clarity I'd never experienced before. And I saw her: the lady dressed in yellow silk, with the long black hair on her shoulders, holding me against her chest and then handing me to Madre Agostina: "Take care of her!" she called above the din, before being dragged away.

"Commander. You said your mother defied your father's orders. What did she do?"

"She went to Viliany the night of the pogrom, Helèna. She wanted to save as many people as she could."

Words got stuck in my throat as they struggled to come out. They fought for precedence and all that came out of me was silence. I saw her—it was her, Elizaveta—she picked me up *and took me away from the fire and the horses. I remembered the silk she wore and her hair, and how I closed my eyes against her chest and struggled when she herself was dragged away, and I was given to Madre Agostina.*

"Did you see her, that night? Do you remember her?" the commander asked, his voice shaking.

It was no use. I couldn't speak. The scene kept playing in my mind, with more and more details—her hand reaching out as she called Madre Agostina to take me away, and she herself was dragged back. There was a ring on her middle finger, shaped like a rose: in my memory, it shone on her blackened hand and sparkled in the soot that pervaded everything.

Another image came back to me: the commander's hands stealing me from the mire.

I took a step toward him now and brought his hand to me: it was there, on his little finger. The ring shaped like a rose.

"Your mother saved me," was all I could say.

"But where are the manuscripts?" Thiago exclaimed. "Argh!"

"Have some patience," I tried to soothe him, but I was frustrated too.

"You know what?"

"What?"

"Instead of reading this, we should ransack the place."

I laughed. "Ransack? I'm sure Lavinia would be delighted, if we did that."

"She'd put the evil eye on us!"

"Stop it. She's not a witch. Wait. Do you think she's a witch?"

"I do!" he said, rubbing his face with both his hands.

"Enough nonsense. Now, read," I said with mock reproach. But he hesitated.

"I suppose..."

"What?"

"I suppose there are advantages to this taking a long time."

"Lavinia's food?" I teased him.

"That too! But what I was thinking of... is that the longer we stay here reading this, the longer I'll be with you."

He said that in an almost whisper, but I heard. And I didn't know what to say, because...

Because I felt the same.

There was a pause.

"So, another *unbelievable* coincidence!" he went on, in a lively tone that sounded more than a little unnatural. "The commander's parents were involved in Helèna's history."

"Coincidence, or destiny, I suppose."

Thiago gave me a long, poignant look. Coincidence or destiny?

That the two of us met, that we were here together?

Oh, Hanna.

I couldn't protect her.

I'm going to try to tell you what happened, though every word hurts so much. When I returned from the library, she was in my cell. She was sitting there, mute and staring. It was as if all life had been drained from her.

A chasm opened in my stomach. "Aurelie?"

"That man found me alone. I was alone." She seemed a marionette, an empty shell who spoke with somebody else's voice.

"Please tell me he didn't... Oh, I shouldn't have left you..." I ran to her and held her in my arms—the way she flinched when I touched her broke my heart.

"It's not your fault."

"He must pay for what he did. The commander must know."

"There's no need," she whispered.

"Yes, there is! He can't get away with this, that beast!"

"I told Sister Giulia. She's prepared them supper."

"What?"

"He was hungry. And so Sister Giulia cooked for him. Maybe for the others too."

I felt cold. I knew that her words had a further meaning. Sister Giulia had cooked for that man, and maybe for the others...

Santia and Emilia are expert herbalists. But it's Sister Giulia who works in the garden. And when we had rats a few weeks ago—when they multiplied to the point of becoming a nuisance—she was the one who got rid of them...

"Amelie. What has she done? What has Sister Giulia done?"

Amelie was silent.

The commander! When we left the library, he said he had to speak to the sentries. And that's what Werner always tried to do—making rounds in the convent, being always in our line of sight, just to intimidate us. Maybe they were together. Maybe they were both eating Giulia's supper! I ran, my shoes slipping on the wet leaves, from the light of the convent to the pitch-darkness outside and then to light again in the circle of the lantern glow. I saw them both, the brute and the commander, both with a bowl and spoon in hand. Werner was dipping bread in his soup, devouring it like the animal he was. The commander was about to bring the spoon to his mouth...

I threw myself on him, pretending to slip as I could—being so strong, he didn't budge, but his bowl and its contents fell on the ground. Werner tried to grab me by the arm, growling something in German, but the commander simply called his name in a voice that made my hair stand on end, even if it wasn't me he was chastising—he didn't even need to move— and Werner let me go.

"I'm so sorry, I slipped, I..."

"Are you alright?" the commander said to me in Hungarian. Werner threw him a bewildered glance, hearing his leader speak another language.

"I'm fine. I'm sorry about the soup. Did you eat any of it, or will I bring you some more?"

"No need. I wasn't hungry, but I didn't want to offend Sister Giulia."

"No, of course."

This man really was an enigma: I didn't want to think about what he'd been responsible for in his army career, not to mention what he'd done to Jacopo's comrades; he was here to steal what did not belong to him, and acted like he owned this place, our resources, us. But he didn't want to offend Sister Giulia by refusing her food?

"Did you have something to tell me?"

"No, no, I just came to get your dishes," I said. I took the bowl and spoon from Werner and hastened to pick up the commander's from the ground before he touched it...

I was losing touch with reality. We'd been stuck in this tiny world of warped interactions between captors who pretended not to be such and captives who'd learned fast to be underhand, and the result of all this was me losing all common sense. No, Sister Giulia was not planning to poison Werner; that was absurd.

"Goodnight, Helèna."

"Goodnight, Commander." Before going, I caught a glimpse of Werner in the light of the lantern—of course, he was fine, standing straight like a rod with that revolting fist-face he'd been given by nature, like a curse. He was fine, of course.

I was making my way toward the convent when I heard a thin moan.

Although it had been barely audible, to my ears it seemed to echo in the night, over the lake and the black hills. At that moment, Sister Giulia came to the kitchen window, her face,

*inscrutable as ever, floating in a globe of light amidst a sea of
darkness.*

*It was at that moment that I truly opened my eyes to the
madness, to the incongruity of the human heart: because my
first thought was for the commander, as I gave a silent prayer
of thanks for having arrived in time to stand between him and
the poison.*

———

Aurelie had asked to be the one to look after Werner in his
agony, and Madre Gloria agreed. I was sure she had no idea
what happened between them—and I couldn't bring myself to
tell her. I knew she'd blame herself.

It lasted longer than we thought. For hours and hours
Werner writhed and screamed in his bed, and by the time he
went, everyone was relieved. I wondered if there was a single
soul in this world who would miss him.

When it finished, a subtle shift had taken place in Aurelie:
her eyes were a shade harder, some of her innocence gone. She
pulled the sheet over Werner's face and stepped out without a
word.

They buried him in a shallow grave among the thickets.
When everyone was leaving, the commander took me by the
arm and whispered in my ear. "Romer told me what Werner
did. I want you to know that had Sister Giulia not seen to it, I
would have done it myself."

I knew that. I was certain. I nodded, my eyes on Aurelie,
walking on the uneven ground, holding onto Giulia's arm.

"You stopped me from eating that soup," the commander
continued.

"Yes."

He wasn't looking at me as his fingers held mine, as his
hand dwarfed mine and swallowed it. I closed my eyes. It felt

good. So good that I took a step forward until my head was close to his chest. The fabric of his coat was rough under my cheek—the scent of cologne and leather enveloped me.

Everything I feel, anything I have felt, be it love or rage or unhappiness or joy, has had to be kept down, controlled, annihilated. By grief, by the Contessa's hold on me, by the desire to be a well-behaved, good-natured girl for Madre Gloria and the sisters. And since the Germans came here, I've been shaped by the willingness and blind need to survive.

But this moment was mine, and mine only. I let him wrap his arms around me, and forgot who we are, where we are and the strife all around us. It was me who searched his lips and me who kissed him, me, the Hungarian girl whom his mother had saved at the cost of her life.

"I told you!" I said triumphantly.

"Okay, okay, you called it. It's strange, though. He represents all that she hates. Even if his mother saved her..."

"It's not just that. I think that was a sort of bridge between them. But she sees the person beyond the soldier. I can only imagine what it would be like to fall in love with the enemy."

"That Giulia, though. And her poisonous herbs."

I shivered. "That was creepy. Do you think they still grow in the garden? Among the roses?"

"Do you think they're in the jam?" He opened his eyes wide, teasing me. I laughed, but thin, cold fingers ran down my spine all the same.

Dear Hanna,

I can barely lay this down on paper. Every fiber of my being screams it's a secret, it's a secret!

Yes. What happened tonight is just for me and Fabian to know. At daybreak, the enchanted time when light wins over darkness, we lay together in the milky light, my head on his chest and his arms around me in a warm cocoon.

It's absurd, surreal, that I felt such joy when I walked back into the convent, and it's equally surreal that I felt no shame.

"We can leave. You can leave all this behind." As I spoke those words, I came to believe them. I would explain everything to Aurelie and to Jacopo, and they would come away with us...

"I can't."

"You never wanted this. You never wanted to be this," I begged him.

"What I want doesn't matter. It never mattered. I can't shame my family name."

"As if your family and your country weren't already shamed! Everyone is, in this war! We can change things..."

"I don't have a choice. And it's too late anyway."

"We always have a choice! And it's not too late."

"It is, Helèna. It's all about to finish. We've been given orders to ruin and destroy all we can, and retreat."

"What? But... I thought you were preparing to take the manuscripts and leave, and..."

"Please. Please, Helèna. Don't say anything else. Don't speak."

"Fabian..."

"These are the last days of my life. But if I spend them with you, I won't have any regrets."

———

Dear Hanna,

The sunrise broke the spell, and we came out of our cocoon to find everything in pieces. My commander disappeared into Madre Gloria's study, and did not allow me in. The radio is jabbering away, and I have no idea what it's saying. The soldiers have lost their arrogance, and they seem to me like coiled springs, ready to lash out.

The sisters don't speak to me anymore—they don't even look me in the eye. It turned out that my secret is not a secret at all. Someone saw me. Only Aurelie hasn't turned against me, but she seems so lost, so far away, I don't know what to do, how to reach her...

How can I blame them? They think I've sold myself in exchange for survival, for safety, maybe even for less—food or money. They have no idea what links the commander and me. They have no idea what the rose ring on my finger means to us.

My heart broke when Madre Gloria grabbed my arm in a way that told me how much she despised me, now. We were on the edge of the cloister, with her study behind us and the garden in sight, with its aromatic plants, its roses. Its poisons.

"What's going to happen now, Helèna? Surely you must know. Surely he's told you?"

I don't recognize the cool, calmly authoritative woman she was when the Germans first arrived. What happened to Aurelie has broken her.

"I don't know anything, Madre. Nothing."

Her green eyes were huge and circled with blue. The radio kept blathering in German behind us, and then Fabian's voice rose and then fell again. His tone was imperious, self-assured— but when he stepped out of the office, his face was bloodless and his eyes were haunted. His self-control was such that there was almost no outer sign of his agitation.

"My superior is on his way. They're going to settle here."

"Why? Why here?" Madre Gloria almost shouted. It made no sense. Events followed each other without logic, following a pattern we couldn't read.

"It doesn't matter why. We need to prepare."

"It does matter, Fabian. Tell us," I said. I'd had enough of *the secrecy and the half-spoken truths and lies and everything in between.*

Madre Gloria stepped closer, and her old strength seemed to come back, because her face was set in determination.

"All is lost, for us," said Fabian. "My superior refused to say it, but it's clear. The Americans and English have come. We have lost and there is no other way open to us but resist until we die."

His Italian was hesitant: I hoped I'd misunderstood. It was good news, the war was over, we'd be free: but God, please, don't let my commander die!

"They'll take and destroy and kill as much as they can. As they sink, they want us to sink with them," Madre Gloria said.

"Yes."

"They'll kill us all."

"I think so, yes. And what they can't have, they will burn," he said.

"The collection," I whispered.

Fabian looked at me. "Hide them. You know where."

He knew!

I'd barely digested the realization that Fabian had known all along when Madre Gloria spoke.

"The manuscripts matter a lot less than my sisters," she said, looking straight at me. Her blame hurt me, and even more her opinion that I cared for the books more than I did for the human beings involved.

But there was no time to explain or argue: because Madre Gloria would take care of the sisters, Fabian would take care of the collection, but my love and duty lay somewhere else. I had to tell Fabian about Jacopo. I knew that now he would help me shelter him.

Angry voices and a woman's scream reached us suddenly— we stepped into the corridor to see one of the soldiers dragging

Sister Santia by the arm, roughly. The commander said something in German, in a voice that was calm and deadly, and the soldier let Santia go as if her skin scalded him. Madre Gloria took the old nun in her arms—Santia was sobbing, and I had to will myself into standing still, instead of scratching out the soldier's eyes. Fabian was in charge—and he showed it. In no time he had the man against the wall and held the man's throat in a vise. The commander could go from poised to lethal in the space of a moment. There was a frantic exchange between the two, and then Fabian let the soldier go, after having muttered what sounded like an apology to Sister Santia.

"I'm sure there was a good reason to manhandle an elderly woman?" Madre Gloria hissed.

"There's never a good reason to do that. He said that she stole his rifle. It's nowhere to be found."

"She stole his rifle?"

"He said someone did. It disappeared."

———

I found Jacopo standing in the middle of the tiny room, all bandages gone—his skin was red and blistered, but he seemed to have recovered almost completely. His energy once again radiated from him, his face determined, his muscles tense and ready.

"Helèna. I'm not staying here any longer," he said before I was even inside, before I could speak. He was like a caged bear.

"No. But let me speak to Fabian first..."

"Who is Fabian?" he said slowly.

Him too. Like the sisters. Nobody, nobody could understand what was between us, if they didn't know that his mother lost her life saving me. My heart hardened. "Fabian is

Commander Von Siegl. Let me speak to him; he will order his soldiers not to hurt you."

"What's happening out there, Helèna? I'm not staying here any longer. Commander or not. Something has changed. I can feel it."

"Yes. More Germans are coming to the island. They've lost, Jacopo! The Allies are here..."

"How do you know? You're cut off from everything!"

"The commander received news. He has a field radio. They'll be here any hour now."

"They've nothing left to fight for. They'll kill us all," Jacopo said. "I will not let them touch you, Helèna. I promise."

"We'll all survive. I promise you. Stay here a little longer. Please, Jacopo. I beg of you."

He didn't answer straight away. He simply turned around and, out of the tangle of his blankets, wrapped in Madre Gloria's shawl, took out the stolen rifle.

"I'm ready," he said.

———

It's all over, now. All over.

I didn't see Fabian for a few hours, so I couldn't speak to him about Jacopo: until it was too late. Much like we saw the boat with the commander standing on the bow like a black crow, we saw Colonel Walder sail on the waters toward us, followed by many boats—so many I could not count.

Colonel Walder hailed Fabian on the shore, while the soldiers greeted each other like old friends. Fabian's men were relieved: they'd been almost frightened to be on this island with us since Werner died. I knew they were spooked.

Fabian and the colonel retreated to Madre Gloria's study, and my heart broke in two: one part hoping that Fabian would pretend he still belonged to the Reich so that his life would be saved, and the other that we could rise up together. Even if it meant being shot. Or worse.

But life is too chaotic, too complicated to plan.

Soon after, one of Fabian's men walked in, pushing a bleeding man in front of him. Jacopo. He looked for my eyes in the small crowd and, when he found them, he made a little gesture with his head—a no. He wanted me to pretend I didn't know him, that I'd had no idea he was hiding there.

He was telling me to betray him.

I cried his name.

It all happened very fast. Fabian took a step forward and began saying something in German, while the colonel barked at him with words I didn't know the meaning of, but I could guess. Then the soldier who'd discovered Jacopo's hiding place forced him on his knees.

"They didn't know. They didn't know I was there," my brother said over and over again.

The colonel took a small gun out of his belt. A tiny, deadly thing. He walked slowly to Jacopo and put the gun to his temple, but then Fabian shouted something, and the colonel turned to him.

The colonel, and everyone else.

Fabian gave me a long, long look—and then took Jacopo's place in the center of the room. Colonel Welder's face was a picture of disbelief. He spoke to Fabian in German, his tone furious, outraged. His gun and his arm were now a straight line, terminating in Fabian's forehead. I couldn't bear it.

My body acted before my brain knew what I was doing, and I leaped toward the men. I heard a shout, Fabian's voice rising and falling, and then I saw blood on my chest and on my hands.

But it wasn't mine.

And it wasn't Fabian's.

Lying between us were Colonel Walder and Jacopo, both prone, both bloodied.

The colonel didn't move again.

I threw myself on Jacopo, my grief too great to be expressed in words. Tears and blood ran down my face and I saw nothing, heard nothing, focused only on Jacopo's body in my arms and his blue eyes open and looking at my face. He was conscious and breathing, but not for long.

He'd kept his promise: he'd saved me. But I hadn't kept mine: we didn't all survive. And none of us would, now, because there were rifles all around us, and I knew this was the final moment of my life.

Jacopo mouthed his last words: I love you.

————

Dear Hanna,

We didn't die.

With all that was happening inside, we didn't notice what was happening outside. Voices and shots filled the air: Italian civilians and soldiers dressed in khaki filled the room. More and more men piled in and almost trampled us—Fabian and I were squashed against the back wall, and I felt a little hand holding mine. It was Aurelie, pale and trembling, but alive and unhurt. I squeezed her hand tight.

Fabian wasn't moving—he was frozen, his hands on his face, folded onto himself. Frozen in fear? It couldn't be, not the commander. A moan escaped his lips as he pressed his hands to his eyes, and then murmured, "Helèna? Are you there?"

He was blind.

"I am. I'm here."

There was a convulsion of bodies in front of me—the Italians, who I now realized were partisans, and the foreign

soldiers were slaughtering the Germans. They would shoot
Fabian too.

I don't know how I could think so quickly, with such clarity, in such a moment—but I did. "Jacopo is saved," I whispered to Amelie, and prayed she'd understand what I was
trying to do. I began to rip the shirt off Fabian, and he didn't
protest. He was floppy under my hands now—he had fainted
from shock and pain.

"Thank God, he is," Aurelie answered, and helped me bare
Fabian's chest.

I reached out for Jacopo's body, lying forgotten on the
ground—my dear brother! An iron rain fell around me, but I
was beyond terror, now; otherwise I would have curled against
Fabian, held Aurelie to me and waited to die from a stray
bullet. I dragged my Jacopo back, took his gray shirt and torn
jacket and, with Amelie's help, I dressed the unconscious
commander. "Forgive me, Jacopo," I said in such a low voice
that nobody heard me but, I hoped, my brother's soul.

Aurelie and I remained there, guarding our dead and our
wounded. I cradled Fabian's head in my lap, expecting his
heartbeat to fade out at any moment. We cowered, deafened by
the shots and the shouting.

Then, silence fell, only broken by the moaning of the
wounded and a feeble voice that was reciting the rosary: I
recognized Madre Gloria's voice. Aurelie joined in, in a whisper. Then, voices rose again: Italian and English, I thought, for
they were American soldiers. An Italian boy who must have
been no older than fifteen noticed us.

"Una suora! E una civile," he called. And then, to us: "Chi
sono questi?" A nun! And a civilian. And then, the dreaded
question: Who are they?

He was trying to sound authoritative, but I saw that he
was scared, and young, and far from home. I prepared myself
to lie.

"Our friends and partisans," I said without hesitation. "Guastatori Jacopo and Fabio. Jacopo lost his life; Fabio was blinded and badly wounded."

The boy nodded—our explanation might be enough for him, but would our act be believed by the others? I didn't want to look as they dragged the Germans' bodies away, but I had to keep my eyes open. Oh Hanna, the things I saw today will stay with me forever!

Like in a dream, I saw Madre Gloria and the other sisters, unhurt, walk across to reach us—there were comforting arms around me, and tears.

"We're saved," Sister Santia said over and over again.

But my relief about the sisters' survival was mixed with grief for Jacopo and fear for the commander.

An American soldier in his brown uniform barked something at us. "We're looking for Commander Von Siegl," the young Italian boy translated, trying, and failing, to imitate the soldier's imperious tone.

Fabian lay in my arms, blind and bleeding. Defenseless.

And then the unexpected happened.

"He's here," Madre Gloria said. "This is the man you're looking for."

She was pointing toward Colonel Walder, who couldn't deny her words, who wouldn't say anything ever again. The Germans were all dead; the only people who could deny her were the sisters. I glanced from Sister Santia to Emilia and Giulia, a silent prayer in my eyes. Nobody spoke.

I burst into tears of relief and pain and shock, and Amelie and I huddled together on the floor—I knew the commander was hurt, and I knew there was still a big chance we'd be discovered, but for now, for the next moment, we were saved. I dug my fingers in Fabian's dark hair, and put my lips to his forehead, cold as ice...

A sudden blinding light filled the room, and there was a

roll of thunder: some ducked, some were knocked off their feet with fear and surprise. I gently laid Fabian down and dragged myself outside, one foot in front of the other, even if my head spun and a painful ringing sound pierced my ears. Again, a light, yellow and orange, and another explosion, with that terrible noise. The body of a German soldier appeared on the water, floating in a burned uniform—and then the unthinkable happened. There was the terrible roar of an explosion, and the shore seemed to roll down in the water, first slowly, then fast, until a whole portion of the thickets beside the church fell and disappeared. More land rolled down and filled what used to be marsh. It seemed to me that land and water had exchanged places: the island changed its face forever.

The collection, the wealth of knowledge and beauty I'd risked my life for, the treasure that had brought Fabian to me— was lost forever.

"It wasn't, obviously!" Thiago exclaimed.

"Please, keep reading," I pleaded, drying my eyes. "I need to know what happens next!"

"This is the last page. There are only a few lines left..."

When we left the island, on the boat that would take me to Lodego and then away, somewhere we could be safe—I turned around one last time and saw her on the shore. Federica, in the white dress she'd worn to escape, standing with her long black hair in the wind, without waving goodbye.

"Thank you," I said under my breath.

Thiago put down the diary and sighed. "That's it... oh, wait. There's something else. A poem."

God's creation opens our eyes
To the sheaves I sowed weeping

And I reaped laughing
In the joy of existence.
—Ippolita Von Oswen, "Angelic Symphonies"

"Beautiful." I was thankful we'd chosen to be here, and alone, when we finished the diary, because tears were falling down my cheeks. Helèna had survived.

"I wonder what Helèna did after, where she went—"

"Is the collection really lost?" Thiago said and rubbed his face with his hands in frustration. "Did Lavinia just play a game with us?"

"Can you imagine? The whole thing, an elaborate hoax. Her rose jam the equivalent of a mind-numbing lotus. It can't be."

"But what if it is?"

"Then how could she have put together that catalog, crappy as it is?" I protested.

"Seriously? You're in art dealing; surely you've seen doctored photos and all that."

"True. I don't know how many messages I got from my boss, only this morning. I have no idea what I'll say."

"Look. Let's assume it's all real and give it one last try. We roam the place until we find the collection."

"There isn't much left to roam. We've seen *everything*. Maybe we should tell Lavinia that we failed."

"We should tell her we want a normal business transaction! I don't even know what I'm doing here, anymore. I suppose the only thing that keeps me here..." Thiago hesitated.

"I know. You want to do this for your family," I said. It had become a struggle to think I was fighting for something Thiago needed too.

"I do. But what really keeps me here is—"

Right at that moment my phone rang and drowned whatever he said next. It was Isaac, and my heart sank. I was reminded of what Lavinia had said to me: that love and joy should go hand in hand... life is short, why suffer?

"Excuse me a moment," I said, and put the phone to my ear.

"Hi, Isaac," I said brusquely. I needed the conversation to be brief: Thiago and I were at a crucial point in our investigation and on the verge of deciding what to do next.

"Hi, you sound busy."

"I am, sorry," I said.

Thiago was walking away with the diary, and I almost cursed under my breath. Even his back looked somehow sad as he went.

"If you want to talk to me about the apartment, this is not—"

"Would it be a problem if I came to see you?" he blurted out.

"You want to come *here*?"

"If you want me."

"Seriously?"

"Yeah. I mean... let's see how it goes. I miss you." And here, he shrugged. I knew he had, even if I couldn't see him. I could see in my mind's eye how his chin shifted to the left a little when he spoke, every time he was nervous.

A million memories flooded me. It didn't make sense. It didn't make sense at all. He was seeing Rowena.

"Francesca?"

"I'm here."

"Can I come over?"

"To Italy? Are you sure?"

"I told you... I miss you. I'm not sure about the choices I made."

"Like... Rowena?"

He sighed. "Like Rowena."

"I need to think about it. I don't even know how long I'll be here for."

"Please, don't leave me hanging." He sounded pleading, but

—what the *hell*? *Me*, leaving *him* hanging? He wanted a trial separation. He asked for space. He found someone else. He hinted at throwing *me* out of *my* apartment. And I was leaving him hanging?

"Give me until tomorrow."

"That's not the answer I was hoping for, Francesca."

"It's the only one I have right now," I said. "Bye."

I should have been happy. Why wasn't I happy? Why wasn't I jumping at the chance to end a separation I never wanted?

I opened the gallery on my phone and began looking through my pictures—a goofy shot of Isaac in our kitchen with a failed pancake, the two of us beside a snowman we'd made at his parents' cabin, our heads close in front of brightly colored cocktails, holding sparklers at a caroling concert Sofia had organized...

But he left me. Because he was tired of our routine, he'd said. He was about to throw me out of the apartment I'd found, I'd rented for us, because he'd met someone else.

The following picture was one he'd sent me from a work dinner, celebrating someone's retirement. Rowena's face smiled at me from the screen.

He'd tried her out, but he realized he preferred me.

Meanwhile, I'd been in despair, sitting there with a bunch of wedding magazines beneath my desk, my engagement ring in my nightstand drawer. An engagement that he'd insisted on.

But after I'd shown my loyalty, my endurance, my ability to suffer in silence and be there for him, I'd proved to him I was worthy of his love. And now he was coming here, to free me from my solitude and save me from the living hell my life had been since he'd left me. Never mind that I was working. Never mind that I was doing something important.

I felt sick.

But I couldn't possibly say no, because what if he changed his mind by the time I'd gone back to New York?

Let's see how it goes, he'd said. Maybe this was a try-out too, like with Rowena.

And Thiago.

I could tell myself my time here with him had meant nothing. That sitting side by side while reading Helèna's story did not create a bond, that I didn't feel butterflies in my stomach, and that ever-present desire to entwine my fingers with his... until it happened.

The sound of thunder in the distance made me jump. A storm was coming to break the sunny, blue day. My phone sang again: a message from Isaac.

> *I'll be away for a few days, family stuff. Will let you know when I'm back. Let's see how it goes.*

What? Is he going away for family stuff or coming here?

Don't understand—I thought you wanted to come here? I typed and was about to send when another message appeared on the screen.

> *Last night was amazing for me. I just need a few days, that's all. Get my head together. Speak soon. I x*

This message was not for me.

It was for Rowena.

Pure rage surged inside me—I thought of Helèna's description when she said she had a volcano inside her. My own personal Vesuvius was erupting.

And then, just when tears had filled my eyes and I was on the verge of crying, a strange peace invaded me. Finally, it was in front of my eyes, what I'd known all along: that Isaac's love for me was another word for selfishness. I knew it, I had known it, but I had been terrified by the truth. I was so determined in my denial that I was filled with fury every time Sofia tried to make me see Isaac for who he was.

At last, there was no longer a need to hold on. The devastation I'd felt when he left me was gone. This text sent to the wrong person was almost... funny. Pathetic. Almost as pathetic as I'd been... Wow, how had I been *so* stupid?

But now, I was free.

It was almost physical: a heavy burden left my shoulders and flew away, up into the sky. I could stand straighter, my heart light, no tears to be shed.

And then I knew.

I knew where the collection was.

CHAPTER 12

THE ISLAND OF SANTA CATERINA

I found Thiago in his room. He was packing.

"What are you doing?"

"What's the point in staying?" he said without looking up. "I'm done playing this game. I'm letting this go."

"Are you giving up so easily?" Perhaps my discovery would reawaken his excitement.

"You'll go back to New York. To... to *him*."

I was astonished. He wasn't talking about the collection. He was talking about me...

"The only person I'm going back to in New York is my sister. Isaac is not part of my life anymore. And he never will be again."

He looked up from his suitcase. "What...?"

"Long story. You need to come with me now." I took him by the hand and led him outside—I ended up running, with Thiago running after me. "I know where the collection is!" I shouted, breathless.

The gloomy atmosphere of the church silenced me. I slowed my pace and reached the spot I was looking for.

"It's here. It must be here!" I fell on my knees on the cold floor, in front of the frescoed wall. I felt the wall with my hands, and the floor, crawling on all fours. There had to be a way in.

"What are you doing?" Thiago exclaimed.

He probably thought I'd gone crazy, but there was no time to argue. I slammed the wall with both hands. "It must be here! I'm sure of it!"

For a moment I thought that night had fallen—the silent garden painted on the walls seemed to sway, and the scent of roses filled the air... I held my breath. And then my fingers felt something—a relief pattern on the stone floor. I followed it, feeling the stone like a blind woman. Thiago imitated me without asking questions—until the stone moved. It was a perfect square cut in the floor—a hatch without a handle.

"We can't lift it with our hands only," Thiago said, and ran outside—returning not long later with a shovel. "Giovanni left some tools outside."

"Did anyone see you?"

"I don't think so. This is what we were supposed to do anyway, wasn't it?" he said, and began to maneuver the shovel around the gaps.

It didn't take long for the stone hatch to lift. I sat back on my heels and rubbed my hand on my forehead, dust and sweat mixing on my skin.

"I *knew* it."

"Don't mean to rain on your parade, but we still don't know what's down there," said Thiago.

"I do."

"How?"

"Federica just told me," I said and threw my legs in the opening.

"Wait!"

Thiago tried to grab me but it was too late, I'd already jumped in. Like a fool. Not knowing how deep it was, if jagged stones would meet me, or dark waters. A leap of faith.

Soft, matted dust met my feet and then my hands and knees.

"For God's sake, Francesca! Are you *crazy*? I'm coming!" Thiago called from the church.

I moved my neck and patted down my arms and legs. I was whole. "I'm okay," I said, just as Thiago landed beside me.

"There could have been anything down here!"

"But there wasn't," I said, and switched on my phone light. The beam illuminated a pile of parcels, carefully wrapped in brown paper and plastic sheets and tied with string. On top was one of the manuscripts, open and covered with transparent plastic. We stooped over it, our lights illuminating the words, framed by exquisite illustrations of plants and flowers.

> *God's creation opens our eyes*
> *To the sheaves I sowed weeping*
> *And I reaped laughing*
> *In the joy of existence.*
> *In the garden of my soul*
> *There grows wheat for bread*
> *Helleborus for sleep*
> *Dreams of life*
> *And life of my dreams.*

My eyes filled with happy tears. At last, we had found the Santa Caterina collection.

———

"Who found it?" Lavinia asked. She'd hugged us both, her rose scent reminding me of the fragrance in the church.

"We both..." I started.

"Francesca did," said Thiago at the same time.

"It clicked when I remembered the frescoes in the church. The wheat and the *Helleborus*."

"I have a question," Thiago said. "In the diary, Helèna talks about hiding the books one by one in a secret place she reached through some kind of marsh. She almost fell in the lake, the first night she went there."

"The explosion destroyed a wing of the convent and changed the very shape of this side of the island. I must admit I despaired for a moment when the wall felt so solid, I almost scratched it with my nails! And then I felt the opening... Well, something happened before then. I think someone helped me."

"Yes. I'm sure she did," Lavinia said.

My jaw fell open—but I didn't have time to ask what she meant, because she moved on.

"So, Francesca. The collection is yours. Congratulations!"

"I..."

"You'll want to let your boss know."

The idea of handing the precious collection to Zil and Cassidy made me feel ill. Also, I didn't find the treasure by myself. "I could have never found it if we didn't work together! It was both of us!"

"But I can't give it to both of you. I certainly can't dismember the collection, half and half," Lavinia said calmly.

"Don't spoil your moment thinking of me, Francesca. You earned this," Thiago said. "You know what? I think I'll go for a swim. I'm a diving instructor; did you know that, Signora Lavinia?"

She smiled her Mona Lisa smile. "Come on, Francesca. Let's go and Skype the good news," she said, and gently pulled me inside.

———

We sat on Lavinia and Claudio's couch, beside a wide window with a view of the water. Cassidy's face appeared on the laptop sitting on the coffee table, and my stomach clenched.

"Hello, hello, how amazing! We never doubted you, Francesca! We never doubted her, Lavinia. She's a most prized member of our team!"

You have me handling your dry cleaning and your hair-dressing appointments, I thought bitterly. *I only came here because Lavinia called me. You only let me because you were busy with your boyfriend.*

"Why don't you go and enjoy your last days in Italy?" Cassidy said with a sickly smile. "Lavinia and I can discuss business."

I saw red. "I'm not giving the collection to you," I said.

Cassidy's smile didn't waver. "What?"

"I'm buying it myself."

Cassidy's expression morphed from condescending to disgusted. "Lavinia, we should finish this conversation ourselves, really. The manuscripts are ours, and..."

"Signora Lavinia. And you're wrong, Signorina Cassidy. These manuscripts are in my possession, and I decide who to sell them to. And I have decided to sell them to Francesca," the Signora said. She was calm and cheerful, as if Cassidy's protests —or anything Cassidy said—were too insignificant a thing to cause her upset. Cassidy was a mosquito, and the Signora was a hippo, not noticing the mosquito's existence. Not a flattering metaphor for Lavinia, but accurate.

"Ha! And how is she going to pay for them?"

That was a good question. How was I going to pay for them?

"That's between Francesca and me."

I was looking from one to the other, trying to digest what was happening.

"You'll be hearing from my lawyers," said Cassidy.

"I'm looking forward to it," Lavinia said, as if it was a much welcome social occasion.

Cassidy was too taken aback to even reply—a symphony of triumph began playing inside me, but a faint melody of worry spoiled it a little.

"Lavinia. She has a point. Without her and Zil, all I have is my expertise. But nothing to buy the manuscripts with."

"I never needed money, Francesca. What the collection needs is a custodian. A guardian."

"In that case, you can trust me."

"It always had to be you, Francesca. And I know you won't do this alone."

She'd done it again: she'd read my mind. With a smile, I left Lavinia to go find Thiago.

———

Thiago had disappeared. I looked for him everywhere, praying he hadn't just left without a word. Finally I found him sitting on a rock on the lakeshore, his long legs folded, his eyes on the blue, blue waters. I hesitated for a moment—only a moment—and then I knew what to say; I knew what to do.

"Hey," I said and sat beside him.

"Hey. Congratulations. I'm genuinely happy for you." He wrapped his arm around my shoulders. "How do you feel?"

I nodded slowly. "I was desperate to prove myself to Zil and Cassidy. And I did. But now, I realize it wasn't the point. I never had to prove anything to them."

He nodded. "Good. Because I don't know about Zil, but from what I heard, Cassidy really is a..."

"Yep. She is. You okay?" I threw a shiny pebble in the water and watched it *ploof* down and disappear.

"Oh, I'm more than okay. You might think you have won,

but that's not entirely true. I win, Francesca. I'm the one who gained the most."

"What do you mean? She's selling the manuscripts to me, remember?" I teased him. I was remorseless because I had a plan.

He took his arm away and looked to the lake. His voice went low, quiet. "I still win. Because I met you." He shrugged. "I don't know what we'll do after this, where we'll go. I just know I want to be with you." He took a deep breath, looking for the right words. "What happened with my brother... it was an accident. Nothing can ever put it right. Not even the collection. I must forgive myself—"

I didn't let him finish the sentence. I didn't want any more negativity, anger, regret. I kissed him deep on the lips, and for a moment, I forgot about everything else.

But then he pushed me away.

"Thiago..."

"Francesca. I need to be sure. Sure of *you*. This is not a... how do you say it in English? A fling? Yes, that's the word I was looking for."

"*Fling* sounds so old-fashioned." I smiled.

"Well, I'm old-fashioned. This is not a fling for me, and I don't want you to be a falling star shooting through my life. I want you to be by my side."

"Me too. I want to be by your side."

"What about Isaac? Is your heart free, Francesca?"

"More than it has been in years, actually."

"Seriously?"

"Yep. I know, it's strange. I loved him very, very much. For years. When he left me, I thought my life was over. I clung onto him. I was up when he gave me some attention, down when he was distant. I waited for him to come back, that was all. My life was on hold. I slept on the couch in my own home because he couldn't possibly move out... the apartment was too convenient for his work. Then he started seeing someone else, and he asked me to move out. Then he changed his mind, and he wanted to come here..."

"Sounds like a man who knows his own heart. Sorry, I don't mean to—"

"Oh, no, feel free to bash him," I said, and I almost couldn't believe how I could laugh without bitterness. "Apparently, coming here was sort of an experiment. Keeping all the options open. At first, it seemed like a dream come true. Then I started having doubts... and then I got the text that wasn't for me."

"What a *pezzo di merda*."

"Quite accurate, I suppose."

"Okay, I don't understand this, Francesca. You seem... happy."

"I'm relieved. I'm free."

He nodded. "What now?" he said in a low voice.

"Now I take my life back."

He gave me a long, serious look, and gently, tentatively, slipped his fingers underneath mine and held my hand. His hold was soft and gentle—there was no possessiveness in it, no sense of ownership; it was the light touch of a new beginning.

"That man is a fool. If you were mine, I would never let you go," he said simply.

I let his words hang in the air as we watched the heavy, waterlogged, stormy clouds march on over the lake, and disappear beyond the hills.

He held me to him, so tight I could only mumble, "You know we sound like characters from Jane Austen, don't you?"

"I don't care," he mumbled back.

And then we were both laughing and kissing, and kissing and laughing, and life was so good, so weightless. It seemed to me that we were one with the lake and the sky, just like Ippolita had said—I was full of a joy I didn't even think possible. I couldn't wait any longer—I was dying to tell him.

"There's only one problem," I said.

"What?" His voice was still muffled in my shoulder—he didn't want to let me go.

I pulled gently away and took his face in my hands. "I can't afford to buy the collection."

"What do you mean?"

"I mean, I told Cassidy that Lavinia gave it to me, not to them. I neglected to say that all I own in the world is half a house in Queens and about three hundred dollars in cash. And a pretty impressive collection of Funko Pops."

Thiago was aghast. "What are you going to do?"

"I have a vacancy for a partner. I know you hate the whole thing, art dealing and everything, but maybe your father might be interested? We could be partners. Casa d'Aste Palladini e Lombardo?"

Thiago stared at me, his mouth half-open for a few seconds, trying to digest what I'd just said.

"Do you think that could work? What do you say?"

"And when you see, you'll see—that you can walk on water," he quoted quietly and kissed me again, for a long time.

CHAPTER 13

THE ISLAND OF SANTA CATERINA

It was time to go—although it wasn't a plane to New York that would take me away from Santa Caterina, but a train to Florence, to Thiago's home.

"There's a question I still need to ask," I said, as we sat at the table on the terrace, waiting for Manuela to bring us the usual coffee, croissants and rose jam.

Thiago nodded. "Why she called us."

"Exactly. She wanted me all along. She saw my name in the brochure, you know, the Zilberstein Art brochure. And when Cassidy couldn't come, she asked for me."

"Had Cassidy been able to come, she would have asked for you anyway. She singled out the Zilbersteins' business because you were there. Think about it. Your boss didn't call her; she called your boss. As she called my father. She handpicked us."

"And we need to know why... Oh, here comes Manuela. Good morning!"

"Good morning," she called in her usual cheerful manner. "*La colazione!*"

"What about Lavinia? And Claudio?"

"They left at dawn," Manuela said. "Dad and I will close

the place now, until you return." We followed her gaze onto the pier, and there was the bright red boat, being readied for us.

"They just *left*?" Thiago exclaimed. "But... did they say anything? Why did they leave before us?"

"I don't know, I'm sorry. I didn't even see them. They left our wages and all the instructions on the kitchen table, and they were gone. They do that, you know. They appear once a year, and then disappear, like that, poof!" Manuela laughed. "They left this for you," she added, and handed us an envelope that bore our names in blue ink, before leaving to finish her work.

Thiago and I looked at each other.

"Better hurry and finish packing. I don't want to inconvenience Manuela and her dad," I said.

"Yes."

In silent agreement, we downed our espressos and grabbed a croissant each—I giggled to myself thinking that neither of us was willing to renounce one last taste of Lavinia's cooking—and made our way toward my cell. Already the rose jam tasted of nostalgia, of things that had happened and passed away.

Our time in Santa Caterina was about to be a memory.

———

Giovanni rowed and Manuela sat near him. Thiago stood at the helm of the boat that was taking us away from the island, while I looked out to the shore, watching it become smaller and smaller.

I wasn't surprised when I saw her standing there, in her white dress, saying goodbye.

"Goodbye, Federica," I said. The noise of the boat drowned my words, but I was sure she'd heard me.

———

We were sitting in Lodego when I opened Lavinia's letter, and read it aloud.

My dear Francesca and Thiago,

I'm sure you want to know what happened to Helèna and the commander when they left the island. I'm happy to say that they found their way to safety, together with Sister Aurelie. Helèna and Fabian got married and had a daughter, Greta, who later in life returned to Italy and married a young antiquarian, Patrizio Palladini, Thiago's grandfather. As for Aurelie, she renounced the veil and married an Italian immigrant to New York, Marco Lombardo—Francesca's great-grandfather.

Now you know why I called you here: to weave the threads of the story of your families.

I'm so sorry for the loss of your brother, Thiago, and I'm sure that you'll make him proud with everything you'll do.

And, Francesca, your great-grandmother Aurelie fought so hard for her happiness: don't give yours away!

In this envelope you'll find another two pieces of the jigsaw, to help you see the whole picture.

With all my love,

Lavinia

"I'm speechless," Thiago said. "Helèna was my great-grandmother!"

"And Aurelie was mine. I don't think anything can surprise me, at this point…"

"What else is there?"

"More letters. And a photograph…"

Copy n.22

To whom it may concern: please help this

***letter find its way to Helèna Szenes, also known
as Helèna Masi.***

My dearest Helèna,

*I sent you so many letters, so many since your adoptive
brother wrote to me! Hope has been thin on the ground during
the war years, but now I pray that this will get to you! I've
addressed them all to Palazzo Masi, but you never answered,
so I knew that the war in Europe had displaced you. You can't
imagine... when your brother's message arrived... my heart! But
let me start from the beginning, or you won't make sense of my
jumbled words.*

Gentilissima *Signorina Hanna Szenes,*

*My name is Jacopo Masi. I write to you in hope that you might
be the answer to our prayers. I'm the adoptive brother of Helèna
Szenes, who came to us as a child after her home village of Viliany
was destroyed, and her family killed. Her whole family was exterminated, but Helèna always believed in her sister's, Hanna
Szenes', survival. I gathered her hope in my hands and looked for
Hanna through contacts among my comrades and family friends,
and I finally came to you. Helèna is not aware of my search and of
this missive, because I endeavor not to distress her should our hope
be shattered. I'm sending you some letters that Helèna wrote
through the years, hoping that should you not be the Hanna
Szenes we're looking for, you could return them to us—but even as
I write these words, my heart tells me that we can call off the
search, that my sister has found her own long-lost sister...*

"Jacopo had worked behind the scenes to reunite the
sisters," Thiago said.

"I hope he succeeded."

"What's the photograph?"

I leaned my head on Thiago's shoulder, just like I'd wanted to do the first night we began Helèna's diary. "It's them! That must be Sister Giulia, tall and broad... Santia and Emilia... Aurelie! And that must be..."

"Madre Gloria."

We looked at each other.

There, among the sisters, stood Lavinia.

EPILOGUE

NEW YORK, SEPTEMBER 1944

Manhattan is crowded, frightening, amazing. A million dreams rise to the sky in this place, some to be broken and lost, some to come true.

I stand with Fabian at my side, his arm in mine to find his way in a world he can't see; and yet his resilience and steadfastness sustain me as much I sustain him. He never once complained about his wounds or the resulting blindness—I know he believes it's his penance. Aurelie is beside us, her chestnut hair, now free from the veil, carefully curled. Dressed like the young girl that she is, she has a light in her eyes that not even the events at the convent could extinguish.

This world is bigger than I'd ever imagined, and full of people displaced by the war. The tides of immigrants ebb and flow around us, and I consider our vulnerability—Fabian can't see, Aurelie's legs are impaired—as for me, the war has written its story on my face. My fingers touch the scar on my cheek—I, too, have changed outside, as well as inside.

The three of us, like the people all around, without a home to go to nor one to return to, are at the mercy of fortune, with only the little money left from the ship passages as a safeguard between us and utter poverty.

But we're free. Fabian is free from the weight of doing deeds he knew were wrong, but he'd been raised to believe were his duty. Aurelie is free from vows she didn't choose, and from her family's belief that her affliction would prevent her from living the life she yearned for. I'm free from the burden of grief and dread that made me want to escape the world, to hide away like a wounded animal: I'm now ready to embrace my life, whatever it brings.

I feel Aurelie's small hand slip into mine, as men and women and children, with their luggage and boxes and sacks tied together with ropes, weave around us. Voices in many foreign languages rise through the air.

A woman comes into sight through the crowds, appearing and disappearing as people step around her. The first thing I notice is her eyes, black, enormous, deep like dark waters; and the second is that she carries a small parcel of letters, tied with a ribbon. She takes a step toward me, and I see tears flowing down her cheeks. One hand holds the letters; the other extends toward me.

I'm too choked to speak—only one word makes its way from my heart to my lips.

"Hanna."

A LETTER FROM DANIELA

Dear readers,

I want to say a huge thank you for choosing to read *The Bookseller's Daughter*. If you did enjoy it and want to keep up to date with all my latest releases, just sign up at the following link. Your email address will never be shared and you can unsubscribe at any time.

www.bookouture.com/daniela-sacerdoti

Thank you to my affectionate readers for being by my side once again with another adventure—and welcome to the ones who pick up a book of mine for the first time! I hope I'll give you a few hours of me-time and a little escape from daily life. Forgive me if there will be a tear or two, often the marks of a good experience!

This time the story takes place in the Italian lakes, a location very dear to my heart for its beauty and abundance of both history and legends. The convent of Santa Caterina is inspired by a real place, and then transported to a dimension between history and imagination, as it always happens in my novels. The Italian lakes are a setting for many dramatic moments in World War II, including Mussolini's murder near the Como Lake. His lover, Claretta Petacci, lived for a while in a pretty villa on the lake called Villa Fiordaliso, which is now a boutique hotel. Also, the last moments of the fascist regime, embodied in the crumbling Repubblica di Salò, enfolded in this area.

In this novel, however, the island of Santa Caterina feels almost suspended in time, in a dreamy setting where history seems far removed, only occasionally touching it with its ripples. I had to take a little liberty with timelines as I set a pogrom against the Jewish village of Viliany in 1930, while the height of violence against the Jewish population in Hungary happened before then, and picked up again with Hitler's rise to power. I hope you'll forgive some poetic license, as I mold both real events and characters' lives to fit together.

One of the two main themes of *The Bookseller's Daughter* is the ability of a woman to climb out of a bog—which in the novel happens both metaphorically and realistically! The ever-present determination of women to rise again after having fallen never ceases to amaze me. To paraphrase the poet Rupi Kaur, our spirit 'crushes mountains' for sure.

The second theme is love of books and knowledge, that ties together Helèna and Francesca and further back, the medieval abbess Ippolita Von Oswen. Most of you will guess that the inspiration behind the fictional abbess, poet, healer and composer Ippolita is Hildegard Von Bingen, a woman whose intensity and mysticism was both blessing and curse to her life. It was so fulfilling, so joyful, to be able to portray a poem as the key to solving a mystery and unknotting a life situation—poems are powerful, often more than we give them credit for. After all, there's little difference between a poem, a prayer and a spell...

Thank you from the bottom of my heart for being here with me, for choosing to spend some of your precious time in my world. I appreciate your support, and treasure the way my readers complete the stories I write through their life experience and perspective. Let's keep each other good company!

A virtual hug to each and every one of you,

Daniela

Made in the USA
Monee, IL
03 August 2023

40407922R00142